ATHENA

Two Years Earlier

T his is fucking stupid.

The same sentence has been rattling around my head since I got out of bed in my new room this morning, since I put on my new uniform, and since I walked the five miles to Blackmoor High in my new, uncomfortable shoes.

In the old days, I would have just taken the bus. I would've worn jeans with holes a little too big for the dress code and a questionable band shirt that some teacher would probably have shit themselves over halfway through the day, and my trusty old Docs. I'd already be at school, chewing through some cardboard breakfast pizza and glaring down any preppy twat of a girl who decided to look down on me because my eyeliner is a little too thick and my parents are a little too poor.

But now, I'm supposed to fit in with them.

The preppy kids. The *Blackmoor High* kids. All because my dad had to go and fuck up, and now my mom is working instead of staying at home with me like a good biker's old lady. Now, instead of helping with book drives for the public high school and palling around with

1

the other old ladies, she's putting on a housekeeper's uniform and scrubbing floors for fucking King Blackmoor himself, the crusty old dude living on the Blackmoor Estate.

Well, not the Blackmoor patriarch exactly. Philip St. Vincent and his family, who I've never seen, are the ones living on the estate these days. For some reason that I don't actually give a fuck about, the Blackmoor family themselves don't live there. At least not anymore.

I've never had any reason to care about any of the founding families of Blackmoor, or their estate, or the prep academy they founded, or the university, or any of the other pies I'm sure they've got their fingers in. They, and everyone like them, would have looked down on my family and me. Bikers. Harley-riding, grease monkey trash. Biker whores. I've heard all the names in the book thrown at us, at my mother and me specifically. At my old friends, back in the school that I can't go back to now. I never gave a single fuck. All it taught me was that I had to be tougher than every bitch that wanted to bring my family and me down. And I was. Athena Saint, queen of the local high school. Everyone knew not to fuck with me.

But in the end, it wasn't snobby bitches and football quarterbacks gossiping that brought my family down.

It was my own fucking father.

Now he's six feet under, and I'm on my way to a place where I know I'll never fit in.

Not that I want to.

In fact, I've gone out of my way on this first day to fit in as little as possible. I rolled the waistband of my plaid uniform skirt so that it ends a little too high up on my thighs, made sure to throw my black polo emblazoned with the Blackmoor High crest into the dryer so that it shrank. Now it stretches tight over my boobs, which over the past summer went from a B to a D cup seemingly overnight, and if I raise my hands at all, it rides up to show a strip of my flat, pale stomach. I made sure to scuff my black flats too on the way out the door, just as an extra measure.

Oh, and I *piled* on the black eyeliner this morning. There's no official rule that I saw about makeup in the little booklet that came home

CRUEL LORD

IVY THORN

with all of the other paperwork to enroll me. But I'm pretty sure none of the prep academy bitches are going to be made up like Avril Lavigne circa 2002.

I hear the early 2000s are back in anyway. Not that I've ever tried to be on-trend.

It's like a different world in this part of town, I realize as I stride quickly down the sidewalk, holding on to my new backpack. I know my mother couldn't really afford any of this shit, not the new uniforms or the shoes or bookbag or anything else, which makes me wonder why she agreed to this at all. I was doing fine at my old school. Well—not *fine*, but my grades were Bs and Cs, enough to probably get into the state college, if I even wanted to do that. And I got into fights, but what the hell else was I supposed to do?

It's dangerous there, after what your father did, my mother had said. *The people who were your friends might not be your friends anymore.*

But it's not like I'm going to have friends at this new school, either. At least at the old one, I might have managed to keep a couple. And as for the ones who might have tried to bully or hurt me over it, I can hold my own. I'm not scared of anyone.

I grew up knowing the world was going to be against me. And I've never seen any reason to think differently about it.

A car drives past, a little too close to the sidewalk, and I jump sideways. I barely heard it coming—it wasn't the roar of a Harley engine or the stuttering growl of a beat-up truck or the groan of a too-old car that I'm used to, but the humming purr of a luxury car, a Benz from the logo that I catch a glimpse of it as it zooms past. I manage to get a brief look at the guy in the front seat—dark hair slicked back, chiseled jaw. There's a skinny blonde girl in the passenger's side, and I imagine she must be his girlfriend, some chick with plumped-up lips and a boob job at sixteen.

I miss everything about my old life already. I miss the homey warmth of our old house and the scent of breakfast cooking, the way that smell clung throughout the day on account of the grease stains on the range vent and the spills on the stovetop. I miss the out-of-date wood paneling, the faded carpet, the way it got hot in mid-August, the only time that it really gets hot up here in New England, and all the scents of the years before seemed to gather in the dusty air, telling stories about meals cooked and drinks had and spilled and people milling about, long before we bought the house and all the years we'd had it.

Now there's nothing left of it. Just ash, cleared away by now by the city. They're supposed to be looking for who did it, but they aren't really. Just like we all know, but we'll never say a word.

Our family home, just another victim of my dad's fuckups.

Sometimes it makes me feel like I should be less of one, just so my mom isn't left alone again. Because God knows if I fuck up too badly, I'll wind up in juvie or jail, and then she'll be alone. I can't let that happen.

I'm the only one who can take care of her now.

I walk through the wrought-iron gates of the school, checking my map to figure out where the administrative office is. I have a first-thing meeting with the dean before I even get to go to homeroom, probably on account of my record back at my old school. I'm sure they're going to have a thing or two to say about it. I've just got to keep my head down and my mouth shut, neither of which is particularly easy for me to manage.

The school campus is huge for a high school, with all ancient stone buildings, manicured grass, and paved cobbled and bricked pathways that I can feel through the thin leather of my shoes. I ignore everyone that I walk past, hating them on sight. I hate their perfectly clear skin and plumping lip gloss and neatly pressed uniform skirts, their perfectly dyed hair, and high-pitched voices. I hate the guys, too, because I know every single one of them is a fucking douche without even bothering to look. Every single person here, born into money and privilege and taking it all for fucking granted. They probably all hate their parents, too, whine about how their daddies didn't give them enough allowance this week or bought them a Bentley instead of a Jag.

I'd give anything to have my dad back, our old worn house, and my comfortable life. The one that I knew the parameters of, understood, was familiar with. Not this strange and gilded world that I know I'll never fit into.

The interior of the admin office is all wood and brick, slick wooden stairs with iron railings, and I go up the four flights to the dean's office. I know it's his because the name is etched on the gold plate on the door reads, *Dean William Edgington.* What a fucking name. Like a lord of the manor or some shit. And when I walk into the office, it's clear that's exactly how he thinks of himself.

He's a short, portly man in a tweed vest and slacks, with a balding head and a mahogany desk and walls lined with books older than this fucking campus. From the look on his face, I can tell that he's going to be a massive pain in my ass.

"Athena Saint." He says my name like it's something exotic and strange as I flop down into one of the dark leather chairs in front of his desk, tossing my backpack carelessly onto the wooden floor so that it makes the loudest noise possible. "A transfer from the public school." The sentence comes out stilted as if he's saying something so dirty he can't quite manage it. "Your mother is a housekeeper at the Blackmoor Estate."

"Yes." I look up at him from where I'm slouched. "My admission was part of her employment package."

"I see. Very generous of Mr. St. Vincent. But then again, he always did have a soft spot for the less fortunate."

I clench my teeth. I can't mouth off to him. I know it. My mom needs this job and Philip St. Vincent's protection. While we're living on and she's working at the Blackmoor Estate, none of my father's old friends will touch us. After all, they work for the estate, too, running protection for the remaining members of the founding families. But if St. Vincent kicks us out, we're fucked.

"Yes, it was very kind of him," I grind out. "We're *so* grateful." I mean for it to sound authentic, but it comes out too syrupy, almost sarcastic. Dean Edgington looks at me from over his papers, his eyes narrowing. They're a little red around the edges, like a rabbit.

"You should be, Miss Saint. Now, as to your record at the old school. I see here that you spent a lot of time in the principal's office. Would you like to tell me why that is?"

I shrug. "Kids like to bully other kids. I don't like being bullied."

"I would say, based on this, that maybe it was you doing the bullying. Fight after fight after fight." He makes a *tsking* sound as he flips through my old school records. "A lunch tray to a girl's head, a boy's nose broken, a skateboard to the face—my, my, Miss Saint, you certainly do have a violent streak."

Once again, it's a struggle not to go off on him. That girl called my mother a whore, the boy whose nose I broke, undid my bra strap and shoved his hand up my shirt. At the same time, he tried to get the other one down my jeans on the bus and then told me that I had it coming, that all biker sluts love being shoved around and taking dick. The kid whose skateboard met his face suggested that my dad was a rat.

Eventually, my dad ended up being a rat, which is why I'm in this fucking situation. But that's not the point.

The point is that I didn't fucking bully anyone. It's always been others calling me names, trying to assault me, trying to hurt my family and me. Names might not hurt anyone in this rarefied world, but in *my* old world, if you don't stop them from calling you names, the sticks and stones come next. Or, in my family's case, a dead father and a house burnt to ash.

"Of course, given your loss, it's understandable why some of your more recent...outbursts occurred." Dean Edgington sets my file down, steepling his fingers. "Setting a trashcan fire in the lunchroom?"

"That wasn't me."

"There are reports of students who say that they saw you."

"Yeah, and teenagers never lie." Nothing pisses me off more than being blamed for things I didn't do.

"Last time I checked, Miss Saint, you are a teenager. And an unruly one." He sits back in his chair, eyes narrowed. "We're not here today to go over your past record extensively. I think it speaks for itself. What we *are* here to do is ensure that this behavior does not continue here at Blackmoor High. Because as I'm sure you're aware, we will not tolerate it here. Do you understand?"

"I think so."

"Let me be clear." Dean Edgington takes a deep breath, ticking off items on his fingers as he goes along. "Fighting is not tolerated at Blackmoor High. Bullying is not tolerated. Name-calling and cursing are not tolerated. Pranks and jokes like trashcan fires are not tolerated. Smoking, alcohol, and drugs are not tolerated, nor is the use of them on or off-campus. Should I continue?"

"Seems pretty clear." I try to keep the sarcasm out of my voice this time, and I think I do an okay job. At least, he doesn't seem to pick up on it this time.

"Very good." He closes my file, slides it away somewhere in his desk. He's finished with me, his expression flat. I was a bullet point on his to-do list, a chore to be completed. He doesn't actually give a shit about me or how I'll be treated here or how well I'll adapt. I'm not surprised, but it does sting a little. I hadn't thought it would, but it does.

"You can go now." He offers a tight smile, and I stand up, making sure he gets an eyeful of my pale belly as my shirt rides up when I sling my backpack over my shoulder. "Oh, and Miss Saint?"

"Yes?" I stop halfway to the door, turning to look back at Dean Edgington, a stout, sad man behind a desk that dwarfs him. I almost feel sorry for him. Or I would if he didn't have such a massive stick up his ass.

"Your skirt is too short, Miss Saint. Please do something about that. Our dress code here is very strict."

I flash him an apologetic smile, one that I'm sure I'll have to perfect while I'm here. "I'm so sorry," I say contritely. "I'll fix it immediately."

"Please do."

I have no intention of fixing my skirt. In fact, I'm already thinking about whether or not I can manage to make it another half an inch higher for tomorrow.

With that meeting out of the way, the day ahead feels a tiny bit brighter, although not much. Looking at my old iPhone, that's four generations out of date, tells me that I've got ten minutes to get well across campus for my homeroom. I'm sure that being late on my first day to my first class is something that the dean will have *plenty* to say about. I rush down the stone steps, not even looking where I'm going as I glance in the direction I'm going to have to quite literally run in order to make it there on time.

The result is that I run smack into someone else coming up the stairs, so hard that the breath leaves me for a second.

Someone who smells like clean laundry and spicy cologne.

Someone with an extraordinarily hard chest and muscled arms that grab me as I totter sideways on the stairs, nearly falling.

When I look up, someone who has a pair of the greenest eyes I've ever seen, like seaweed underwater, fringed with dark lashes. His skin is faintly tan, that pale brown that very pale people get after spending a huge amount of time outside, the darkest they'll ever manage. And his hands are still gripping my upper arms.

When I manage to pull back far enough to get a good look at his face, I realize something else.

He's absolutely fucking gorgeous.

Enough to make it take a little longer for me to get my breath back and forget that I hate every single person here.

Including whoever this Adonis is that I just crashed into.

"I'm sorry," I manage to stammer out, and I instantly hate myself, too. I've never been the kind of girl who *stammers* in front of a guy. I despise girls who get like that around guys, who flutter their eyelashes and stutter and pretend to be stupid just to attract them.

Except I'm not pretending. I'm fairly certain a number of my brain cells just...stopped working.

It was probably the impact against his rock-hard—chest.

Oh my god, shut the fuck up!

The guy is looking down at me now, an arrogant smirk on his face. "You should probably watch where you're going," he says, those green eyes locked onto mine. It sends a shudder down my spine because he has a look in his eyes that I recognize, that I've seen on the faces of way too many men already in my life.

A look that says he's a predator...and I'm the prey.

The difference is, I'm used to seeing that look on the faces of *men*. This guy is my age. So why the fuck is he looking at me like he could own me if he wanted to?

I stiffen, glaring at him as I step back. And that's when I see the other two guys coming up behind him.

Two equally gorgeous guys. One is tall and well-groomed, with slicked-back hair and icy blue eyes that look like they could freeze you with a glance. The other is a little edgier, with black hair that's shaved on the sides and long down the top and eyes that are equally dark—so brown that they almost look black. Even his uniform is a little sloppy compared to the other two, wrinkled in places, and his polo is untucked. In fact, he looks ridiculous wearing a polo at all— this guy was made for ripped black jeans and faded vintage tees. The school uniform looks like a costume on him. On the other two guys, it seems tailor-made.

"Who's the chick?" the black-haired guy asks, a similar arrogant smirk on his face. His eyes slide up and down my body with a posses- sive glint that makes me shudder, although I manage not to show it. "Nice tits."

"Nice legs, too," the other guy says, the one with the slicked-back hair. His icy eyes make something knot in my stomach as he comes up the stairs a step, and I can see his shoulders tense under his school jacket, like something preparing to pounce.

I feel small, hunted like a frightened, cornered animal.

I don't like it at all. This is when I lash out. When I fight. But I don't know what to do against guys like this. I don't know what their weaknesses are, what will make them back down. And more than that, I just came from a lecture in the dean's office, telling me *not* to fight back.

Mine and my mother's lives might be literally on the line. I have to keep my mouth shut.

Even if it means taking shit from entitled little dicks like these.

"I don't know." The guy who I initially ran into lets his eyes run over me too, taking in my outfit, my pale skin. I suddenly wish I

9

hadn't hiked my skirt up so short. "What's your name?" he asks, his gaze still appraising.

I can't seem to speak. I really, really don't want to give these guys anything. But something tells me that they'd just find out anyway.

"Don't you have a name?" the black-haired guy jeers, still smirking. "What is this, your first day here?"

Somehow, that jolts something loose in me. "My name is Athena Saint," I snap, glaring at all three of them. "And yes, it's my first fucking day. And now you've made me late. So how about you get the fuck out of my way unless you're going to write me a note?"

The guy in front of me looks slightly taken aback, which is the most satisfying thing that's happened to me all morning. "Well, Athena Saint," he says slowly. "I wouldn't be a gentleman if I didn't welcome you properly to our lovely school. And I'm nothing if not a gentleman. Right, *gentleman*?"

"Sure thing," Slicked-Back Hair says, grinning wolfishly.

"Fucking right," Black-Haired-Guy agrees.

"See?" Guy-I-Ran-Into looks down at me, his muscled arms now at his sides. "They all agree."

"And how are you going to do that?" I snipe, preparing myself for all sorts of lewd suggestions about how they might "welcome" me to the school. But his answer is surprisingly tame.

"I'm throwing a party tonight. Back to school and all that shit. You should come. In fact, I'm personally inviting you." He grins, and it *almost* seems genuine. "Whaddaya think?"

"I'll think about it," I snap. "But for now, I need to get to class. Unless you like to welcome girls by holding them against their will?"

His face darkens, and that expression, coupled with the way the guys behind him suddenly look at me too, their eyes dragging over me again, makes me wish that I'd said anything else. Offered up literally any other comeback.

But all he says is, "See you tonight, Athena Saint." And then he jerks his head, motioning for the other two to follow him up the stairs, which they do. But not before giving me one last long look.

ATHENA

J hurry down the steps, trying to push the entire mess out of my head. At this point, I might as well skip homeroom altogether and just go straight to my first class; I'm so late. And as for the party Muscles is throwing, I have no intention of going. Some booze and drug-fueled blowout in that dickhead's mansion, while his parents are out of town, doesn't hold any appeal for me. Hell, his parents might not even be out of town. They might just not give a shit. He was probably raised by nannies. They probably don't even pay attention to anything he does.

"Oh my god, I can't believe you just did that."

What the fuck? I nearly jump out of my skin, whirling around to see a girl about my age and height, with her hair in two braided pigtails and freckles dotting her nose beneath her round glasses staring at me as if I just killed a dragon. She looks like the poster child for a school uniform, everything about her screams *nerd*. She's as far from the fake, glossy prep girls who occupy every corner of schools like these as you could possibly get.

"Did what?" I snap, immediately annoyed. *Am I destined to meet the entire school this morning?* I can't even seem to get to class without running into people who want to talk to me. My whole goal here was to be as off-putting as possible, and that seems to be failing terribly.

Maybe I don't have as good of a resting bitch face as I thought.

"Told off Cayde St. Vincent," she breathes, looking up at me as if I'm her hero. "*No one* talks to him like that. *No one.*"

Now it's my turn to stare at her. "What did you say his name was?"

She looks at me as if I'm stupid. "Cayde St. Vincent," she repeats slowly. "What, are you new here or something? Everyone knows Cayde."

Oh my fucking god.

St. Vincent.

The guy I just ran into on the steps, the guy who for a second made me feel like I couldn't breathe, is a St. Vincent. The same family my mother works for. Possibly very closely related.

Maybe even Philip St. Vincent's son.

Which means I live on the same property as him.

I'm definitely not going to that fucking party now.

"And he invited you to the *party*," the girl says, her voice slightly awed. "He must really like you, especially after the way you talked to him. I mean, you're beautiful and all, but *Cayde...*"

Me? Beautiful? I frown. No one has ever called me that. Guys tend to use words like *hot,* or *slutty,* or *fuckable,* and girls just get pissed because I'm a junior in high school and have bigger tits than some of their mothers. But the way this girl is looking at me, you'd have thought I was a supermodel.

"Let's start over," I say, pushing the fact of exactly how fucking late I'm going to be *again* out of my head. "I'm Athena. And you're not the first person to ask, but yes, this is my first day. What's your name?"

The girl sticks out a hand bare of nail polish, with short-bitten nails. "Mia, Mia Grayson," she says quickly, flashing me a smile that shows a mouth full of braces with bright pink bands. "It's so nice to meet you, Athena. I—"

I cut her off quickly, my mind racing. I need an ally if I'm going to survive this place. I'm not about to suck up to any of the plastic bitches that infect it, so I'd resigned myself to going it alone. But this nerdy little girl looks promising. She's nothing like my friends back at my old school, but I was never going to find girls like those here. At least Mia seems halfway normal. "What's your first class."

"English, with Mrs. Allan—"

I sigh with relief. "Me too. Come on, we're both going to be late. You don't look like the type that's usually late, either."

"I'm not," Mia says cheerfully. "I'm always on time. But I just had to watch you take down those guys, I mean, *Cayde*—"

"What about the other two?" I interrupt her, not wanting to hear more about Cayde St. Vincent. I have a sinking feeling that I'm going to see and hear more of him than I want to, living on the estate. "What are their names?"

"Jaxon King and Dean Blackmoor," Mia supplies helpfully, and I screech to a halt, staring at her.

"Blackmoor? Like Blackmoor High? Like Blackmoor Estate?"

"Yup." Mia shrugs. "He's Cayde's sidekick these days, along with Jaxon, now that the Blackmoors are out of favor and the St. Vincents hold the estate. I don't think Dean takes it very well, though—"

She keeps rattling on, but I tune her out. I have questions, but I remind myself that I don't care. I don't care about this town, the founding families, or why the people the entire town is named after aren't running it or living on their family estate. The only family I give even the smallest shit about is the St. Vincents, and that's because my mother and I are depending on them to keep us safe.

Still, I'm not letting Cayde St. Vincent get the best of me.

And I'm definitely not going to his party.

* * *

"I can't believe we're going to the party!"

I wince. Mia's voice can apparently reach a pitch that I'm sure only dogs can properly hear, and it's painful.

That aside, over the course of the day, I think we might have actually become…friends? We have all the same classes, and despite the fact that I'm clearly a fuckup from the wrong side of the tracks who has no business even being at Blackmoor High, Mia doesn't seem to care. In fact, she seems like the most well-adjusted person I've encountered there, or probably ever will. She's legitimately happy to be at the school, not because of the glamor or attention, but because it's a good school that will get her into a better college, maybe even Blackwood University, which is one step under an Ivy League. She cares about her grades, and one glimpse inside her backpack when she unzipped it in English revealed that it was stuffed full of books that weren't even on our required reading list.

In short, Mia is exactly the kind of person I need in my life right now.

However, she did manage to convince me to go to the party, right when she figured out that I'm living directly adjacent to it.

"You live *on the estate*," she'd said at lunch, by which point I'd figured out that we were just going to be spending the rest of the day joined at the hip. "And Cayde invited you. You can't *not* go."

"I definitely can," I'd insisted.

And yet, here I am.

I don't have anything appropriate for a high school party thrown by the guys who apparently run the entire fucking place. Then again, Mia doesn't seem to either. She's wearing high-waisted jeans and a polo shirt with her glasses pushed up her nose, her curly hair pulled back into a ponytail, and sneakers. Her sense of style is completely non-existent, which is just another of the things I'm rapidly starting to love about her.

"Here." She throws me a black cropped t-shirt—cropped by yours truly, complete with ragged and fraying hem—with a skeleton of a dinosaur on it and a pair of well-ripped black jeans. "Wear these and…those combat boots." Mia points at a pair of very-loved Docs. "And then do a bunch of makeup. Like the eyeliner you have on now but…more."

"That doesn't look like anything the other girls wear." I purse my lips. I know exactly what the girls are going to be showing up to the party in, trendy short shorts and tight little dresses, their heeled sandals alone expensive enough to have paid a month of the mortgage on my old house. Plenty of fruity-flavored, sticky lipgloss and blush high on their cheeks, eyes lined to look big and doll-like, their blonde hair highlighted to perfection.

In short, the opposite of me in every way.

"That's the *point*." Mia huffs. "You're never going to look like them, right? You don't want to, and neither do I. So wear what you like, and fuck 'em." She grins at me, displaying her mouth full of braces, and I can't help but smile back despite myself.

"Fuck 'em," I echo, and take the clothes out of her hand. I like her more every second.

Soon as nightfall hits, we hear the trickling of voices and music coming out of the big house across the massive lawn that separates the Blackmoor mansion from the servants' housing. The main part of the estate itself is huge and sprawling, with a sparking, Olympic-sized pool out back that's now still and deep blue, reflecting the lights all around the back of the house. There's a hot tub out there too, and as Mia and I approach, I can see tons of kids hanging out back there, some of them already making out in the hot tub. They all have drinks in hand, and I can see a flicker of anticipation in Mia's eyes as she pulls me forward. "I've never been to a party here before," she says, her voice full of nervous excitement.

"Cayde didn't invite you." I glance at her. "Is that going to be a problem?" I don't know how any of this works, and to tell the truth, I don't really care. I'm definitely not going alone.

Mia shrugs. "If anyone asks, I'm your date, and you swing both ways." She grins at me, laughing. "Then we'll both be mysterious and exciting."

I choke back a laugh, looking at her. There's never been a person who looks less "mysterious and exciting" than Mia, but the fact that she clearly doesn't care is one of her best traits. She's just here to have fun, and she's not about to let anyone stop her.

We walk into the house without anyone asking why we're there. And it's not really a surprise; the party is already well underway. And holy shit, is it a party. It's not anything like the couple times I've gone to ones that kids at my old high school threw when we all drank bottom-shelf vodka out of red Solo cups and danced in someone's living room to a Spotify playlist the host threw together of whatever was most popular at the moment.

There's a DJ in the main room—an actual, live DJ, with lights and everything, spinning requests, and the major hits. The room is dark, clogged with bodies swaying and grinding together, still holding those red cups, but I bet they're not full of charcoal-filtered vodka. That's just confirmed when Mia and I push our way into the massive kitchen and see the alcohol bottles scattered over the marble-topped island—it's all top-shelf stuff. Some of the brands are ones I don't even recognize. Hell, there's even a bottle of Laphroaig scotch there, as if high school kids drink scotch, and I know how much a bottle of that costs because I heard my dad get upset at my mom once when she bought him a bottle for his birthday. But for these people, that's probably bottom-of-the-barrel shit.

I grab the bottle and raise it to my lips, turning it up and taking a huge swig. "Athena!" I hear Mia gasp, shocked, but I'm suddenly really pissed. This is the kitchen my mom works in, the house she helps clean, and tomorrow after they've trashed it, she'll have to come in and clean up their vomit and their spills, the sticky-sweet red stains on the marble, and the trash already on the floor where someone was too drunk to get it into the garbage can. None of these rich, privileged assholes are going to clean up after themselves. They're going to pass out and then let the people they think are lesser than them pick up the mess.

I've never had scotch in my life. Still, I gulp it down, the smoky, spicy heat swamping my senses, burning all the way down into my gut. I'm so angry that the bottle is just left out like it's nothing when I clearly remember my mom crying in the bathroom years ago because she'd just wanted to surprise my father with his favorite liquor, one that he hadn't had in a long time. She'd spent most of the utility money on it. We'd been without lights for three days, and she'd cried every single one of them.

My father never did drink that bottle. It gathered dust in a cabinet all the way until the house burned down. I wonder, as I swallow down the fiery gulps of alcohol, if the bottle made it through the fire, if the people who cleaned it up found it and someone took it home, if someone right now is drinking a glass of the scotch that caused one of the only fights I ever remember hearing between my parents.

The bottle is half empty before I give up, slamming it down on the counter so hard that for a minute, I think it might break.

"Let's get the fuck out of here," I tell Mia, already feeling a little woozy from drinking so much, so fast, when I never really do. "I don't want to be around these people a second longer."

"O-okay," she says hesitantly, and I can see the disappointment in her face, but I can't bring myself to care. Mia is nice and all, but I've known her for less than twenty-four hours. Right now, that's not enough to stop the boiling rage in my gut or the fact that I wish I could set *this* house on fire, burn every one of these fuckers to the ashes that my old life is in.

We start to push our way through the throng of people in the rooms between the kitchen and the back deck, but it's hard to get through. I change direction, Mia still following in my wake, going straight for the first gap in the crowd that I see. This place is packed, and I haven't even caught a glimpse of the guy who invited me in the first place.

"Where *is* Cayde anyway?" I mumble as I push through the doors in front of me, stumbling into a huge room that's blissfully, gloriously almost empty. It smells like leather and paper, and as I sway a little in the center of the room, Mia behind me, I feel my stomach turn over, still burning from the scotch.

In retrospect, I probably should have eaten before we came.

"Right here, sweetheart."

The bemused voice makes me spin on my heel at the same moment that I hear Mia squeak, and I see Cayde himself standing in front of me, leaning against a leather armchair with a smirk on his face. How is he so fucking hot? I think blearily, looking at him for the first time out of his school uniform. He's wearing black joggers that look casual but probably cost an obscene amount of money and a tight grey t-shirt that outlines all of the muscles on his chest and abdomen, the sleeves tight around his bulging arms. *He must play some kind of sport.*

And then, in the next moment, as he pushes himself off of the chair and walks towards me, I shake my head, trying to clear the fuzzy feeling. I hate guys like him. Arrogant, self-obsessed pricks, all of them. I shouldn't be attracted to him. I'm *not* attracted to him. It doesn't matter how chiseled his jaw is, how his arms flex when he crosses them over his chest as he stops in front of me. He's super tall, his dark blond hair falling forward a little as he studies me. "You smell like alcohol," he says darkly, and I glance around to see where Mia is, but I don't see her.

"It's a party," I manage, mustering every bit of defiance I have. *Fuck, fuck, fuck. What if he's pissed? What if he tells his dad to fire my mom and kick us both out? I should never have come—*

"Word is that the new little goth girl at Blackmoor was chugging down half a bottle of scotch in the kitchen. Expensive scotch, too."

I stifle a laugh that turns into a hiccup. That was hardly expensive in Cayde's world. But I can tell that he's trying to shame me, make me feel small. *I'm not going to let him,* I think to myself, but I can't seem to get my thoughts straight. "I'm not goth," I manage, looking up at him with a mouth that suddenly feels dry.

His eyes rake over my body, and I suddenly feel hot and uncomfortable. "Could have fooled me," he says, his voice low and dark, taking in my cropped t-shirt, my ripped jeans, my boots. The thick black eyeliner around my eyes. "You have pretty eyes," he says, reaching for my chin as he tips my face up. "Shame they're hidden with all that crap."

"I like it," a voice says from behind me, and I jerk my head around, out of Cayde's grasp, to see who spoke. It's one of the guys who were with Cayde earlier, not the one with the ice-blue eyes but the other guy, the one who looked so out of place in his uniform, with his hair shaved on the sides. I notice now that his ears are slightly gauged, not too big but about the size of a pencil eraser, and he has a ring through one side of his lip. "She looks like a *bad* girl."

There's such raw lust in his voice that it jolts something deep inside me, something I haven't felt before and definitely don't want to feel now. As I sway on my feet, as Cayde grabs my chin and pulls my face back around to look at him, I realize that the other guy is behind me too, the one with blue eyes. They're caging me in, moving me closer to Cayde, and I have an instinctive, gut feeling that I need to get out of this room. But I can't seem to move. My stomach does a flip, and I swallow hard.

"Are you a bad girl?" Cayde asks, his voice deceptively low.

If anyone else had asked, someone from my old high school maybe, I would have said a resounding yes. I've always been a bad girl in everyone else's eyes, everyone but my parents. Even my friends thought so, and they loved me for it. Athena Saint, queen of the bad girls, daughter of a biker enforcer, willing to put her fist in the face of anyone who had anything to say about it. But I know that's not the kind of bad girl Cayde means. He's not talking about the girl who knocked a guy out with a skateboard or broke a guy's nose for feeling her up.

When he says "bad girl," what he really means is "slut." And that I'm not, and never have been.

The truth is, I'm still a virgin.

"No," I whisper, feeling my stomach turn over again. I look up at him, and I know my eyes must be huge, begging, and I hate myself for it. I can feel the heat of the other two guys at my back, their muscled, large bodies boxing me in, keeping me here for Cayde's pleasure. Because the part of me that is sending alarms throughout my entire body, the knowledge that all women have deep down, knows that's where this is going.

That's probably why he invited me to the party in the first place.

"I think you are. I think only bad girls chug scotch in other people's kitchens and then try to leave without even enjoying the party. You just wanted a little taste of the high life, right?" He grins. "I know who you are now, Athena Saint. You don't belong at Blackmoor. You're just my father's latest charity case." His expression darkens. "But I don't do charity. And I don't like being tricked. Do I, boys?"

"No," the voices behind me answer, and I can hear humor in them both. They're enjoying this, enjoying my humiliation, enjoying the power they all have over me.

"There was a time when girls like you would have to kneel to their betters," Cayde says, his grip loosening on my chin so that he's almost stroking my face, the gentleness of the gesture at odds with the darkness in his voice. "I think it would be a good time to get back to that tradition. Down on your knees, little Saint. I think it's time to find out just how much of a sinner you really are."

"Fuck you," I snap, reeling back. I feel sick, the scotch turning my empty stomach to acid, but I have enough of my senses left to know that there's no way in hell I'm kneeling down for this asshole. I'll kick him in the balls before I let him force me onto my knees, or to do anything else.

"Ooh, keep going," Cayde says, grinning at me. "You're getting me so fucking hard. Keep fighting, little girl. It's a nice change from the ones that go down before I even ask them to."

"The only one going down is you," I spit. "When I tell someone what you're trying to make me do when I, I—"

"When you what? Don't want to? Don't pretend you don't want my cock. Every girl in the school wants a taste of this dick." Cayde reaches for the waistband of his joggers, pushing them down. I choke back another wave of nausea as he springs out, hard and thick and bigger than I'd ever imagined a man might be in person.

I've never seen a naked dick before, and I hate that this is my first.

"No." The word slurs, but I get it out anyway. "I'm not—"

"You are, or I'll go to my father tomorrow and see about the circumstances under which you came here. After all, I hear you and your mother are in quite a mess. But maybe, since you're so tough, you'd rather not have my father's help." His erection bobs in front of me, the head red and angry and already wet with precum, and I shrink back.

But there's no use. "Get her down, boys," Cayde says, his voice suddenly impatient. "I'm tired of this game. I get her first, and then once she swallows my load, you can shoot yours wherever you want."

I feel hands on my shoulders, heavy hands, forcing me down to my knees. I land harder than I meant to, and the wood of the library floor bruises my skin, bringing tears to my eyes as I look up at Cayde.

"That's right," he says darkly. "Beg all you want. Cry, like a bad little girl who needs to learn her place." His hand wraps around his thick length, angling it towards my lips as I press them tightly together, and then—

The nausea that I've been fighting back for the next several minutes rushes up, hot and burning at the sight of Cayde pushing his dick towards my mouth. I can't stop it this time, and I don't even want to. I open my mouth for him, alright.

And vomit all over him, hard cock and all.

"*Fuck!*" Cayde shrieks and jumps back, and for a moment, he's almost comical, his joggers around his broad thighs, his splattered dick still bouncing as if it hasn't quite caught up to what's happening, still engorged. "You fucking *bitch!* Disgusting cunt! Get out! Get fucking *out!*" He's still screaming when the other two haul me to my feet, and as they spin me around, my stomach revolts one more time, just enough to spew another round of vomit over them both. I hiccup once, more bile spilling down my chin and onto my shirt, and I feel the room tilt.

Oh. So this is what it's like to blackout from drinking.

That's my last thought before my head bounces off of the library floor, and everything goes dark.

* * *

I WAKE up in the wet grass of the back lawn. Someone is shaking me, and there's a voice in my ear. My head is pounding, and my mouth feels cottony. I open my eyes blearily to see Mia's face wavering over me, her eyeliner streaked with tears and her face a mask of worry.

"Athena! Athena!"

It sounds as if she's calling my name from down a long hallway, the echo of it just barely reaching my ears. The world is still spinning sickly around me, and my aching head flops back into the grass.

I just barely manage to register that I'm topless, in just my black bra, jeans, and boots, before I pass out again.

* * *

WHEN I WAKE UP AGAIN, it's in my bed, and my alarm is shrieking, splitting my head open with the obnoxious jangling sound.

I groan, swiping at the clock and sending it tumbling off of my nightstand onto the floor. Thankfully my room is carpeted, so it doesn't crack, but I sit up anyway, suddenly guilty that I might have broken it. We can't afford to just replace things, especially when the sleek digital alarm clock next to my bed was already there when we moved in and probably costs a stupid amount of money. The kind of people who live in a mansion like the one I saw last night is the kind who would think a hundred-dollar alarm clock for the servant quarters is cheap.

I've never been hungover before, but if this is that, then I don't want it. My head feels like it's going to split open, and as I stand up slowly, pressing one hand to my forehead, I realize that there's still vomit on my chin and in my cleavage.

Gross.

As I stumble out of my room and down the hall to the shower, hoping that my mom is already at the main house and doesn't see me like this, bits and pieces of the night before come back to me. My sick anger when I stood in the kitchen with Mia. Chugging the bottle of Scotch. Wandering into the library and finding Cayde there. What he'd tried to do to me.

Waking up in the wet grass, my top gone.

At least the rest of my clothes had still been on, which means that my throwing up must have grossed them all out enough for them to not carry on with their plans for me. I grit my teeth as I strip out of my clothes and turn on the taps of the shower, trying to wrap my head around how anyone could be so entitled as to think that he and his friends have a right to have a girl suck their dicks because he invited her to a party and she drank some of his booze.

It's not like I've never seen male entitlement before, of course. Bikers tend to have the same sense of ownership over women's bodies as rich men do. But there was something different in the way Cayde looked at me, something not quite like the lewd glances and possessive comments that I'd heard around the clubhouse where my father used to hang out. Something that had made me feel small and trapped.

Just forget about it, I tell myself. If any guy back at my old school had done something like this, I'd have done something to make sure he regretted it. But here, I don't have that option. This isn't my world. I'm out of my depth, and more importantly, Cayde's father holds sway over my mother and me. His decision to keep us here or not could quite literally mean the difference between life and death for us.

So really, my only recourse is to pretend it didn't happen and hope that Cayde and his "boys" were disgusted enough by me blowing chunks all over them to stay far away from me for the rest of my time at Blackmoor.

I spend longer in the shower than I probably should, scrubbing myself until I'm as pink and raw as I can be, getting every trace of last night off of me. And then I get dressed, putting on a different uniform skirt, one that's the correct length. However much the rebel in me wants to flout the dress code, I want Cayde St. Vincent to notice me less. And if I blend in until he moves on to someone new, maybe I can avoid any more of his attention.

Fat chance. I see him before I can even get off the property, striding towards his black Bentley with his keys in hand. I swerve to one side, hoping that I can duck behind a row of hedges until he's gone and then continue my walk to school, but apparently, when it comes to Cayde, I can't catch a fucking break.

Here in the light, in the stupid school uniform, he looks a little less threatening. But not much. He's still tall and more muscular than any guy I've seen up close, his green eyes still piercing as he catches mine.

But he doesn't say anything. He just looks at me, his face carved from stone, and my heart starts to thump wildly in my chest.

Oh fuck. He's pissed. He's pissed that I puked on him and pissed that he didn't get a blowjob, and now he's going to have his dad throw us out. I can't let that happen I can't—

"I'm sorry," I blurt out, knotting my hands together in front of me. I hate this, I hate every second of feeling like a begging child in front of this guy who is literally the same age as me, and I can feel my cheeks flushing red with the shame of it.

I'm not the queen of anything anymore. I've never felt so low.

His eyes sweep over me, taking in my bare face without any makeup today, my black hair tumbling loosely around my shoulders, my normal-length skirt. His lip curls up as if in disgust, and then he turns on his heel, clicking the button to unlock his car before sliding into the dark, cool interior.

I jump when the engine turns on, the purr of it filling the air as he peels out of the driveway. My heart is still pounding, my throat tight with anxiety.

Okay, I reason with myself as I walk. He's pissed, but that doesn't really mean anything. Surely he's not going to admit to his dad that he tried to get me to blow him in the library, that he told his friends to hold me down while he did it? And even if he did, would his father really throw us out for that? I don't really know Philip St. Vincent, I've only just barely seen him, but he's given my mom a job and given me a free ride to one of the most exclusive schools in the country.

But he could lie. He could make some shit up, and who is going to say different? You?

I try to push it out of my head, but I feel sick the entire way to school. One day and I've already managed to make things even worse than they already were.

Mia is waiting for me at the gate, her curly hair braided back and her glasses sliding down her nose, and she looks worriedly at me as I catch up to her. "Are you ok? You didn't look so hot when I got you home."

"Did my mom see me?" I glance over at her.

Mia shakes her head. "No, she was already in bed. It was hard, but I managed to get you inside and in bed. You were sort of in and out, so I didn't have to carry you the whole way." She laughs. "It's a good thing you're skinny."

"So are you," I say absently, as if to assure her, but she's not looking for that.

"Are you sure you're okay? What did they do to you in there?"

It's then that I remember that I'd looked for her, and she was gone.

"Where did you go?" I look at her, frowning. "What did they do to *you*?"

"Nothing." She shakes her head. "Cayde's friends just pulled me out of the library and shut and locked the doors. I waited outside, but I couldn't hear very much over the music. And then I didn't see you again until they dragged you out. You were unconscious, and your shirt was gone, and I tried to yell at them, but they just ignored me. I followed them outside until they dumped you on the lawn and then tried to wake you up. It took a while."

"Thanks for staying," I say quietly, gripping the straps of my back-pack a little tighter. It makes me like Mia even more because I know a lot of people wouldn't have hung around. She was as out of place at that party as me, but she waited to make sure I was alright. Or as alright as I was going to be, anyway.

"Did they hurt you?" she whispers. Her face is pale, her freckles standing out more than usual.

I shake my head. "No. Not really. I'm fine. I puked all over them before they could get do much."

Mia starts to laugh, clapping a hand over her mouth. "Oh my god —oh, I'm sorry, I shouldn't laugh. But oh my god, you *puked* on Cayde St. Vincent?"

I feel a tiny flicker of a grin starting at the corners of my mouth. "I puked on all three of them," I confirm. "*All* over them. And all over Cayde's dick, too."

Mia splutters with laughter, so hard that we have to stop walking for a minute. "I wish I'd seen that. Not his dick," she clarifies. "But everything else. They so deserved it. They're such assholes to every-one. That's amazing."

I wish I felt amazing and not terrified that I'd fucked everything up by agreeing to go to that stupid party at all last night. But for just a minute, it feels good to laugh about it, to feel like I did something good and brave and cool, and not something that could potentially get my mother and I killed if Cayde twists it badly enough.

"Just forget about it," Mia continues, seeing my expression. "Don't think about him or his stupid friends. They're not worth it. They'll move on to something else before long, and until then, just try to stay away from them."

"That's what I was thinking."

We're halfway down the hall towards our lockers by now, and I glance away from Mia, only to see a crowd of students gathered around the spot where my locker is. "What the fuck?" I mutter, apparently loudly enough for several of them to turn and see me approaching.

"Oh my god, that's her," someone says, and the rest start laughing, some outright, others covering their mouths and giggling.

"That's so fucking gross," someone else says.

"Hey whore!" another guy yells. "Don't you know better than to beg to suck a guy off and then puke on him?"

My face goes red, and my first instinct is to bolt, to head straight out of the halls and as far away as I can get from all of this—from Blackmoor, from Cayde, from his sidekicks, from the group of kids gathered around my locker, all of them laughing more and more as they look at me and back at whatever drew their attention in the first place.

But I can't. Even if I were willing to back down, I have nowhere to go.

Behind me, Mia is silent.

"Get out of the way." Cayde's voice booms through the hall, and the crowd splits. He stops in front of my locker, the other two guys behind him, that same arrogant smirk plastered over his face. And then, with the students slightly dispersed, I'm able to see what they were all looking at.

My shirt from the night before, now covered with dried puke, is taped to the front of my locker. And someone has written in bright red paint across the front of it, *whore.*

The sight of Cayde standing there, looking down at me the way he did the night before, like he owns me, like he can do anything he wants with me, makes me feel sick all over again. And angry.

So fucking angry.

Everything I'd thought earlier, about keeping my head down and letting it blow over, fizzles away in a rush of pure fury as I stalk towards Cayde, my hands in tight fists as I stare up at him. "Really?" I glare straight into those sea-green eyes, feeling myself start to shake with how angry I am. "You're telling everyone I *begged* to suck you off?"

He grins down at me. "Well, that's exactly what happened, little Saint." He raises his voice, so everyone can hear him. "You followed me into the library, drunk, and begged to go down on me. Said you wanted to pay me back for everything my family has done for yours. And then when my friends Dean and Jaxon here came in to see what you were doing in the library, one of the rooms that's supposed to be off-limits during parties, you said you'd blow them too, as long as they didn't throw you out." His smile is hard, cruel as he backs me towards the lockers, right next to where my filthy, stinking shirt is hanging.

My back hits the cold metal of the locker, hard. He's close to me, too close, sneering down at me with the perfect arrogance of a man who knows he's untouchable.

"No," I whisper. "No, that's not what happened. You tried to force me to go down on you. You told me I belonged on my knees. And you tried to get your friends to hold me down while you did it." To my horror, I can feel tears at the corners of my eyes, and I bite my lip hard, willing them not to fall. I can see the other two guys watching, Dean and Jaxon; I know their names are now. Dean is looking at me with the same smirking arrogance as Cayde, but something in Jaxon's face is surprising. He doesn't look like he's enjoying this as much as the other two.

"You wanted me," I whisper. "You wanted me enough to lure me to your party and try to force me. So don't make it sound like I'm the whore."

"But you are, little Saint." His smile is so cruel, so full of the assurance that he'll never have to pay for any of this. That it'll always be girls like me who take the brunt of his desires and then get thrown away. "You and your mother and all the girls like you. You would have loved it, my cock in your mouth, pushing down your throat. You would have loved tasting my cum. You would have swallowed it all down and then begged for more."

His voice is dark, almost rasping, and I know he's turned on. I know this is making him hard, and I cringe away from him, but there's nowhere to go. "You would have begged for them, too," he says, and Jaxon clears his throat.

"Come on, Cayde, we're gonna be late."

Cayde doesn't move. "Say it louder," he dares me. "Try telling everyone that you didn't want it."

I should know better. But I try anyway. I've never been one to just back down, and this is no different.

"You tried to force me!" I say louder. "I didn't want any part of it. I told you no!"

Cayde starts to laugh, straightening and looking down at me, and the rest of the students join in, all of them laughing at me as my heart sinks. As I glance sideways, I see Mia standing away from them, clutching her bookbag, tears streaming down her face.

"Like I would bother trying to fuck the help." His face is sneering, disgusted. "I can have anyone I want. I could ask any girl here to drop down and suck me here in the halls, and they'd do it. No one would say no. No teacher would tell them to stop. No one would send me to the principal's office because anyone who tried to tell me no would be fired by the end of the day. Our families own this town and everyone in it. And that includes you, little Saint." His green eyes fix onto mine, pinning me against the locker as he digs his phone out of his pocket. "Look." He holds up his iPhone, and I try to focus on what's on the screen. It takes a second for me to understand what I'm seeing. As the images that he flips through come into focus, I can see that it's two blonde girls on the bed, bent over, still in part of their cheerleading uniforms with the skirts pushed up, legs spread so that I can practically see inside of them. All three of the guys are in the photos—Cayde, Dean, and Jaxon, all of them with their hard dicks out, in varying stages of having sex with the two girls. Mouths, hands, pussies, the guys sharing them, inside of them in every possible way, and then finally the money shot, the photos of the three guys jerking off over their faces, streaking lips and tongues with their cum. All of it lewdly displayed in front of me, and I feel a rush of anger, of shame for those girls.

Maybe they liked it. "Did they know you were taking those photos?" I challenge him, looking away from the screen. I both want to look away and don't, because as disgusting as I find all of it, there's also a strange heat flushing over my skin, a dampness between my thighs at the sight of something so blatantly pornographic, three men sharing two girls, both of whom looked ecstatic. Orgasmic, even.

"Sure." He shrugs. "But it doesn't matter. Their fathers work for mine. They'd have done anything we asked. One of them even took it in the ass. She loved every second of it. Me in her ass, Dean in her pussy, Jaxon in her mouth." He grins lasciviously down at me. "You think you could handle that, little Saint? All three of us inside of you at once. We love sharing, after all. Most of the girls in this school have taken at least two of us, and the rest are just dying to."

I fight to keep from reacting, but I can't help it. My face blushes bright red at that, at the thought of three men touching me, fucking me, when I've never even had one. My body feels tight and strange, and I swallow hard, my mouth suddenly dry, as I look up at the muscled Adonis of a boy looming over me, talking about fucking a girl with his friends like that's a totally ordinary thing to do.

"Holy shit." Cayde looks down at me, and suddenly he starts laughing. He takes a step back, his shoulders still shaking with laughter, and points at me. "You're a fucking virgin."

"What? No!" I exclaim, wanting more than anything for him to not know that, to not know that there's something of mine that's precious, untouched, something else that he could try to take away from me.

29

"No wonder you couldn't even get a cock in your mouth. You're probably a fucking dyke. That's why you puked all over it." Cayde snorts, shaking his head. "God, I didn't know it was possible for a virgin to be as whorish as you."

"I didn't—I—" I start to stammer, not knowing how to fight two such opposing things at once, his ridiculous accusation of me being a whore and also not letting him know for sure that I really am a virgin.

But it doesn't matter because he's clearly already tired of this game. "Clean that shit up," he says, pointing at my locker. "God, you really are fucking pathetic. Come on." He jerks his head to Dean and Jaxon, and they follow him as he pushes through the crowd, leaving me there slumped against the locker as the other students disperse, following him like some kind of pied piper.

Mia rushes towards me, but I hold up a hand, needing space for a second. I rip the shirt off of my locker, crumpling it up and stuffing it in the nearest trash can, and then I turn towards Mia, my jaw set.

"Once I graduate," I say with conviction, staring after the disappearing crowd. "I'm going to do every single fucking thing I can to make sure I never see Cayde St. Vincent, or either of those other two, ever again."

CAYDE

Present Day

*S*ometimes I hate my fucking life.

It's the end of the summer, and the rest of the newly-freed seniors are out living it up, sunning on the Newport beaches, taking boat rides, getting drunk with fake IDs, partying in Boston. But am I doing any of that?

No. I'm sitting in the back of my dad's Towncar, flanked by Dean and Jaxon, being taken down to the warehouse district to, and I quote, "prepare to take up my rightful place in the family business."

I can feel the tension in the car, on one side of me at least. My father is cold and stern as always, sitting across from us and staring out the window without the slightest glance in my direction. Jaxon is slumped on my left, seemingly not giving a single shit about anything going on. But Dean, on my right, is practically vibrating, sitting up stiff and straight.

I always knew it was going to be like this, that after high school, there'd be a tension between Dean and me that wasn't there before. The weight of our families' expectations, pulling us in two different directions, made that inevitable. But the truth is that I hate it. Dean is my friend, as much as Jaxon, and I'd like for that never to change.

If I had it my way, we'd have stayed in high school forever, fucking vapid cheerleaders and playing sports and drinking underage while we threw ragers at the Blackmoor mansion. None of the responsibility of being adults and all of the fun.

But now we're all eighteen, pushing nineteen since all of us have winter birthdays, and it's time to start "acting like men," as all of our fathers would say. As if they don't do the same shit—fuck and drink and cheat and lie.

What's the point of money and power if you don't get to use it to make others do what you want?

The car rolls to a stop in front of a huge metal warehouse, and I can see other cars parked out front, as well as several Harleys, and I know then what we're going to find inside. The bikers being here means they've found someone, or someones, who need to face our fathers' particular brand of justice. Someone who's fucked up in a very significant way.

Seeing the bikes makes me think of something else, though, or rather—*someone*. Someone who shouldn't take up even an ounce of space in my head, but who I haven't been able to shake loose since the first time I literally ran into her two years ago on the steps of Blackmoor High.

Athena Saint.

She's the daughter of one of these bikers, or rather, was. I did a little digging into her past after that fateful night when she made an enemy out of me, and figured out who her father was. A rat, someone who turned state's evidence and who paid the price. I'm not sure why my father chose to shelter her and her mother rather than let the club do what they wanted. I'm equally unsure as to why he chose to not only do that, but give Athena a free ride to Blackmoor.

Something about her had piqued my interest from the second I saw her on those steps. She wasn't anything like the girls I was used to, girls with sticky gloss on their lips and high-pitched voices who were all too easy. I was sick of them, sick of the way they rolled onto their backs without my even having to ask, sick of their sloppy blowjobs, and the way every hole in their bodies was easily mine for the taking. Mine, and Dean's and Jaxon's.

Fucking stops being fun after a while when it's just handed to you. When it doesn't take any real effort.

All I'd had to do was take one look at Athena Saint to know she'd take some effort. That she'd put up a fight. And that had made me instantly harder than I'd been in months.

At first, when I first saw her, I'd thought that she was the daughter of some rich family, a black sheep, someone who liked to pretend to be edgy and rebellious. I hadn't thought that she really *was* that girl, lowborn trash, the daughter of a biker and the new housekeeper.

But in a way, that had made it even better. I'd been into the idea of forcing some rich fucker's daughter to bend over for me, but knowing Athena was no better than the help had really gotten me hard. She was meant for me, meant to kneel and service me in any way I pleased. After all, my father had brought her and her mother to the house. What better reason than so I could have a girl to meet my every demand at a whim, not one who did it because she wanted to cling on to my status, but because she had no other choice?

That whole fantasy had been shattered when she'd not only fought back, but fucking puked all over my friends and me. She'd almost made a laughingstock out of me. The only thing I could do then was shame her until she'd become a pariah at the school, an outcast, the laughs, and name-calling following her all the way to graduation. The dirty little slut who got drunk at a party and puked on *me*, Cayde St. Vincent. It really was a story that wouldn't die.

But unfortunately, that meant not getting to fuck her. Once I dragged her through the mud, it would have looked too bad for me to actually stick my cock in her.

That should have been the end of it. I should have washed my hands of her and moved on to my next target, my next conquest. But I couldn't seem to get her out of my head. Every time I fucked some simpering cheerleader after that or some hanger-on after a game, all I saw were Athena's blue-grey eyes staring up at me defiantly when I backed her up against that locker telling me that she hadn't wanted it. That she hadn't wanted *me*.

What a fucking joke.

Everyone wants me. I'm fucking Cayde St. Vincent. And most of them want all three of us—myself, Dean Blackmoor, and Jaxon King. The rulers of Blackmoor High, for all four fucking years. And it's going to be no different tomorrow when we head to Blackmoor University and pretend to give a shit about our grades for another four years until we walk across another stage and then go on to our respective places in the family business.

But the best part is yet to come.

I shift in my seat as the car comes to a stop, thinking about the other part of all this, about the girl who will be literally at our whim for four years. There's no telling who she will be, but just the thought of that, of having the girl that's chosen for us at our beck and call while we play the game, makes my cock twitch.

God, it's fucking good to be me.

I'm going to win, of course. There's no chance in hell that I'm letting control of the town go back to the Blackmoors, or God forbid, the Kings. My father might literally kill me. He won the estate and the town back for our family when he was the one at university, and it's up to me to make sure it stays that way.

The August heat burns into my back as we walk towards the warehouse, falling in step behind my father. Two bikers are guarding the door, guns in hand, and I can hear the screams from inside. Whoever's in there, they're working him over good.

Or rather, *them*. When we step inside, the heat inside the metal building nearly suffocating. There are *three* men tied to chairs, all of them blood-soaked. They're sweating profusely, their shirts sticking to them, and I can see that whatever information they had, whatever they did, they've already given it all up and paid almost in full. They're all slumped forward, bearing the marks of a dozen wounds and far worse.

The hefty man in front of them wearing the leather cut emblazoned with the *Devil's Sons* patch on the back and *Blackmoor* below it turns to face us, his heavy beard dark with sweat and his long hair plastered back against his head. "They're all but done, boss," he says, glancing at my father. "We've gotten all we're going to get."

"We know who shorted us on the shipment?" My father looks coolly at the three men, his face impassive. There's nothing about his bearing or expression that indicates he's in the slightest bit alarmed by the state of the three men, who are all whimpering faintly, flanked by two more bikers.

"This one, Mr. St. Vincent." The man standing behind the one in the center nods. He's taller than the rest, with dark blond hair and narrowed blue eyes. "He stole the drugs. He'd planned to sell them on the side, make a little extra money. As if you don't pay him enough already." He cuffs the man hard on the back of the head, and the man lurches forward, blood dripping onto the floor from his mouth.

I feel a faint quiver in my stomach, but I ignore it. This is the least of the things I'll see as a man in the St. Vincent family. Glancing at Dean and Jaxon next to me, I can see that Dean is as unaffected as my father, his face completely impassive and his ice-blue eyes hard as gems. Jaxon, on the other hand, looks slightly green. He's visibly affected by the sight in front of us, and I grit my teeth.

"Get it together," I hiss at him, and Jaxon glances at me, his eyes troubled.

"This is—" he starts to speak, but my father starts talking, drowning him out before he can say anything more, which is probably for the best.

"Just the one in the middle?" My father sounds almost disappointed.

The other two bound men take that opportunity to start pleading, through mouths mostly divested of their teeth, the words thick and sloppy. "Please, Mr. St. Vincent, we didn't—we didn't know, we were just there helping unload the shipment, we didn't have shit to do with it! Please, we told the others, we didn't know, we didn't—"

"Shut them up," my father growls, and the two bikers flanking the three chairs deliver solid punches, one to the jaw and one to the gut, leaving the two men sobbing and gagging.

Jaxon looks like he might throw up, too. "If they didn't—"

Once again, he's interrupted. "Give them the guns," my father says coldly.

My suspicions are confirmed as the hefty biker hands us each a gun, his face as blank as anyone else's here. These are his men, but he's tortured them almost to death. I can't help but wonder how that makes him feel, if he's burning with anger under that carefully neutral expression, if he wants my father dead. Especially if the two others are telling the truth about having had nothing to do with it.

Dean's uncle and Jaxon's father step up then, next to my father. Mark Blackmoor and Nathan King, both of them dressed like my father in expensive tailored suits, looking entirely out of place in the bare, hot warehouse.

"This is your rite of passage, boys," Mr. Blackmoor says, his gaze fixed coldly on us. His eyes are the same hard ice blue as Dean's, impassive and emotionless. "The first step in becoming men, and the true heirs of the founding families. These men have been found guilty of working against us after we brought them into the fold, gave them the means to make a living and support their families. The punishment for betraying the families is death." He looks at each of us in turn as if to drive that last point home.

"No! We didn't—tell him, we didn't have anything to do with it! Please, it was Corey, not us, don't kill us, we didn't—" The men are still begging, saliva and blood dripping onto the floor, tears making dirty tracks down their cheeks. No noble death for these men, they're willing to plead and cry for their lives, and after all, would I really do so much better in their place? I can't imagine the kind of pain these men have been through this afternoon. I can't help but wonder if my father—all of our fathers—would be so careless about it if they had to inflict the torture rather than just come in at the end to oversee the results.

Something curdles in my stomach at the whole thing, especially since I can't help but believe that the men on either side of the one in the center—Corey—actually had nothing to do with this. They were just in the wrong place at the wrong time. Unfortunately, the ones picked to go along with Corey to pick up the shipment he decided to short. And as a result, they've become part of the grotesque passage that our families put us through. My father did this, and so did Dean and Jaxon's, their fathers before them, and theirs before them. It's how things are, and these men are only guilty of not being us.

But I know better than to argue. And in the end, maybe it's better for these men to die. Their lives weren't great before this, and they certainly won't be worth living now after the injuries they've sustained.

It's a mercy, really, like putting down a sick dog.

I tell myself that, because it's easier than looking the truth head-on for what it is, that we're about to kill three men so that we can begin to take up our place as potential heirs to our fathers' lands, estates, and wealth. It's *my* first step down the path towards retaining the St. Vincent hold on the town of Blackmoor and all it holds. It's my job to make certain that it stays in my family's hands, and that's been made clear to me since I was old enough to even vaguely understand. To make certain that Dean and Jaxon continue to be *my* backup, my side-kicks, and not the other way around.

The bikers move out of the way, leaving plenty of space for us. Our fathers stand to one side, and then there are only the three men seated in front of us, spaced out so that we each have our own clear target. We weren't assigned one, but as we stand, I've got the one in the center, Dean the one on the left, and Jaxon the one on the right.

This means I have the easy part in this, mostly. I know my target's name, which makes it a little more personal, but I have the satisfaction of knowing that he's guilty. That he stole from my family. He committed an unforgivable crime, and that will make it easier to pull the trigger.

In the end, it's almost *too* easy. I know how to shoot, I've been taken to target practice since I could hold a gun, and I push every thought and emotion out of my head as I level the gun at Corey. He isn't crying, not like the others. He seems to know there's no way out of this. Maybe he's even grateful for the bullet that will put him out of his misery.

It comes down to one single motion, pulling my finger back. Too simple a gesture for taking a man's life. It's a split second's decision, the signal from my brain running down to my index finger and telling it to press down, and that's the difference between living and dying.

The sound echoes in the warehouse, almost too loud. I hit my target spot-on, I can see the proud look on my father's face, and I let it warm me, let myself feel that instead of the sick knowledge that I just killed a man. My first, and possibly not my last.

"Please, no, I—!"

The second shot goes off. Dean's. Quick and efficient, his face cold and hard. Not a trace of emotion, a perfect hit, just like mine. He lowers the gun to his side, motionless, and Mr. Blackmoor nods. No pride for Dean, just the weight of expectation. Sometimes I think he has it even harder than I do.

Now there's only Jaxon left. His target is blubbering still, pleading, his words almost nonsense now from his sheer terror. I can see Jaxon's hand wavering, his fingers trembling around the grip of the gun.

"Fucking get it together, Jaxon," I hiss. "Remember who you fucking are. You're a King. A founding son. This man is nothing."

"He didn't do it." Jaxon's voice is a whisper.

"It doesn't fucking matter. The wasps outside of my window didn't sting me, but I killed them all the same. You've been given an order. Do it. Or do you want to take his place?"

Jaxon swallows hard at that.

Closes his eyes.

The third shot goes off.

And then another.

His target is a mess. He missed the first shot, or rather—he hit the guy but didn't kill him. The second shot finishes it, but his wasn't a clean kill, and I can see the rage in his father's face at Jaxon's failure.

"He suffered more because of your weakness," I hiss at Jaxon, looking at his pale face. And then his father grabs him by the collar, hauling him outside of the warehouse, his expression furious.

"You did well, son," my father says, walking up to me. I turn away from the bodies to speak to him, not wanting to watch as the bikers close in to remove them. I can't think too much about it, about how seconds ago they were living, breathing, begging men, and now they're nothing. Just sacks of meat and bone.

"You've accomplished the first step," Mr. Blackmoor says quietly to Dean as he and my father guide us towards the door. "The rest is easier. Congratulations, boys."

"Thanks," Dean says gruffly. I can't quite form words yet, but I feel a sense of relief that it's over. I always knew this was coming. Now it's behind me. It will never be quite this hard again.

Outside, Jaxon is bent over, wiping his mouth. There's a puddle of vomit on the concrete, and his father is nowhere to be seen.

"You alright?" I narrow my eyes at him, pausing as he straightens up, his face still pale.

"He's pissed at me. But I'll survive." Jaxon shrugs, his mouth twisting with humor that I know he doesn't really feel. We've spent too much time together for me not to know him well, grown up side by side our whole lives. I might be an asshole, but I notice things about my friends.

"You need to get it together," I tell him flatly. "Our families don't have any place for weakness. And that's exactly what that was."

"Oh, for fuck's sake. Sorry I had a hard fucking time blowing the head off of an innocent man." Jaxon spits the words out, a red flush of rage appearing high on his cheekbones. "You might be chill with all of this, Cayde, but I'm fucking not."

"And what are you going to do about it, then?" I glare at him. "What, judge Dean and I for doing our duty? You fired your shot, too, in the end. Two of them, and you put your target through more pain because you couldn't get your shit together."

"He was a man. Not a 'target.'" Jaxon shakes his head in disgust. "Maybe you can disassociate all this, man, but I can't."

"It's part of this life. What are you going to do, leave?"

Jaxon presses his lips together. I know he wants to fire back some retort, but I know he's also wise enough to know the dangers of that. Being his father's son doesn't give him much protection that he

39

doesn't have to earn, not anymore, anyway. Now we're on the path to being men. Our fathers expect us to reflect on the brutality and cold-decision making that got our families to where they are.

"You know I don't care about the inheritance."

"I do." My voice is flat and cold. I don't have time for Jaxon's emotions. "And Dean does. So get with the program, Jaxon, or get the fuck out. I won't have use for you otherwise."

There's a long silence, and neither one of us speak. Jaxon's dark eyes look troubled. "See you tonight," he says finally, turning away from me and walking back towards his father's car, his hands shoved in his pockets and his shoulders hunched forward.

I let out a sigh, letting him get several paces away before I follow. It's going to be a long four years if Jaxon balks at every little thing.

The ride back to the estate is silent. My father doesn't seem to have any other words of encouragement or advice for me, at least not now. He looks lost in thought, and I'm fine with it. I don't really have the capacity to make conversation right now, either.

There's a long night ahead of us all. Then tomorrow, I'll make the drive to Blackmoor University on the coast, along with Dean and Jaxon, to settle in before the semester starts. We'll be living in the main house on campus, the envy of all the other students.

It'll be good to be the lords of campus again, to wield our power and influence over the others. To be in a place that feels comfortable, natural, and right.

Today I felt out of my depth. That's not something I enjoy.

"Don't be late tonight, son," is all my father has to say as the car comes to a stop in front of the mansion, and he steps out. He doesn't give me so much as a backward glance as he walks up the steps, but it's something I'm used to. My father has never been the warm and cuddly type. Then again, neither has my mother. There's always been something reticent about her, slightly pinched, especially when my father comes into the room. She keeps to herself more often than not.

Some say our family is cursed since we took over the town from the Blackmoors.

I think that's fucking ridiculous.

There's the sound of dishes clinking together as I pass the massive kitchen. I glance sideways and catch a glimpse of one of the house-keepers, a slightly pudgy woman with long, braided black hair, putting them away. But it's not her that I notice so much as the girl standing next to her, helping.

Athena.

My cock lurches in my jeans, an almost Pavlovian response to her at this point. It makes me boiling mad with rage every time because there's no fucking reason I should want her as much as I do. No reason why just the sight of her thick black hair pulled back in a high ponytail makes me think about wrapping it around my fist while I force her mouth down onto me or drive into her from behind.

I can have any girl I want, but for some reason, this one just won't stay out of my fucking head. She never has, not since the day I ran into her on the steps, and definitely not since the day I pinned her up against those lockers. She still defied me, in front of half the student body, no less.

I want to punish her for it. I want to master her, to finally see those wide round eyes look up at me while she pleads for my cock. I want to reduce her to what every other girl I've fucked is, just a series of holes for me to pleasure myself with and then toss aside.

That's the only way I can think of to satisfy the desire for her that just won't fucking go away.

Except—I'm hoping there might be another way. For the last two years, I've thought about her pretty face and perfect body every time I jerked myself off. Still, I haven't fucked her—not just because she flat out refused, but also because I couldn't let it get around that I'd fucked the same girl whose reputation I'd turned to shit, who I'd told everyone was a disgusting whore that I wouldn't let near my cock if she was the last girl on earth.

But tomorrow I leave for university. A new start, a fresh crop of girls from freshman all the way to senior to fuck. Surely there'll be at least one of them there that won't drop to her knees the second she sees me. Someone who can give me a little bit of a challenge.

I'll get through tonight, I tell myself as I stride towards my room, forcing myself not to look back for one more glimpse of Athena. *And then I'll leave for university tomorrow, and that glimpse I just got will be the last time I ever see her.*

I'll be the prince of the whole fucking school again, the heir to everything Blackmoor, and I'll fuck Athena out of my head. I'll never think about her again.

All I need is to put some distance between us, and I'll be able to forget about her.

I know it.

CAYDE

*D*espite those assurances to myself, I'm still hard when I get into the shower to rinse the blood off my face and arms from the work earlier, Athena's face swimming in my thoughts. The combined stress of the day and the anticipation of the night to come has my body humming with eagerness, and seeing her on my way through the house only added fuel to the fire.

I know I don't have much time before I need to get dressed for tonight, but my cock doesn't seem to care. I'm so hard that the head is nearly brushing my abdomen, pre-cum leaking from the tip as I try to ignore it, forcing myself to think about anything else in an effort to get my stubborn erection to deflate.

It doesn't work. No matter what I think about, Athena's face flickers back into my head, that thick dark hair and those full lips, the defiance in her eyes that makes my balls tighten and ache every time I think about it.

Fuck. I reach down, gripping my cock tightly in my hand. *Just a quick stroke.* It never takes me long when I think about her—less time than I'd like to admit, really, but if I got my hands on her, I'd make it last. I'd savor every second, fucking her until she was quivering, weak from orgasms—or maybe I wouldn't let her come. Maybe I'd pin her down, make sure her slender fingers couldn't get to her clit, fuck her hard until I was ready and she was on edge, and then take her ass. Unless she turned out to be one of those girls who came from anal, a truly bad girl. My little sinner Saint.

"Oh fuck yeah," I mutter under my breath, stroking harder. "That's it. Fuck yes." My old standby is to picture her up against the locker that day, her lips parted, eyes indignant. I imagine shoving her down to her knees, pulling my cock out in front of all the students there and feeding it to her, forcing the swollen head between her lips and seeing her mouth open for me, feeling her tongue sliding down my shaft, her throat tightening around me as I choke her with my thick length.

But today, I have a new fantasy. I think about her in the kitchen, in those tight black leggings she had on. I picture myself bending her over the marble-topped island, yanking them down to her thighs so that she can't move, so that they're squeezed together, her pussy lips poking out as I press my cock against them. I picture them, puffy and pink, dripping with the arousal she swears she doesn't feel. But of course, she does. All girls do, there's not a girl in Blackmoor who wouldn't beg for my cock, and Athena Saint will do the same, she'll beg for it in her mouth and her pussy and everywhere else, she'll beg and beg, until I fuck her hard until she's screaming, and then I'll watch my cum drip down her thighs and over her lips and ass and—

"Fuck!" I shout, almost loudly enough to be heard above the spray of water in the shower, my hand a blur on my cock as my balls tighten, that last electric surge of pleasure before my orgasm filling me, and I groan aloud.

And then someone bangs on the door, loudly enough to jolt me out of the fantasies of my cum oozing out from between Athena's full lips…and just in time to ruin my fucking orgasm.

"Cayde! Are you in there? Hurry the fuck up, man, you're going to be late!"

Fucking Christ. Nothing ruins a good orgasm like hearing your buddies yelling your name on the other side of the bathroom door. It's too late to stop, but I'm so distracted that I barely notice the streams of cum shooting out of my cock, splattering the shower floor without much pleasure, the repetitive pounding on the door taking me completely out of the moment.

"Fuck you!" I yell. "I'll be out in a minute."

"Oh, sorry, man, you were jerking it, weren't you? Thinking about the girl tonight?" Jaxon is laughing on the other side, and I grit my teeth.

"Fuck off. I was just washing my hair. Got some soap in my eyes."

"Sure." Jaxon snorts. And then: "Leave me alone, Dean! Mr. St. Vincent sent us to get him."

"He'll be out in a minute. Come on, let's go."

Dean sounds as humorless as I would have expected. He's the most uptight of the three of us, and with good reason. There's a generation's worth of weight on his shoulders, his father's failure to keep my father from taking ownership of the town, and the expectation that he should be the one to get it back. Beyond that, he's the only one of us with a true title—Lord Blackmoor, passed down since his father's death. And he acts like it, too, with all the straight-edged, stick-up-his-ass attitude that you'd expect from someone with a proper English title. It's irritating as fuck, most of the time. Almost more than Jaxon's carelessness.

I finish showering quickly, turning off the water and drying off at an impressive speed. I don't want to deal with how pissed off my father will be if I'm late, though. At least for now, my dick is leaving me alone—my orgasm might have been shitty, but it at least cleared my head.

A suit is required for the night, which is annoying in and of itself. It's hard to get one tailored correctly to fit me, as muscled as I am, and they always feel too tight, even if they look perfect. *Especially* if they look perfect, honestly. It's my least favorite thing and yet another reason to look forward to leaving for university. Joggers and t-shirts all day, baby.

Neither Dean nor Jaxon is waiting for me when I walk out into the hall, and I'm glad. I'm in no mood to deal with their teasing, and all I want is to get the evening over with. I've never been particularly fond of the pomp and ritual that our families so enjoy.

45

The Blackmoor mansion is hundreds of years old, and the layout reflects that—complete with a great hall and a ballroom that is reserved for events just like this. Everyone who is anyone, from Newport to Boston to Manhattan and everywhere in between, is in attendance. It's only the oldest sons who vie for the right to be heir, which means that the children born after that, sons or daughters, are sent out into the greater world to do great things—make money, build a business, make profitable marriage alliances. The Blackmoor roots have spread over the centuries, and the hall is full tonight, families seated at the round tables in a way that encourages mingling and brokering deals. This is the biggest fucking network event of the generation until Dean, Jaxon, and I have sons of our own to start the cycle all over again.

Which is a weird thought. I love sex more than just about any other fucking thing in existence, but the idea of having a kid is so foreign to me that I can't even really imagine it. Still, it'll happen eventually. There would be no way around that, even if I wanted to avoid it. It's my duty to produce an heir, just as it was my duty to kill that man this afternoon, and it's my duty to participate in what will happen here tonight.

We're not seated with our families. Instead, we're seated with others who share some of our interests, who might make good connections, who we can strike up a conversation with. For instance, I'm seated at the table of a former IRB World Champion of the Year for Rugby, his *much* younger wife, and their daughter, who can't be more than eighteen if she's a day. She's looking at me like she's starstruck from the moment I sit down, her thin cheeks flushing, her pointed chin dipped down as she looks at me with wide, sparkling blue eyes.

Normally, that would be enough to make my dick twitch with definite interest. She looks like the shy type, maybe even a virgin, the type who would pretend not to want it until I had her impaled on my cock, and then she'd start squirming, yelping, squealing with pleasure. She'd come without my even trying, her submissive nature awakened by my muscled bulk pinning her down to the bed.

46

"Nice evening for a party, isn't it?" The girl's father, Richard Cushing, smiles politely at me. "I heard you're headed for the rugby team at Blackmoor."

I answer his questions, ask a few of my own, make small talk with his wife, all the while wondering smugly if he knows that I'm thinking about splitting his daughter open in bed. It's that moment of conquering that really gets me off, knowing that I'm the one in control, the one with the power. Your daughters aren't safe with me. Maybe not even your wives.

I'm Cayde St. Vincent, and my father owns this town.

One day I will, too.

But even looking at the daughter—her name is Alice, I think—I don't feel the things I usually would. And the reason for it makes me fucking furious because it's not that I'm not attracted to her. She's my usual type, frail and blonde and pretty, with a full bottom lip that begs to be bitten in the throes of passion. No, I'm pissed because looking at her, all I can think about is a very different girl, one with black hair and sharp, piercing eyes, one who looked at me as if she wanted to break me instead of fuck me.

The dinner is delicious, of course, and I make a point of enjoying it. Once I leave for university, I'll be back on a strict training diet for rugby, but tonight I stuff myself on Caesar salad, chilled gazpacho, roast lamb, braised scallops, crisp vegetables, and fudge cake, all washed down with plenty of the best wine my father could bring up from the cellar. I don't actually like wine all that much, it's either too achingly sweet or annoyingly drying, and I feel pretty much the same way about champagne. Beer or tequila would be my preference any day. But for an event as exclusive as this one, only vintage bottles of wine will do.

After dinner, there's still the "reception" to get through, which is really just an exceptionally classy afterparty. That's held in the ballroom, with servers carrying around trays of champagne and dessert wines and very small desserts on very miniature plates. I catch a glimpse of my mother gliding through the crowd, in the latest by some famous designer, I'm sure, convinced of her beauty and usefulness for this one night at least. My father is next to her, and while tomorrow he'll go back to ignoring her as he usually does, for tonight at least they're the picture of wealthy romance.

That'll be my future, I think grimly. A wife I don't love, possibly even one I hate, but who fits my needs and the needs of my family. Plenty of pussy on the side when I want to actually get laid. And then—

"Cayde!" Jaxon slaps me on the back, jolting me out of my thoughts. "Hell of a party for us, huh? Not your usual graduation blowout." He looks around the room with a smirk. "To be honest, I think I would have preferred a kegger and some strippers."

"You and me both."

"Neither of you have any taste." Dean slides up next to us both, the picture of elegance in his perfectly pressed suit. He's a runner, so he never has a problem finding a tailor who can make a suit to his exact specifications.

My father didn't really want me to play rugby. He said it was a brutish sport, not gentlemanly, and he'd pointed to Dean as an example of what I should have done instead—track or soccer. He'd gone on and on about head injuries and how he wanted a son with brains, not brawn, and all that other shit. But in the end, I'd gotten my way.

Rugby is the one thing I can control. The one thing in my life that I've chosen for myself. And it's a good feeling to have that.

"You look like you're looking for someone," Dean says, following my gaze as I look around the room.

"Just some good pussy," I say carelessly. I don't want to admit, not even to myself, that I can't stop looking for Athena to appear in the crowd, even though she has absolutely no reason to be at a party like this. Her mother—and probably her, too—will be cleaning up after us tomorrow, scrubbing the mansion from top to bottom. The thought of Athena on her hands and knees, scrubbing up champagne spills from the gleaming wooden floor makes me both oddly uncomfortable and strangely horny.

Of course, my brain put her in a French maid's outfit, the short skirt riding up that full ass of hers—

"Earth to Cayde." Jaxon elbows me. "Man, you are really out of it tonight. You're not usually this preoccupied."

"Just thinking about later." I shrug. "It's not like we really know what's going to go down."

All three of us are quiet for a moment. It's true that none of us know what will happen after midnight when my father will take the three of us down into the labyrinth below the mansion, where none of us have ever been allowed to go, and begin the ancient ritual.

I imagine that it's all just as archaic as that sounds. But really, there's no way to know. There are no photos, no stories. It's all shrouded in deep mystery, far more than the mason's lodges and other tamer societies that rich families in other places belong to. All we're ever told is that the firstborn sons, when they're eighteen, will be taken deep below the mansion after the banquet and reception and that we'll be initiated into the ancient rites of the Blackmoor, St. Vincent, and King families.

And that there will be a girl involved—and that she'll somehow be the key to which one of us inherits the town.

"I hope we're not all supposed to fuck her in front of everyone, or some shit like that," Dean mutters, as if reading my mind. "Who do you think the girl is, anyway? Someone here?"

I look around the room. *What if that's true?* It's hard for me to imagine, exactly. Would Richard Cushing agree to have his frail little Alice tied to an altar, spread open and waiting for the three heirs to fuck her raw? I can't deny, the thought gets me a little hard, even with Athena still in my head, distracting me.

But most likely, it's not going to be anything that insane, I tell myself. Probably just some old men chanting and trying to feel important, passing an old cup around or some shit. Nothing really dark. I can't imagine my father, or any of ours, being that cool, to be honest.

Still, I'm intrigued by the thought that it could be one of these girls in this room. The idea sounds hot enough to distract me from Athena, even if only momentarily. One of these privileged, spoiled girls, forced to do as we wish, for our pleasure. That definitely gets me hard.

Not as hard as the thought of Athena begging for it, but it'll do.

I see my father pushing through the crowd, heading towards us, and I steel myself for whatever comes next. There's no telling what kind of weird rituals the families have cooked up over the years, but we'll get through this, just like anything else. And then tomorrow we'll be off to Blackmoor, and four years of sports, fucking, and getting hammered whenever we want.

"Come on, boys." My father's face is stern and serious, and I stifle a smirk. Of course, he's going to act like this is some super-important, super-sacred thing. *Whatever.* I'll keep a straight face, and then Dean and Jaxon and I can all laugh about it later.

He leads us through the ballroom, past the crowds of laughing, dancing, drinking guests, and all the way to the kitchen. It's hot and stifling in there, the air still thick with the scents of cooked meat and roasted vegetables, oil and grease and fat lingering in the air. We're taken all the way to the back, and my father pushes open a heavy door, showing us stairs that lead down into the dark.

"Follow me," he says simply.

CAYDE

*W*e all exchange a look, but in the end, there's nothing to do but obey. This is how things are, how they've always been, and besides, we're not afraid of the dark.

If anything, what's down in the darkness should be afraid of *us*.

We have to almost feel our way down the winding steps; it's so dark. When we reach the bottom, my father reaches up, and there's a clanking sound as he brings something down from the wall.

A moment later, he lights the torch he's holding, and we're able to see the narrow hall we're standing in.

It's made of grey stone, damp in places, and beneath the bracket where the torch hung, there's a small, carved wooden table with what looks like strips of fabric laying across it. My father reaches for them and holds them out to us, his face still as impassive as if it were carved from the same stone that's all around us.

"Put these on," he intones, and we all exchange a glance.

"What is this, a fucking blindfold?" Jaxon asks, and my father glares at him, his gaze cold.

"Yes," he says crisply. "And you will wear it until you enter the hall of ritual. You will also watch your language, Jaxon King." He says the last word as if it tastes bad, a reminder that out of the three families, the Kings have failed more often than not.

Jaxon's lip curls up slightly. "I don't like the sound of any of this." He takes the blindfold from my father's hand but holds it limply, like a dead fish. "Wandering around down here in the dark?"

"You'll be led."

"Even worse."

"Fuck it." I grab my blindfold out of my father's hand. "Can we just get on with this shit already?"

I don't see the slap coming. My father's hand connects with my cheek, hard and stinging, and I recoil back from the blow. I was punished plenty as a kid, but my father has never hit me before. He said he didn't believe in hitting children when my mother wanted to spank me once.

"You're not children anymore," my father says in a low voice, as if reading my thoughts. "And you will respect this place."

Or else. I can hear the words hovering in the air, and I shiver slightly as I lift the blindfold to my eyes. I can see Dean putting his on quickly in my peripheral, and Jaxon reluctantly raising his as well.

After that, there's nothing but darkness. My other senses are keener, and I can feel the damp chill down here, smell the faint mildew in places, the stale air where there's nothing to stir it. I can feel the shape of the stones under my fine Italian leather shoes. I focus on the sound of our footsteps until, at last, I feel a shift in the air, as if the space around us has opened up, and then my father brings us to a halt.

When the blindfolds come off, it takes my eyes a moment to adjust. When they do, I'm momentarily taken aback by what I see—what's been under this house all along without my ever knowing it. We're in a large stone room, in a circular space surrounded by carved stone pillars, and there's a flat table in the center made out of—you guessed it, more stone. It can only be described as an altar, and I feel a sort of detached curiosity about what it's going to be used for. Animal sacrifice? Human sacrifice? A place to fuck one of the girls from upstairs, turn by turn?

The last would be my preference, obviously.

Dean and Jaxon's fathers are there already, shrouded in dark green robes with the hoods down. There are others there, too, the grandfathers that are still alive, and my uncle as well as Jaxon's.

I suddenly hope that there isn't any sex involved in tonight's rituals. The last thing I want to do is fuck in front of Uncle Alfred and Grandpa Oliver.

Three hooded figures that I don't recognize—mostly because I can't see their faces under the dark green, draping hoods—step up behind us, draping similar robes over our shoulders. The fabric feels heavy, and for a moment, all the humor leaves me. Whatever is going on here, *they're* taking it seriously. It seems that maybe we should, too, at least for now.

It's hard to believe that all of this is down here. All my life, I never knew. Generation after generation, men of our families have stood in this small space and performed the rituals we're about to perform. I'm only just now finding out about any of this.

It feels truly insane.

My father produces a cup out of nowhere, a huge pewter goblet with a skull embossed on three sides. Above each skull is the initial of one of the families—**SV**, **BM**, and **K**.

"Wine," my father says, his voice deep and grave, and Dean's father hands him a bottle of wine, uncorked. He fills the goblet to the brim, the dark liquid shimmering in the torchlight all around us, rippling like blood. For the first time, I start to feel something queasy in my gut. Anxiety, I guess, about what's to come. I don't dare look sideways at Dean or Jaxon to see if they're nervous, too, but I can feel Jaxon shifting on one side of me, and I know that he at least is.

"Knife."

It's Jaxon's father that hands him the knife, a long dagger with a hilt bearing three gemstones—a ruby, diamond, and what looks like black onyx. I swallow hard, hoping that no one notices. I was trying to be chill about all of this, but long sacrificial-type daggers are a reason for concern.

"Step forward to the altar."

All three of us hesitate, and the robed figures behind us put a hand on each of our backs, pushing us forward towards the altar. One by one, the men surrounding it put out their right hands, all around the goblet that's now in the center of the altar.

My father is the first to slice his thumb with the knife. He runs it around the edge of the goblet, and he doesn't wince, not even once. Not when the blade cuts into his flesh, and not when he presses the fresh wound against the pewter rim.

The knife goes to Dean's father next. And then Jaxon's. To the grandfathers, the uncles, and then at last to Dean, who is on my right. Each of them did the same, each slicing the pad of his thumb and running it along the rim of the cup.

Dean does the same without hesitation. He doesn't even flinch. His eyes are icy cold as he smears the blood atop the mingled stain of all the others, and then he hands the knife to me.

What the fuck? I wasn't prepared for this. All thoughts of ritual fucking have flown straight out of my head. I hate pain. I like *inflicting* it on others, particularly emotionally, but I don't like receiving it. The entire point of ruling is to not have to experience pain, or so I thought.

But they're waiting, and I know that if there's one thing my father truly hates, it's being kept waiting. Especially when it's important.

I'm not sure that there's anything more important to him than what happens here tonight.

I have to fight not to wince when I press the knife down against the pad of my thumb, pulling it across the flesh and watching it split in the wake of the blade, blood blooming against the gleaming silver. Swallowing hard, I reach out, hoping my hand doesn't shake as I run my thumb around the rim of the goblet, the crimson joining the rest and dripping down the sides.

I hand the knife to Jaxon.

"You've got to be fucking kidding me." His voice is dry and sarcastic, and I tense. *Shut the fuck up*, I want to hiss. But I don't. I stay quiet as I wait for my father's response.

"Do not mock the sacred ritual." His voice is low, dangerous, a warning evident in it. "Mingle your blood with the rest of the families', or be excommunicated from this place and this town forever."

The silence that follows is heavy, weighted down with the import of what he just said. Jaxon's refusal would mean being ejected not just from the ritual, from his place at my side, and in competition for the rulership of this town, but entirely. Thrown out, never allowed to return.

None of us realized that tonight held that weight, but I guess we should have.

"Well, shit," Jaxon mutters. He jerks the blade across his thumb unceremoniously, the blood welling immediately and spilling down his finger. Reaching out, he swipes it around the rim, his jaw set. It's patently obvious that all of this is making him uncomfortable—even more so than any of us. I can't help but wonder why. Is it because his family has so rarely had any real power here? Or because he doesn't actually want it?

My father reaches out, raising the goblet up with both hands. "With our blood mingled, drink from the sacred cup, and be bound forever to the rites and laws of this town and these families. Let the blood of the St. Vincents, the Blackmoors, and the Kings touch your lips, and know that your fealty is ordered, from now until your bones are dust."

"From now until our bones are dust," the others echo as my father lifts the cup and drinks.

I feel like I'm in a dream. I watch as he lowers it, his lips stained with wine and blood, and hands it to Dean's father.

"From now until our bones are dust." Our voices join in this time, Dean's clear and loud, mine slightly hesitant, Jaxon's muttered under his breath. It's repeated with each drink as the goblet passes from hand to hand, until at last, it's in Dean's grasp.

He drinks deeply, our voices rising and filling the small caverned space.

"From now until our bones are dust."

I have to take a deep breath when the goblet is passed to me. I'm not squeamish, but something in me balks, just a little, at putting my lips on a cup that's smeared with the blood of several other humans, family or not. But I know there's no choice. And at the end of the day, what's a little blood between family members and friends?

The edge of the cup tastes metallic, the wine too sweet. My stomach turns over a little at the mingled flavors, but I force myself not to think about it, handing the last of the wine to Jaxon.

He grins as he takes it, raising it up as if he's making a toast. "From now until our bones are dust," he says, and then he tilts the goblet back like he's taking a shot, swallowing the rest of the wine in one long gulp.

I can see the simmering anger in my father's eyes. Still, he says nothing, only takes the goblet when Jaxon is finished and sets it down in the middle of the altar again.

"Wine," he repeats, and Dean's father hands him the bottle once more. My father pours the last of it into the goblet, and my stomach wavers again. *I sure as hell hope we're not going to repeat that?*

"Bring in the sacrifice!" His voice echoes in the room, and I freeze, my head spinning.

Animal sacrifice? *Shit, if I'm asked to drink that blood too—*

But when the door opens, it's not an animal that's brought out.

It's a girl, shrouded in white. Her hands are bound in front of her. Her face and hair are covered in a thick, opaque white veil that's impossible to see through.

"If we're killing a girl, I'm fucking out," Jaxon hisses, too low for anyone else to hear. Or so I thought, but clearly, my father does hear him.

"Centuries ago, we sacrificed a virgin on the night of the ritual. It was her blood we would drink instead of the wine, to cement our bonds and bring our sons into manhood. New life, through the sacrifice of death. But now, we sacrifice her in a different way."

The girl makes a muffled sound, squirming in the hands of the hooded figures who flank her, but they hold her tight.

"Silence, girl!" My father's voice thunders from the room as she's pulled forward to the altar, her bound hands stretched in front of her so that she's clasping the goblet. "It is an honor to be sacrificed to the princes of Blackmoor. It is an honor to be the gambit that is thrown down so that one of them may take up their rightful place as heir."

She's still struggling, but as the hooded figures take her hands, raising the goblet to her lips with it in her grasp, she's forced to drink the wine through the veil or suffocate. It's plastered against her nose and mouth with the weight of the goblet, and as the liquid flows through the fabric and into her mouth, I hear her choke and splutter.

But they get it down her. And a few moments later, I see her sag in the figures' grasp.

"Place the sacrifice on the altar."

The lackeys do as they're told, lifting the girl and laying her on her back, the white fabric of her dress clinging to her body in a way that I can't help but notice. She has full breasts and a narrow waist, but my gaze keeps flicking back to the red wine stain on her veil, splashed grotesquely where her lips are like a slash of blood.

"This girl's sacrifice will determine the future of this town," my father intones. "She will be installed with you at the house at Blackmoor University, your pet to treat in whatever way you please. She is bound by the terms of her agreement to accept all treatment and punishment that you mete out and to service you in any way you choose—up to the point of taking her virginity." He pauses, looking at the three of us. "Whichever of you claims her virgin blood will be the next ruler of this town. So it has been since we first changed the nature of the sacrifice. The proof will be displayed here, in this place, and the future of Blackmoor will be secured."

He smiles, but there's no humor in his expression. "She has been handpicked for you. May the best man win."

And then her veil is pulled back.

My world spins around me and comes screeching to a halt.

The girl on the altar is Athena.

ATHENA

*W*hen I wake up, for a moment, I'm completely disoriented. I feel like I don't know where I am, my head aches as if a dozen nails are being driven into it, and my mouth feels dry and cottony. My eyes are sticky when I try to open them, and I have to blink several times before I get them all the way open, sitting up slowly in bed.

That's when I realize I don't actually know where I am. The sheets under my hands aren't mine, smooth and soft, and many hundreds more thread count than the ones I sleep on back in the little house my mother and I share. The mattress feels spongy, like expensive memory foam, and the pillow I was just laying on—

I turn, my eyes still bleary with sleep, and press my hand into it. Sure enough, it's fucking down. Soft like a motherfucking cloud.

My bed at the house on the estate is nicer than the one I used to sleep on back home, but it's definitely not as nice as this. This is *luxury*.

I force my eyes all the way open, rubbing the sleep from them as my heart speeds up in my chest. *What the hell is going on?* I don't recognize the room I'm in, either. The bed is a mahogany four-poster, the wooden floor is covered in a thick sheepskin rug, and there's what looks like an antique wardrobe against one wall. Next to the bay window, there's a desk with a pad and several pens and an expensive-looking leather chair. Across the room, I can see a door to what's probably the closet and another chair, this one a plush velvet wing chair with a soft-looking throw tossed over the ottoman in front of it. There's a bookshelf too, empty, but there nonetheless.

What happened last night? Did I get drunk? Did I blackout? Did I go home with someone?

But that's not like me at all. I don't go home with guys. I never have. There's a reason I'm still a virgin when I'm pretty sure every other girl in my class except for Mia, and all the ones above and below lost it already. I don't even drink all that much, not since that awful night at Cayde St. Vincent's party. That pretty much taught me the consequences of getting too drunk in unfamiliar places.

But my mouth feels thick and dry, and my head hurts like I have a hangover. My stomach is twisted in sick knots that only get worse as I frantically try to remember the night before and can't. I can't even remember the *day* before, I realize. I don't remember what I did yesterday, and even the day before that feels foggy. Everything in the last forty-eight hours or so feels like a white, noisy blur inside of my head. The last thing I remember is watching a rom-com with my mother, which I think was a couple of nights ago. But I'm not even entirely sure how long it's been since then.

My heart rises into my throat, and I fight down panic. This isn't my room. This isn't anywhere I even recognize. Shoving back the heavy, plush duvet, I scramble out of bed and over to the desk, looking at the pad of stationery set neatly in the center of it, just below the daily calendar.

On the top of it, beneath an elaborate crest, are the entwined initials **BU**.

I know that crest. I know those initials. Everyone around the town where I grew up does.

Blackmoor University.

But that's not possible. I don't know how I could even be at Black-moor. There's no way I could afford tuition there, and *that* wasn't extended to me as part of my mother's employment package. I'd applied at the public university about an hour away, and I'd been accepted. I remember that much. I was supposed to leave...soon? Yesterday? Tomorrow? I have no idea what day it actually is, and I don't know where my cell phone is.

In fact, I don't see any of my belongings anywhere. No phone, no purse, not even shoes. This doesn't make any sense. I'm always careful about my things. I've never had many of them, so it wasn't like I could just be careless like so many of the rich girls at Blackmoor High. My parents couldn't just replace things I broke or lost, especially not now, when it's just my mom.

What happened last night? I try harder to remember, squeezing my eyes tight as I sit back down on the edge of the bed, trying to force some kind of memory to swim back to the surface. But it feels like being deep underwater, trying to claw my way up and finding nothing to grab onto. Somewhere deep in my mind, I hear some strange, garbled voices, but I can't make anything out of them. It feels like a memory I have but can't access, like it's locked away.

The sound of the doorknob turning breaks through my train of thought, and I jump, grabbing for the sheet to cover myself. In the same instant, I finally realize what I'm wearing. I look down at myself in horror as I realize it's nothing but a thin white slip nightgown edged in lace, like something you'd buy at fucking Victoria's Secret.

That sense of panic claws at my throat again. I don't own anything like this. I never have. I definitely don't fucking *sleep* in something like this. I'm more an oversized t-shirt and panties to bed kind of girl.

The door opens, and as I stare at it with growing panic, a man who must be seventy years old if he's a day steps in. He's wearing pressed black trousers and a crisp white shirt, and his iron-grey hair is combed back neatly. He looks like a fucking butler, and that's only emphasized when he starts to speak in an English accent, introducing himself as Geoffrey.

"Who the fuck are you?" I demand, forgetting any hint of manners

I've ever had. I don't know why this old guy is standing in the bedroom I apparently slept in, but this is getting fucking weirder by the second, and I want out.

Now.

"I told you, Miss Saint, my name is—"

"Not your name," I spit out, my fists balling up in the sheet that I pulled over my chest. "Who are you? What is this place? What the *fuck* am I doing here?"

"Language, Miss Saint," he says crisply. "But to answer your questions, I am the house manager here for the Blackmoor heirs. You are in the heirs' home, Blackmoor House, on the university campus, the main residence where the three heirs reside."

"The three heirs?" *He can't be talking about who I think he's talking about.* Why would I be in their home?

"The eldest sons of the founding families, miss." His voice is terse and formal, and I shift uncomfortably on the bed. None of this makes any sense.

"Why am I in their home? Is it just them living here?"

"Yes, miss. The house is exclusively for their use, except when other pledges come to celebrate here. The Fraternity of the Heirs is highly sought after. Membership in the fraternity and good standing often leads to opportunity and wealth after graduation." He speaks like he's reading off of an informational pamphlet, rote and emotionless. "Do you have any other questions, miss?"

"Yeah." I glare at him. "You haven't even answered the main one. Why am I here? Why have I woke up in this bed, in this stupid nightgown, without any of my things and any memory of the last two days at least." I clench my jaw, trying to keep my voice level, to not show just how scared I am. "It doesn't make any sense for me to be here. I don't even go to this college."

"That's where you're wrong, Miss Saint." Geoffrey smiles patronizingly at me. "You are a student at Blackmoor University."

"No, I'm not," I insist. "I never applied. And anyway, I could never afford it—"

"Your admission was completed for you, and your tuition is covered."

"How—" I trail off, confused. "What—"

"It's all part of the contract you signed, miss?" That same patronizing smile stays glued to his face. "Or don't you remember that, either?

ATHENA

"*W*hat fucking contract are you talking about?" I demand, still staring at him. Now, this *really* doesn't make any sense. "I didn't sign any contract."

"But you did, Miss Saint." Geoffrey strides across the room and opens the top drawer of the desk, pulling out a few sheets of paper and handing them to me. "Here it is, in black and white."

With a sinking feeling in my stomach, I start to read. A lot of it is legal jargon, but some phrases stand out to me, leaping off the page and slapping me in the face.

Ms. Athena Saint, hereafter referred to as "pet," agrees to obey Mr. Cayde St. Vincent, Mr. Dean Blackmoor, and Mr. Jaxon King, hereafter sometimes referred to as "owner," or "owners," in all things, to conform to orders immediately and follow all instructions given, including but not limited to:

1. *The clothing (or lack thereof) that the pet is permitted to wear*
2. *What the pet shall eat, and when and where that food shall be consumed*
3. *Where the pet is allowed to go when not attending classes*
4. *Who the pet is allowed to associate with outside of the house, and normal classroom interaction. The pet is not allowed to interact*

with other men at any time unless they are her professors, and
then only in a classroom setting. If the pet must go to office hours,
she must be accompanied by one of her owners.

The pet agrees to perform all services requested of her. This may include
running errands, preparing food, cleaning the home, etc. The pet will do it in
the manner requested and the type of clothing (or lack thereof) requested
without complaint.

The pet will provide sexual satisfaction to her owners in any way they
choose, without complaint. She will do so without requesting her own satis-
faction or experiencing orgasm without express permission, which will be
granted at the whim of her owners and at no other time.

The pet will not pleasure herself, touch herself intimately outside of
normal hygiene, or bring herself to orgasm without the express permission of
her owners.

The pet will not engage in sexual activity with any other person of any
gender except her owners.

Failing to abide by these rules will result in reprimands and/or punish-
ment(s) of the owners' choosing. The pet agrees to accept this and present
herself willingly for punishment if so ordered. Punishments may be punitive
or financial.

The pet will check in with her owners at all designated times.

The pet is allowed to choose her own major, minor, and classes while
attending Blackmoor University. All other decisions are under the power of
her owners.

By signing, she willingly surrenders all bodily autonomy over to her
owners for the duration of her natural life.

I can feel all the blood draining out of my face. "This is bullshit," I
splutter. "I never signed anything like this."

"But you did, miss. Look there. Your signature is at the bottom."

He's not wrong. It is there, in black and white, my bold scrawl.
Athena Saint. But I can't believe it.

"It's forged, then," I say flatly. "I would never sign something like
this. Have you read it?"

"I have not, miss. But I know the gist of it. I am aware of your...

position in the house," he says delicately as if just thinking about it offends his sensibilities in some way.

Well, it offends my fucking sensibilities, too.

"It basically makes me a slave," I spit out. "A *sex* slave, no less. So it must be forged. I would never agree to something like this."

"It is not forged, Miss Saint," Geoffrey says tersely.

"Then I was under the influence of something. It's not legally binding if I wasn't coherent when I signed it."

Geoffrey lets out a long-suffering sigh. It's clear that his formal patience with me is coming to an end, but I could not give less of a shit. I'm not going to just sit here and let this happen to me.

"I assure you that the best lawyers money can buy put this contract together. It is absolutely enforceable. And you are bound by your signature."

"No." I cross my arms over my chest, holding the sheet in place. "I refuse. I'm not going to be anyone's fucking *pet*, and I'm certainly not going to *service* any of those assholes. They bullied me all through the last part of high school, and they're not going to get away with it now. I won't do it. So if you can just give me back my things, and my clothes, I'll be leaving. Please," I add for good measure, just in case it might help.

It doesn't. Geoffrey looks unmoved. "I have to inform you that if you try to refuse the terms of the contract you signed, Miss Saint, your mother's position at the Blackmoor Estate will be immediately terminated without severance, and her bank account frozen. She will be turned out into the streets, and you will be removed from campus immediately to join her. I have also been instructed to remind you, Miss Saint, that your father committed sins against his brothers that are unforgivable and that none of them will let either of you live for long without the protection of the estate." He smiles coldly. "I believe, in layman's terms, your father was a rat. And I believe that you know how well the men your father called brothers can exterminate a family of rats."

I can't breathe. My blood feels like it's turned to ice in my veins as I stare at him, unable to speak. The full horror of what's happening settles on me, weighing me down until I feel like I'm drowning. Of all the things I could have imagined, it wasn't this.

I shouldn't have been surprised, really. If there's anything I've learned, it's that rich people are into way more fucked up shit than you'd ever imagined. And really, in the end, it makes sense. When you can buy anything and anyone you want, have everything handed to you on a golden platter, what's the point of simple pleasures like going to a movie or having a drink out at a bar or going on a date? No, when you have the kind of wealth that lets your family claim ownership of an entire town, that means being into way weirder, worse shit. Like colonizing. Big game hunting. Or, apparently, blackmailing a girl into sexual subservience.

"The contract is legally enforceable," Geoffrey repeats. "There are punishments for breaking the rules in it, Miss Saint. Some are up to the boys to enforce, the punitive ones mostly. Others are financial—and I assure you that neither you nor your mother could afford the fines that you could incur by refusing to be compliant."

"So that's it?" I demand, finding my voice again. "I'm sold into slavery in exchange for my mother staying safe?"

"The benefits are actually quite extensive, Miss Saint," Geoffrey says primly. "You will live here at Blackmoor House, free of charge, with your room, board, and tuition covered in full. Your clothing will be provided for you, and you will want for nothing unless, of course, you lose your privileges by failing to comply. Your mother has received a raise, a hefty monthly stipend added to her pay for your service to the family."

I stare at him open-mouthed. "She knows what's happening here?" I manage, my voice cracking at last. I can't imagine my mother knowing that I'm being forced to *service* the boys she cleaned up after, that I'm their sex slave. It's too humiliating to even think about.

"She believes that you're on scholarship, that's all. And taking a full load of very difficult classes, so you won't have much time for visits home."

That's probably not the only full load I'll be taking soon. The minute the gallow's humor flickers through my head, I have to stop myself from bursting into hysterical laughter. I'm pretty sure I won't be able to stop if I do, or I'll just burst into tears. Or both.

"So I have no choice." I look at him with one final shred of hope that he'll tell me this is all a prank, one last way for Cayde to embarrass me, to frighten me, to get the upper hand because I once refused to suck his dick in high school and then puked all over him.

But Geoffrey doesn't laugh. The door doesn't fly open, and no one rushes in to tell me I've been pranked. Instead, Geoffrey just looks at me, the tiniest shred of sympathy in his face at last.

"No, Miss Saint," he says finally. "I'm afraid that you do not."

DEAN

I'm waiting downstairs in the living room with Jaxon, who is sprawled in a leather recliner as we wait for Cayde to come down from his room, and then at some point, the guest of the hour.

Athena Saint.

Not who I would have picked, really, for our prize. Our *pet*. Our sacrifice, as our fathers liked to call her, to get around the pesky little detail that she's really, for all intents and purposes, our slave. She signed the contract, sure, but does it really count when she doesn't remember it?

I would say probably not. Not that I give a shit.

There was a time, centuries ago, when men who held the title of Lord got to have their way with girls like Athena whenever they wanted. She's nothing but a servant girl, after all, or the daughter of one anyway, which is basically the same thing. I should have had the privilege of taking her if I wanted her—but now I'm forced into this ridiculous game, competing to take the virginity of someone so far beneath me in order to win a prize that should have always been mine by rights.

It's ridiculous that the other families were ever given a chance to rule. The town was founded by Blackmoors, it bears the name, and the St. Vincents and the Kings were merely supporters. The town should go to me regardless, without all of this childish stupidity. It's my birthright, and yet here I am, battling Cayde St. Vincent for it.

Jaxon isn't a threat, really. The Kings haven't been in charge for generations. But Cayde will cling to it, even though his father living in my ancestral home is an insult to my family. The fact that I grew up in a different house and not on the estate is an insult.

He's my friend, but he's also now my rival. And I resent that I have to play this game at all.

"So, Athena, huh?" Jaxon drawls from where he's slouched in the recliner. "Not who I thought they'd pick, to be honest."

"Philip picked her because he knew Cayde is obsessed with her," I retort sharply. "He knew it would prime Cayde to fight harder to win than he might, otherwise. He's not stupid. He knew that seeing us go after her would drive his son crazy, push him over the edge. He'll do anything to pluck that biker whore's cherry, though I can't imagine why. She and her mother are nothing but jumped-up trailer trash."

"So you don't want to fuck her?" Jaxon eyes me.

"Of course." I shrug. "But I don't much like the idea of competing for her. I *do*, however, like the idea that she doesn't have much of a choice in the matter."

"So, what are you going to do if you win?" He looks more curious than anything else. "You know we're supposed to keep her."

I shrug again. "Keep her as a servant, I guess. Or maybe as a pet, to give to anyone who deserves a reward." I smirk. "I'm certainly not going to *marry* her like Philip St. Vincent did with his pet. Honestly, if there was ever any indication that they don't deserve what they've been given, it's that. Imagine. Marrying a pet."

Jaxon rolls his eyes. "I don't know why you care so much. Maybe he fell in love with her or some shit."

"That's disgusting." I can feel my lip curling up just at the thought. "Men like us aren't supposed to *love*. We conquer. We take. We claim. We don't let someone else take anything from us."

He doesn't say anything, just slinks deeper into his seat, looking away from me.

I suppose I shouldn't have said that to Jaxon, of all people. I know his sob story, of course. Everyone does. He was in love—or as *in love* as a teenager, especially one from a family like ours can ever be.

But she's gone now, and as far as I'm concerned, so much for the better, in terms of what's good for Jaxon. As far as what's good for me, maybe it would have been better to serve as a decent distraction if she were still around.

Jaxon doesn't seem to care anymore about renewing his family's glory now than he did before, though. Maybe even less, to be completely honest.

Which is more than fine with me. And Cayde too, I'm sure.

"Athena is mine by right," I say finally. "Just like this whole fucking town. I'll take her and the prize, and then you can keep being you, and Cayde can be *my* right hand instead of the other way around."

"Fine by me, bro." Jaxon shrugs.

"The St. Vincent's are upstarts. Claiming a town that doesn't even have their name on it."

"Sure."

"It's all named after my family. The academy, the estate, the college, this fucking house we're living in."

"Yep. It is." Jaxon's eyes are half-lidded as if he's considering taking a nap.

"Don't you give a single shit?" I glare at him. "Don't you care that your family has done nothing but serve since this town's inception? That only *once* has a King occupied the estate?"

Jaxon laughs. "No," he says flatly. "To be honest, Dean, I don't give a shit. I never have. Sure, we only ran the town once. Good for whatever great-great somebody that was. I don't fucking want it. It's too much goddamn responsibility. Do you think I'd be able to do the things I do now if I ran this fucking place? Nah. Hard pass."

"So *you* don't want Athena?"

Something flickers in his eyes. "I didn't say that. She's fucking hot. I'd love to be the first cock she takes."

"But you can't have both. You can't have the girl without the responsibility of the town."

Jaxon grins. "I do like breaking the rules."

I let out a frustrated sigh. "These aren't rules that can be broken, Jax." I use his nickname, though I rarely do. When we were all younger, I had a lot of affection for Jaxon, before it really sank in for all of us that we were destined to be rivals one day, despite our brotherly love for one another. "You really pushed it at the ritual. Philip St. Vincent was pissed."

"Let him be. You think I give a shit?"

"You're too rebellious." I shake my head. "You're going to get yourself in real trouble one day. Trouble that none of us can fix."

"And you've got a stick up your ass bigger than my cock," Jaxon retorts, though his tone is light. "You—"

He trails off because Cayde walks into the room then. He's dressed in his usual joggers and a sleeveless rugby jersey, his sandy brown hair combed back. "Geoffrey says she's on her way down," he says casually, flopping onto the couch next to us. "I guess she's getting ready."

"There was no fighting?" I ask curiously. "No pushback?" That seems out of character for Athena. We all saw the way she reacted to Cayde's demands at that party years ago. And we also saw the way she stood up to him the next day at school. "She doesn't seem the type to look at a contract like that and just agree."

"Unless she's into *way* kinkier shit than we thought," Jaxon adds with a smirk.

Cayde glares at him. "Geoffrey told me that she was not pleased. In fact, she tried to refuse."

"Did she?" I look at Cayde, mildly curious. "What finally convinced her to agree?"

Cayde shrugs. "I guess the part about turning her mother out onto the street. And promising her mother a stipend for the "work" that her daughter is doing." He laughs coldly. "Man, the look on Mrs. Saint's face if she knew her daughter was our sex slave."

"But no one will tell her," I caution Cayde, frowning. "It's part of the agreement. Parents of the sacrifice are not told about it, or what it entails."

"Of course not." Cayde rolls his eyes. "Doesn't mean I can't enjoy the thought of how she'd react if she did know."

"She can't know that we're competing for her virginity, either." I look between Jaxon and Cayde. "That part is always to remain a secret. It ruins the game if she knows that we're competing for her."

"Duh." Jaxon glances towards the door. "I won't tell. It'll be more fun to watch you two fight over her if she doesn't know what's going on."

"Why would I want her to know?" Cayde grins. "It's definitely not as much fun. It'll stay between the three of us."

"Until I win." I smile coldly at Cayde. "Make no mistake, I'm taking this town back for the Blackmoors."

Cayde meets my gaze, his smile just as icy. "Only if the best man doesn't win."

ATHENA

$\mathcal{G}$eoffrey left me with pointed instructions to get ready as quickly as possible and meet the boys downstairs for my first "inspection." Just that word makes my stomach curdle, but it's clear that I don't have a lot of options.

I'll figure a way out of this, I tell myself. *But first, I have to get a grip on the situation.* I avoided Cayde and his sidekicks for as much of high school as I could after that embarrassing incident at his party and the fallout the next day at school. He made me a laughingstock, but that hadn't been as terrible for me as it probably would have been for some girls—I hadn't expected to be popular or well-liked at Blackmoor High anyway. And I hadn't cared about making friends. In fact, I'd very much wanted the opposite. Cayde making me into a social pariah just meant I had to deal with less bullshit up until graduation, at least from the girls. A lot of the guys gave me hell, telling me they'd "fix my gag reflex" or that they'd "let me puke on their dicks any day." "If I'm hitting it from the back, I won't get any on me." That kind of shit. But I'd had Mia, so I didn't care. I'd just kept my head down and ignored most of it. It wasn't like I wanted to get on any sports teams, be a part of clubs, date anyone, or make friends. I'd just wanted to graduate and move on to college and then get my mother and I both the *fuck* out of Blackmoor.

I'd really thought I was so close to just that. But now I'm here, trapped at Blackmoor University and contractually obligated to be the pet of the same three guys that I tried so fucking hard to escape. I don't know why the hell this is happening to me, but I'm definitely going to try to figure it out.

And then I'm going to make the Three Stooges downstairs wish they'd never tried to pull this shit on me.

I discard the stupid silk nightie that I slept in, tossing it aside and going to the closet to see what my options are.

They're not good. I've always been a jeans, t-shirt, and Docs kind of girl at home, never mind that stupid uniform I used to have to wear to the academy, and then some oversize t-shirts for bed and my workout gear.

The closet has literally none of that. It's stuffed with tight, low-rise jeans, pleated skirts that would probably barely cover my ass, mini-dresses—and when I go over to the wardrobe, it isn't any better. Crop tops, skimpy shirts, see-through everything.

Is it too much to hope for a pair of cotton boyshorts in the underwear drawer?

Apparently, it is. That particular drawer is stuffed full of lace and satin, and what is cotton is skimpy—ribbed cotton thongs edged in lace, thigh-high socks, cheeky panties that will crawl right up my ass crack. None of it is what I would have opted for at home, which I suspect is precisely the point.

I pull out a pair of soft lace boyshorts, a matching lace demi cut bra, and shimmy into them, reaching into the drawer with the tops for something that I won't completely hate. The closest thing I can find is a leather crop top, so I slip that on and dig in the closet for a pair of jeans. I come up with a low-rise skinny black pair and knee-high, high-heeled black boots. I'm going to feel fucking ridiculous in this, but it's better than going downstairs in a mini tennis dress. *Who the fuck wants me to wear that?*

I have a feeling I'm going to find out at some point.

A line in the contract stated I was expected to wear minimal makeup and keep my hair down unless the boys specifically request otherwise, but fuck that. It's a small act of rebellion, but I have to do *something*. I can't just fall in line. It's not in my nature. There are none of my actual clothes here, or I probably would have worn those downstairs just to see what kind of stupid punishments they'd try to mete out. But since that's not an option, the best I can do is a smoky eye with some thick liner and putting my hair up.

While I'm doing my makeup, though, it's hard not to think about what waits for me downstairs. Anxiety twists my stomach into knots, trying not to go crazy with imagining, but that's almost impossible. The contract said I'm supposed to *service* the guys however they please, which makes me wonder—do they know I'm a virgin? Does it matter to them? Is that some part of this sick twisted setup, that they all get to take my virginity at the same time, or some fucked-up shit like that? How does that even work? Does it count for all three if it's in the same night, during the same…session, or whatever you'd call it?

Is that part of why I'm here? Because I'm still a virgin?

It would make sense for Cayde to know that—he figured out pretty quickly that day he got me up against the locker that I was. And he had enough control over the school to know that no one had gotten to it since then. But there were summers and the months after graduation—surely he doesn't know everyone in the whole freaking town. True, I'd rarely left the estate. But he and his family can't have that much control. I could have lost it to anyone outside of the school, and he'd never know.

Right? Right.

But if that's not it, and they think I'm sexually experienced at all, what's going to happen when I'm forced into doing something, and they're disappointed—because I have literally no idea what I'm doing? Are they expecting me to want it? Surely not—every other girl in the school wanted their dicks, but all three of them knew very well how I felt about it. There's no reason to think I've changed. Is that part of it? Do they *like* that I'm being forced into this?

I don't know how to handle the unknown parts of any of that. It makes me sick to my stomach that they might be looking forward to forcing me, and I don't know what to do. *Should I just give in and do it all happily, so they don't get to have that pleasure?* Inwardly, everything in me rebels immediately against that. I can't picture myself pretending to fall at their feet, to actually *want* them.

I mean, they're gorgeous. There's no denying that. But that's not what matters to me. Their looks can't conceal how ugly their souls are, how dark and twisted they are on the inside. I don't want them or this. And already, I feel all out of sorts, anxiety creeping up and starting to make my skin crawl, making me feel twitchy and uncomfortable.

At home, I've always kept to a routine. Growing up the way I did, and then losing a parent and having your home burn down and being forced to live in a house that doesn't in any way feel like yours can... really mess you up. I've struggled with anxiety and panic attacks since my father died, and my personal routine was a way of keeping control of that. I got up at the same time, ate basically the same things, wore the same clothes, went to school, went to the gym, studied, did it all again. It helped to keep me grounded, kept me from feeling like my world was spinning out of control any more than it already had.

But now everything has been thrown completely out of whack, and I don't really know what to do.

I don't even know what major to pick or what classes to enroll in. I'll have to do all that today, after waking up in a strange bed in strange clothes and being told that I've basically been sold into slavery. The price of that was my mother's safety and mine, and more money in her bank account. Which she fucking deserves, don't get me wrong. But she'd be horrified if she knew what was happening in order to keep us safe and for that money to appear.

I've always considered myself tough. I've always tried to be strong. I knew that I had to be, growing up the way I did. But for the first time, I feel so out of my depth that I'm floundering. I'd managed to handle the curveball that was living on the Blackmoor Estate, going to Blackmoor High. But this is nothing I could have envisioned, nothing I could have anticipated. I didn't even know shit like this happened in the real world. This is something out of some twisted Lifetime movie, but it's not a movie. It's real, and it's my life.

And for the first time, I have no plan. No clue how I'm going to turn this to my advantage or even just get through it like I'd done with the prep school. Then it had been to keep my head down, keep to myself, and just make it to graduation.

But now I can't keep to myself. And as far as I know, this continues after graduation. *For the rest of my natural life,* the contract had said.

That's not possible. I can't live like that.

I look in the floor-length mirror that's next to the wardrobe. I hardly recognize myself. I look hot, sure—I'm fit and healthy, my body just curvy enough to fill out the crop top and skinny jeans, my stomach flat and pale. With my black hair up in a high ponytail, the muscle I've built on my shoulders and arms is visible—not enough to be a female bodybuilder or anything, but enough that I can lift a good amount of weight and hold my own on a martial arts floor or in a boxing ring.

"You're strong," I tell myself, looking at my reflection. "You're not going to let this rule you. You're gonna do what you have to survive, and keep your mother safe, and then when you have a chance…the first time that chance presents itself, you're gonna get the fuck out."

It feels silly talking to myself in the mirror like this. But it's all I can think of to do. The sound of my voice does calm me; hearing it out loud does soothe me. I feel a little more prepared to go down and face whatever is waiting for me.

I'm a survivor. My mother and I both are, and she didn't raise me just to give in to men who want to hurt me. She's serving the families, and now I'm expected to do the same thing. She'd expect me to be smart about it. To bide my time and then figure out what to do when the time is right.

With my chin lifted, I head for the stairs. The memory of what happened in high school, of Cayde trying to force me to blow him in the library, of our standoff the day after, lingers in my mind. This is his ultimate chance for vengeance, I suppose.

I'm upset about the past. I'm scared for the future.

But more than anything else, I'm determined not to show it.

JAXON

*H*onestly, this whole situation feels sort of surreal.

Like the other guys, I knew that there was some sort of girl that would be mixed up in all of this. But I hadn't expected *this*. I hadn't expected us to be competing to try to take her virginity, that she'd be our *pet*, that whoever won would be responsible for her afterward, too, as well as the town.

I do know that I for sure don't want all that fucking responsibility. But I can't help but be intrigued by Athena.

Since we were kids, Dean and Cayde have been like my brothers. But that doesn't mean that I don't know that they're both assholes. I'd kind of enjoyed watching Athena fight back in high school when Cayde tried to make her suck him, and she said no. It was kind of funny watching her puke all over him, although not as funny when it got all over me, too. And her fighting spirit was, to be honest, pretty fucking hot.

I don't give a single shit about winning the town, but I *am* interested in Athena. If the girl we'd been given had been one of those rich heiresses, I'd have sat back and munched on popcorn while Cayde and Dean fought to the death over her. But now that it's Athena, I'm both ready to be entertained by Cayde spiraling out of control every time Dean touches her...and interested in touching her myself.

If there's a way to take Athena for myself without having to get the town along with her and all the bullshit that comes along with it, I'd be down for that. Getting to pluck her cherry while she claws and bites, and I fuck her hard over the side of my bed, in the shower, on the floor, right up her ass before I come?

Yeah, I'd be really into that. I'm getting half a chub just thinking about it.

I'm even more interested when she finally walks into the room.

We're all lounging on the chairs when the door opens, and Geoffrey announces her. She walks in with her chin up, her eyes defiant, and I feel my cock twitch. She's clearly not going to take this lying down—or at least not without a fight, and I like that.

I like how she's dressed, too, in that leather crop top and those tight jeans that mold her ass into a perfect shape, and the high-heeled boots along with it, and the dark makeup. It's a look that really screams—

"Biker slut." Cayde sounds disgusted as he gets up, striding towards her. He starts circling her like a predator, his gaze raking down her face and her body, his upper lip curled. "I think the contract was clear about your makeup. You look like a whore."

Personally, I think the makeup is hot. But I'm not about to throw my opinion out there. I'm staying out of this fight for a while until I decide just how much I want to participate.

Cayde squeezes her ass in the tight jeans, and to Athena's credit, she doesn't flinch. She stays very still, letting him make a circle around her until he comes to stand in front of her, his gaze raking down her yet again.

"Are you aware of the situation you're in?" he barks, his voice sharp and almost angry.

"Yes."

It's the first time I've heard Athena's voice in a long time, and I'm surprised by how much I like the sound of it. It's crisp and clear, almost musical, but her voice is steady.

"Do you understand the situation, and what's expected of you?"

"I think so," she says carefully. And then, cutting her eyes sideways at Cayde with just a hint of defiance in her voice. "But I don't like it."

Cayde smiles coldly at her. "See, that's the thing, *Athena*. I don't give a fuck what you like or don't like. You're a pawn. A *pet*. Our pet. And that's just how things are now."

She says nothing, looking straight ahead now. I have to admire her gumption. A lot of girls would either be fawning over Cayde right now, or us, trying to get into our good graces and see what they could get out of the situation for themselves, or they'd be sobbing and pleading, depending on how they felt about the whole thing. Athena is doing neither. She's not begging us to change our minds—probably because she knows it'd be a cold day in hell before *that* happened—but she's also not pretending to like it.

She's got balls, and I have to respect her for that.

"All that matters," Cayde continues, circling back behind her, "is what *we* like." He smiles, and I know she can't see the look on his face, which is probably for the best. She'd probably be more terrified than she already likely is if she could. "And," he says, grabbing another handful of her ass. "I don't know about the other two, but I haven't seen enough of you to know if I like it."

She must know what's coming. Cayde isn't exactly being fucking subtle about it. But she doesn't move a muscle. Her emotionless expression doesn't change, not even as Cayde drags down the zipper in the back of her crop top and then pushes it off of her shoulders. Her arms are at her sides, and the straps slide down until it lands on the rug at her feet.

"Take off your boots," he orders. "I'm not getting on the fucking floor for you."

Athena obeys. She doesn't act as if she hates it or loves it, and I realize this will be her strategy for now. She's not going to act as if she wants it, but she's not going to give us the satisfaction of pleading and crying, either.

Smart girl.

She's just going to frustrate the hell out of us by being non-responsive and see how long she can get away with it.

With me, probably forever, since it's been a long time since I've wanted anything badly enough to really try for it. With Dean, maybe a little while. He's not so concerned with how she feels about it as just winning. If that means she lays there like a cold fish while he pops her cherry, he probably wouldn't care so much.

But Cayde? She's playing a dangerous game with Cayde. He doesn't just want to win. He wants *her*. And he wants her crying. Begging. Pleading either for his cock or his mercy, and he's only planning on giving her one of those. The longer she holds out and doesn't give him the satisfaction of any emotion, the angrier he's going to get.

And the worse it's going to get for her.

Athena stands on the rug in bare feet now, and Cayde reaches around, unbuttoning her jeans as she stands there motionless. He yanks them down her hips, revealing the black lace panties she's wearing, and I feel my cock twitch at the sight in front of me.

Athena is very much my type. Medium height, fit as hell, even a little muscular. She obviously does some lifting at the gym. Pale, dark-haired, dark-eyed—it's like she was custom made for me, almost. She's a tough, hard-edged girl, and that just adds to the appeal. I like a girl with a mouth and some sass, a girl who doesn't let the world fuck her in the ass bareback. Athena is all of those things, so far as I can tell.

I liked her all the way back in high school. But there was another girl for me back then. And there hasn't been another since.

It's sure as hell not going to be Athena. But she is a hell of a temptation, that's for sure.

Cayde reaches for her bra strap, and I see the first flicker of emotion in her eyes. Cayde can't see it, thank god, but it's a twinge of fear. I can see her fighting back the desire to resist, to tell him no. She doesn't want to be stripped naked in front of everyone in the room—hell, I don't know any girl who would. I'm sure there are a few out there, but I've never met them.

"Cayde—" I start to tell him no, that he's going too far, but Dean catches my eye and shakes his head firmly. I sit back, chastened. I know what Dean's trying to tell me without his having to say it—a lot worse is going to happen to Athena before the end of all this than just being stripped down in front of us. And anyway, we're all likely to see her naked at some point or another in our quest to take her virginity —if I decide to participate, that is. I'll have to at least make a show of trying. So this is mild, as punishments go.

If I'm going to ever fight to keep something from happening to her, it's going to have to be when it's something really bad. I can't show that card too early. If I'm painted as her white knight, it's going to be hell for both of us around here.

Not that I'm about to be that for her.

Nope. Not a chance.

The bra falls to the floor, and we're treated to our first view of Athena's naked breasts. My cock lurches in my jeans, half-hard and rapidly approaching the point where there's not enough room for it in my boxers. I can feel the head starting to slip out, rubbing against my fly, wanting to escape. Wanting *her*.

She's got full breasts but not too big, the kind I could really get a handful of, with some left to spill out. A C-cup, maybe. Her nipples are the perfect size, a soft pink, and they harden quickly in the air-conditioned room. Seeing them like that, stiff and poking out, I have the sudden urge to press my mouth against her, nibble and lick at that hard nipple and see if she'd be so stoic then.

And just like that, I'm fucking rock-hard.

Cayde wastes no time stripping off her panties and then stepping back to take a good look. "Turn around," he says curtly, spinning a finger. "Let's get a good look at all of it."

I can't help but take note of how the other two are reacting to her. My competition, if I want her. Cayde has a bulge in the front of his joggers, but I know he's getting off on the power trip more than anything else, as Athena mutely turns in a slow circle, her expression still blank. She's fucking gorgeous, with a pert ass that looks like she does her squats, firm thighs, and a narrow waist, and...

Her pussy isn't shaved, which is how I usually like it, but even with the tight black curls that cover the space between her legs, my mouth waters a little despite myself. I can't help but wonder if it's ever been licked, if she's a virgin in every way, or just unfamiliar with cock.

I fucking love eating pussy. And I'd love to hear Athena scream while I ate her out.

Dean is clearly aroused too, but he has a haughty expression on his face, like he's looking at some fucking art at an estate auction. Some shit he wants to possess but doesn't have any real emotion about. All it takes is a title, I guess, to make a guy act like a ruling lord every fucking moment of the day.

I see his gaze flick to Cayde, and I can tell that the real competition is going to be between the two of them.

Between the guy that wants to own her and the one that wants to break her.

Athena stops turning and looks at the three of us. "Are you pleased, my *lords?*" Her voice is sarcastic, and I smother a grin. *Goddamn, this is gonna be fun to watch.*

Cayde is at her side in an instant, her hair wrapped around his hand as he pulls her head back. "You're going to learn what that mouth is for," he hisses in her ear, loud enough for the rest of us to still hear. "I could make you suck my cock right here, in front of the other two. Is that what you want? I could make you wear my cum on your face to your first day of classes. Is that what you want?"

Athena swallows hard. I can see the struggle on her face, the desire to defy him mixed with the *very* strong desire not to have that happen to her. "No," she says finally."

"No, *what?*" Cayde snaps. He moves closer to her, grinding his hard-on against her ass. "Hurry up, little Saint, before you end up on your knees. And puking won't save you this time. I'll just make you wear it along with my cum."

"No, sir," she whispers.

"Louder!"

This time, it's Dean that speaks up. "Cayde, as fun as this is, we can't be late for class."

Cayde lets go of her hair so fast that she stumbles forward, nearly falling. "Go upstairs and get dressed in something appropriate. And wash that mess off of your face."

"I like what she was wearing," I interject. "And her makeup."

Cayde's face flushes with rage. "Is everyone going to fucking argue with me this morning?"

I shrug. "I'm pretty sure that we're all allowed to speak up if we're happy with our pet's appearance. There are three of us here, with three different tastes. And she fits mine today. So I say let her get dressed, and let's fucking get to class."

Athena looks over at me, and I can see the surprise on her face before she can hide it. She wasn't expecting anyone to stick up for her.

Don't get your hopes up, little girl. I don't plan to make a habit of it.

Athena scrambles back into her clothes, and as Dean and Cayde start to head towards the door, she shoots me a grateful look.

"Thank you," she mouths.

I shrug. "How're you getting to class?" I ask, letting my gaze rake over her just enough that she can see that I'm not going to be altruistic about this. I'm just as interested in fucking her as the next guy.

I'm just not quite as cruel as the other two.

"I was going to walk." Athena's voice is flat again, her face carefully blank.

"In those shoes? Nah." I grin at her, winking. "Come on. You can ride on my bike."

ATHENA

*M*y head is spinning as I follow Jaxon outside. It's been all of fifteen minutes since I met my new "owners," and already I've been stripped naked, stared at, and threatened. I tried to use the time to get a handle on the guys and who they are now versus who I knew in high school. Still, it was difficult…what with Cayde stripping me like that and the other two looking at me like hungry wolves.

Jaxon wasn't looking at me like Dean and Cayde did, though. I'm downright terrified of Cayde. He seems as if he hates me, as if he might actually want to hurt me. I'm not entirely sure that he doesn't have something to do with me being here in the first place. On the other hand, Dean looked at me like I was something that was owed to him, like he was just tolerating the other two until he inevitably claimed what was his.

Dean's arrogance practically oozed out of every pore. I don't know which I disliked more, Dean's attitude or Cayde's.

But Jaxon doesn't seem to hate me or think he ought to own me. He wants me, that's for sure. I saw the size of the hard-on he had in his jeans. But he looked at me differently than the other two did. I'm definitely not about to trust him…but I'm not as afraid of him.

He might be the closest thing I have to an ally in this house, which is honestly fucking terrifying.

His motorcycle, though, is *magnificent*. Even better than the guy, and that's saying something, because if the circumstances were different and I were actually going to go for one of these assholes, I'd pick Jaxon. Not just because he's what I'm familiar with—all black jeans and biker boots, denim button-down, and a leather motorcycle jacket—but his physical appearance, too. His dark hair, long on top and shaved on the sides, those almost black eyes, his chiseled jaw with a hint of stubble—all that is right out of the playbook of what I'd describe as the type of man I'd really like to fuck.

It's a shame he's part of this shitstorm. There's no way I'd ever give in to a man, or worse yet, *want* a man who would agree to be a part of owning me.

It's just a little disappointing because while they're all really, really hot, Jaxon is fucking *smoking*.

And his bike, which is a matte black Triumph Bonneville brat, is just as drool-worthy.

He drops me off in front of the main building on campus, where I'm supposed to go to register for classes. "Good luck," he says with a smirk. "Don't be late after school. Daddy St. Vincent and Daddy Blackmoor will be pissed if you are."

I wince. "Please don't call them that," I say before I can stop myself and then flinch, hoping he won't be pissed at me for speaking out of turn. For all that there's a detailed contract, I don't exactly know what the rules are. I have a feeling Jaxon is going to be laxer than the others, though.

He laughs, and it actually sounds genuine. "Alright then. Cayde and Dean will be pissed. And you definitely don't want Cayde angry with you."

That's for fucking sure.

"Thanks for the ride," I say quickly, grabbing my bookbag. "I won't be late."

"Sure thing." Jaxon settles back onto the seat. Then he's gone, the motorcycle growling away with the smell of exhaust lingering behind.

It makes my chest tighten a little. I grew up around men that always smelled like that, the scent of sweat and grease and oil clinging to them long after they'd showered and changed. I hadn't expected to ever leave it. To be honest, I'd thought that I'd wind up dating one of their sons, marrying into the club. I'd be an old lady like my mom was, riding on the back of some hot guy's Harley, all the way until I had kids and he grew a beer belly, and we got old together, unless he died on a run, like some of the guys.

My life has taken a *very* different turn.

The next hour is taken up with registering for classes. There's no embarrassing meeting with the dean like there was my first day at the academy. Though my advisor seems wholly confused as to how I could have gotten into Blackmoor University without having any real idea about the classes I wanted to take here or what my major was going to be. I can't exactly tell her that I hadn't planned on it, that I hadn't even applied, and that my plan had originally been to go to the public university and just kind of coast for a while on gen ed classes until I figured out what the hell I want to do with my life.

No one just "ends up" at Blackmoor University.

But then she opens my file and sees where my residence is. And her whole face changes.

"Oh," she says, and her tone gets very strange. I can't tell if it's disgust or sympathy in her voice, but I'm not particularly interested in figuring out which. I just know this meeting got a whole lot more awkward.

"You can take whatever you want, really. Just declare something as a major. It doesn't really matter what you graduate with after all." She shrugs, closing my file. "Do you like to read?"

"Um...yes?"

"Good. English it is." She taps away at the computer for a moment as I stare at her, slightly dumbstruck, and try to make sense of what she just said.

It doesn't matter, after all. Why? Because I'm always going to be a Blackmoor pet and never have a life of my own again outside of that?

That thought is so utterly terrifying that I can feel my stomach knotting, a ball of ice settling somewhere deep in my gut. *I'm not going to let that happen,* I think to myself. *I'm not going to spend the rest of my life serving one of those assholes. I'm going to get free of this, whatever it takes.*

Even if it means putting up with it for a little while.

The advisor gets up, walks to a printer, and then returns, handing me my class schedule and a map. "There you go. Your first class starts in fifteen minutes, so you better hurry. And good luck," she adds, glancing at me briefly before turning back to her computer.

* * *

I GET SLIGHTLY LOST TRYING to find my first class, English 1101, but not so much that I don't slide in right as the professor is getting ready to start. It means the only seats I can find are closer to the front, but I just grab an open one, sliding down in my chair, and fishing a notebook out of my bookbag. My advisor seemed to think that I didn't need to really pay attention, that none of it will matter in the end, but I'm not going to listen to that "advice."

I'm going to make sure that when I *do* get out of here, I got something out of this fucked up situation.

As I open my notebook, I realize every set of eyes except for the professors is on me. *It must be this ridiculous outfit,* I think, sliding down in my seat a little more. I'm definitely the only student here wearing skin-tight jeans and leather. Most of them are still in some form of pajamas or yoga pants. And the girls *definitely* aren't wearing full faces of makeup. I look like a fucking sideshow.

But then a skinny blonde girl comes to sit next to me, her eyes wide with awe, and she leans in close. "You're so lucky you belong to Prince," she whispers, her voice low enough that the professor can't hear her, and I stare at her, entirely confused.

"Prince?"

The girl looks at me as if I'm a complete idiot. "Cayde? St. Vincent? You belong to him?" She rolls her eyes. "Don't act shy. Everyone knows you're his."

"I don't belong to him." I narrow my eyes. "There are three guys in the house, anyway. None of them own me." *The contract would suggest otherwise,* I think grimly, but I'm not about to say that. I'm already weirded out enough that this girl—and apparently a lot of others—know anything about it.

"You're the Blackmoor House pet. So I guess they all own you, but we all know Cayde is the head of it. Anyone who went to Blackmoor High has stories about him." She sighs dramatically. "You're so *lucky,*" she repeats. "I mean, everyone has heard rumors about what happens to the girls that are picked to be the pet, but I'd let those guys do *anything* to me if it meant getting to belong to them. *Especially* Cayde."

I can't keep my mouth shut. I was prepared to handle what was going to happen in the house—as much as I could ever be, anyway—but I was *not* prepared to deal with idiots like this girl coming up to me and actually being fucking *jealous* of me. Jealous of the fact that I'm a pet, that I'm basically a slave. It's so moronic that I can't even quite come to terms with it or come up with an answer that isn't:

"I guarantee that it's not all it's cracked up to be," I snap at her. "Now, can I pay attention to the professor? I'm actually here to learn."

Her mouth literally drops open at that. I'm about to helpfully tell her that she looks like a fish, when I hear someone clear their throat behind me.

The girl gasps softly, her entire demeanor changes. Softening. She pushes her hair back, simpering a little, and I know before I glance around that it must be one of the three heirs.

I just hope it isn't Cayde.

When I look over my shoulder, I see that it's not. It's Dean, and although I can't quite read his expression, I know he heard everything I just said.

And I don't think he's happy about it.

So much for paying attention to the lecture. My stomach is in knots the entire time, and I can barely focus on what the professor is saying because I can feel Dean's eyes burning into my back the whole time. The moment class is over, I grab my backpack, forcing my way down the aisle and bursting out into the hall. I hurry straight for the ladies' room before Dean can catch up to me, thinking that at least there, I'll be safe from dealing with him for now. Maybe he'll cool down before I get back to the house tonight.

I turn on the faucet, splashing cold water on my burning cheeks, careful not to get my eye makeup wet. It's not even halfway through the first day, and I'm already probably in trouble.

I've never been particularly good at staying *out* of trouble. So how am I going to manage now?

The door swings open, and I look up, expecting it to be some other girl or a pack of them. But instead, to my horror, Dean walks in instead.

He casually pushes a chair in front of the door, tilting it under the knob so it'll be almost impossible to open.

"You can't be in here," I blurt. "This is the ladies' room. You're not allowed—"

Dean snorts, laughing as he shakes his head. "Oh, little Athena. You're going to learn very soon that we three heirs are allowed wherever the fuck we please."

I stare at him. *The fucking arrogance!* He's obviously handsome, dressed in jeans and a charcoal grey tee with a brown leather jacket thrown over it, with his dark brown hair and icy blue eyes, but he's so arrogant that it cuts into that. He's looking down at me as if I'm nothing to him as if I belong to him—and I suppose in a way, I do.

"You need to leave," I say before I can stop myself, lifting my chin. "I don't care who you are. You can't be in here."

Dean chuckles, taking a step closer to me. I back up, but he keeps coming, backing me up further and further until suddenly I'm against the cold stone wall. The chill of it seeps into my bare skin underneath my crop top and leaks into my blood, freezing me from the inside out as I look up at Dean, looming over me now.

I'm in a lot deeper shit than I realized.

"You've got quite a mouth on you," Dean says, his lips curling up in a cold smile as he reaches for my chin. I try to jerk my face away, but his grip tightens, holding me so that I can't look away from him.

"Cayde warned you about it this morning. He didn't have time to teach you a lesson then, but I think I have time for one now.

"I—" I try to say something, but he squeezes tighter, cutting off my response.

"You mouthed off to Cayde this morning," he says, his voice hard. "You spoke badly about us to that girl earlier. And now you're talking back to me. I think it's time you learned what better uses there are for that smart mouth of yours."

He tugs on my chin, opening my mouth. "Pretty lips," he muses. "But I bet you've never given a blowjob in your life, have you? You look like you're terrified at the very thought. I can see that you're trying to hide it, but I'm better at reading people than Cayde is. Better than Jaxon, even. You'll find that you can't hide much from me." Dean laughs then. "You probably don't even know how," he says mockingly.

I can't answer, but even if I could, I'm speechless. My heart is pounding in my chest like a frightened rabbit, and I'm frozen against the wall, unsure of what's going to come next, hoping that it's not what I'm thinking.

But it definitely is.

"Get on your knees, Athena," Dean says carelessly, letting go of my chin. "Now."

I shake my head, moving my jaw around a little now that he's let go of it. I know it will be sore tomorrow, but that's not what I'm worried about. I'm worried about what happens when Dean finds out that I really don't know what I'm doing.

He undoes his belt, and the slithering of leather is a sound I'll remember for the rest of my life. As his belt falls open, Dean slides his zipper down, and in a matter of a second, he has his hard cock out and in his hand with a practiced motion, gripping it at the base as the red, angry head stares right up at me.

He's fucking *huge*. I've never seen a dick this close before, but I've watched porn. He could be a porn star, easy. He's long, and maybe there are thicker guys, but he's still big enough that I know it's going to be an effort to get much of him in my mouth. My heart rises into my throat, and I feel the fear crawling over my skin, taking over my better sense.

"Uh-uh." I shake my head. "No. I can't. Please, Dean—" I hate myself the minute the plea comes out of my mouth. I told myself I wasn't going to beg, wasn't going to give them the satisfaction. Still, as I watch the pre-cum pearling at the tip of his cock and realize what's about to happen, I can't help myself.

This is too much, too fast. "I only found out what was happening this morning. Give me some time—" I stop talking abruptly as Dean's face hardens, and I realize numbly that I'm making a fool out of myself for nothing. He's not going to be swayed.

None of them are. Even Jaxon, probably, if he decides to have his way with me. And there's nothing I can do about it.

Dean strokes himself once, slowly, his palm rubbing over the head and gathering some of the fluid there, smearing it down his shaft so that the skin is tight and gleaming. He sucks in a breath between his teeth, his hips jerking forward a little, and I can tell that he's enjoying this.

And somewhere, deep down, I feel a tingle. It's covered up by fear and shock and dislike of everything Dean and the other guys are, but I can feel a warmth between my legs, seeing his thick, hard cock up close. Hard and dripping with pre-cum, for *me*. He wants me. I can see the desire in every inch of him, his body straining to keep control of the situation, to not just grab me and spin me around, forcing himself inside of me. He could if he wanted to, I know that. He's stronger than me. He could have my jeans down around my ankles and his cock inside of me in a matter of seconds.

So why doesn't he? Why doesn't he just fuck me and get it over with?

Because he doesn't want to get it over with, you idiot. This is about a power trip. Not about fucking you.

Dean strokes himself again, long and slow, his mouth set as he looks down at me. "Remember the contract, Athena," he says, his voice deadly quiet and thick with arousal. "Do you remember what happens if you break it?"

Slowly, as if he's a snake that might bite, I nod.

"Good," he says with satisfaction. "So get on your knees."

I have no choice. I know that. And so slowly, fighting back the tears of hopelessness, I slide down to my knees on the tile in front of him.

His cock is right in my face. It looks even bigger up close. I can smell him, the warm, musky maleness of him. I was too drunk to really notice anything with Cayde. I barely remembered any of it the next day. But now I can take in all of it. The ridged, pulsing veins along the top, the head that's a darker, flushed color than the rest of the shaft, the liquid at the tip, sliding down as Dean holds himself firmly in front of my face.

"Open your mouth," he says, his voice harsh and rough, and I obey.

Like a good little pet, I part my lips and stay there kneeling, waiting for instructions.

"You're not good enough to suck my cock yet," Dean says hoarsely, beginning to slide his hand up and down his length. "You haven't earned the right to have this dick in your mouth. You argued with me when I wanted to give you my cock. So now you're just going to sit there and watch and take my cum in your mouth, like a good little whore." He's stroking faster now, his breath coming in short, hard pants. "Little whore. Little biker slut. You don't deserve my cock anywhere in you. You don't even deserve my cum."

I stare up at him, dumbfounded, holding my mouth open, too afraid to move or speak or even make a noise. I've never heard anyone talk like this. I can feel my face flushing, embarrassed, and I wonder if someone is going to walk in. Dean is stroking himself faster; still, pre-cum dripping from his cock faster now, lubing it, and some of it drips onto my chin as he jerks it.

"Beg for it, little whore," he says, looking down at me, his blue eyes darkening with lust. "Beg for my cum. Tell me how badly you want it. Beg me to come in your mouth and not all over your face."

I'm still speechless for a second. I don't even know how to begin. I've never imagined doing something like this. Maybe some girls fantasize about it—I can even see how it could be hot under different circumstances. And despite *these* circumstances, I can still feel that warm tingling between my legs, hinting that my body might have very different ideas than my mind about what's going on right now.

"I'll come all over your tits and face if you don't," Dean murmurs, his hand a blur now. I can hear the wet sound of it, the slap of his hand against his flesh, sinking down to the base and back up again as he fists himself hard. "You'll have to wear it all day. If you wash it off, I'll fucking spank your ass red and then come all over you again. Beg for it, Athena. Fucking beg—"

I realize with shock that he's about to come, and the last thing I want is to go to class with it on me, streaked with it, smelling of it...

"Please," I whisper and then look up at him, speaking louder, faster. "Please come in my mouth, Dean. Please, I want to taste your cum, please, let me have it. I know I'm not good enough, but please come in my mouth, please—"

"Fuck!" Dean groans aloud. "Stick out your fucking tongue!"

I do it immediately, opening my mouth and sticking out my tongue, trying to remember what I've seen girls do in porn, gripping my thighs with my hands as I see him angle his cock towards me. I feel the head brush against my tongue just as the first hot spurt shoots down my throat.

"Fucking hell, god, Athena—" he groans, bracing one hand against the windowsill as he strokes himself, spurt after spurt of thick hot cum coating my tongue and sliding down my throat. I keep my mouth open, half-choking as it pools at the back.

Dean shoves the head between my lips. "Suck it, ahh—swallow it all like a good girl, fucking *yessss*—" he groans. I wrap my lips around the tip, sucking hard as he groans above me. I swallow convulsively, the salty taste of him everywhere in my mouth as I feel the last drops of it leak out.

He pulls out of my mouth, and I kneel there, stunned as he tucks himself back into his jeans and zips up. When his belt is buckled again, he looks down at me. "There's cum on your lips," he says. "Lick them."

Numbly, I obey, and he pats my head.

I stare up at him in shock. "Good pet," he says with a small, tight smile. "Maybe you'll do alright."

I nod, speechless.

Dean pauses. "If you behave like that more often, you'll be rewarded," he says. "Now, get to your next class before you're late."

And without another word, he turns and strides out of the room.

I stare after him. I can still taste him in his mouth, still feel the phantom shape of his cockhead between my lips. My face is flushed with embarrassment from being patted on the head, and I desperately want a drink of water. But besides that—

Very slowly, I slide my hand into my jeans, underneath the lace of my panties. My clit twitches under my fingertip as I slip one finger between my folds, all the way down to my entrance, and I pause, shuddering a little. And then I jerk my hand out before I can admit that I want to touch myself or give in to the forbidden temptation.

I hadn't known what to expect. But I know one thing for certain.

I hadn't expected Dean Blackmoor jerking off into my mouth to make me soak through my fucking panties.

CAYDE

*S*omehow I make it through the day without having to sneak off to the bathroom to masturbate. I spend most of the morning half-hard, trying not to think of Athena so that I don't have a stiff fucking boner all day long.

Every time I think of stripping her naked this morning, not only do I get hard as hell, but I want to fucking rub my hands together with glee. A couple years ago, she thought she'd won. She thought she could get away with refusing to suck my dick, puking on my friends and me, and then defying me in front of everyone else, and just spend two years as the school outcast before moving on. She hadn't even seemed to care that much back then.

But my father gave me the best fucking gift. He gave me Athena, contractually obligated to follow my every command.

And now I can really get my revenge. I can humiliate her any way I want. I can force her to do anything I want. And if she doesn't obey, I can ruin her whole fucking life.

Maybe revenge really is a dish best served cold.

Seeing her embarrassment this morning, when I stripped her naked in front of Dean and Jaxon, was just the beginning. I'm going to make her life hell before I finally take her virginity, break her down in every possible way until she's begging for me to fuck her just so it can end. And then she'll find out the best part—that she's mine forever. Mine to keep, mine to own, mine to do any fucking thing I want with.

That lingers with me until the end of the day when I finally get out of my last class and can head to the gym to meet Dean and Jaxon. Jaxon is unsurprisingly already there, doing some bag work. I start warming up, but when Dean walks in, he's got a shit-eating grin on his face that can only mean one thing.

"What did you do with Athena?" I glare at him the moment he drops his gym bag. "You got something out of her, didn't you?"

"Don't tell me you already got her to let you fuck her." Jaxon grins, and at that moment, I want to punch it right off of his face. He doesn't really give a shit about any of this. He might want Athena because he thinks she's hot or because it turns him on to think of being her first, but he doesn't care about winning the town back. He's *enjoying* watching Dean and I go back and forth.

"Fuck no." Dean grins. "On the first day? Even if I could have, where's the fun in that?"

"So, what did you do?" I grind out, still glaring.

Dean eyes me. "Maybe I don't want to say."

"Part of the agreement is that we don't keep it from each other. If someone does something with Athena, they have to tell. Just so we know where everyone stands with her," Jaxon points out. "So 'fess up, Dean. What base did you get to?"

"I jerked off and came in her mouth," Dean says, shrugging. "I liked humiliating her, telling her that she wasn't even good enough to suck it. Just to be a receptacle for my cum, that's all. Barely even good enough for that."

I can feel my blood boiling. "I should have been the first one to do anything with her," I snap. "If you hadn't stopped me this morning, I would have! Is that why you stopped me, huh? So you could be the first cum she tasted?"

Dean laughs. "No. I stopped you because you were going to push the poor girl over the edge five minutes after she found out she's going to be our slave. I'm all for tormenting her, but you can't make her actually lose her mind. Then she won't be any good to anyone. I didn't plan to do that, but she mouthed off about us to some random bitch in English. I had to teach her what her place is, what that mouth is for."

"I had the first right to her," I snarl, and Dean shakes his head.

"There's no such thing, buddy, and you know that," he points out. "You're just mad that she didn't swallow your cum first. But hey, at least now she's a little broken in for you, right?"

I'm seriously considering knocking one of his perfect teeth out then and there when Jaxon sidles up between the two of us, looking back and forth.

"Hey now," he says, holding up his hands. "In the end, it doesn't matter, right? All that matters is who gets to be first for the main event. And I'd bet she's pretty pissed at Dean here, so maybe you've even got a bit of an advantage, Cayde." He shrugs. "Let's not start fighting over her for real on the first day."

"To be honest, I think it kind of turned her on," Dean says with a grin, and I clench my teeth.

"Do you even care about this?" I demand, wheeling on Jaxon as he tries to separate us again. "Do you give a shit about winning back the town for your family, or are you just getting a kick out of watching us?"

Jaxon goes very quiet for a moment, stepping back from us both. "The Kings, despite their name, have never had very much power," he says quietly. "I know my history, as well as you two do. We were always the runners-up, the ones who took to the background, who did the labor while the St. Vincents' and the Blackmoors took the glory. Some in my family were fine with it, and some chafed against it, but I can tell you for my part that I know we're the least of the three families, and to tell you the truth—" he heaves a sigh, shrugging. "I don't give much of a shit about changing that."

"If you don't care about your *family*," I bite out, "you should at least care about getting to be the one who takes Athena's virginity."

"Nah." Jaxon grins. "I like a girl with some experience. One who knows how to fuck me right."

I can't tell if he's bluffing or he really feels that way. It's completely foreign to me—since the day I ran into Athena Saint, I haven't been able to get my obsession with being her first, being the one to break her in, out of my head. But Jaxon looks as if he might actually mean it.

"I could probably have Athena right now if I wanted to." Jaxon looks at me. "I'd bet money, if I felt like making that bet."

Dean laughs, but Jaxon doesn't. "At least I'm probably her type," he continues. "She's probably not into arrogant assholes or guys who like to brag about their title of 'lord,' like we're in fucking England still or some shit."

"You're the real asshole," I grind out between my teeth. "Treating this like it doesn't matter."

"We've been friends all our lives," Jaxon says calmly. "As close as brothers. And we're going to let a girl and a power trip come between us? We're better than that."

Dean shakes his head. "Pussy and power, man," he says grimly. "That's come between men and brothers for all of history."

Still, Jaxon's comment lightens the mood a little. I'm still sullen that Dean got to be the first one to really do anything with Athena, but Jaxon was right about one thing. What matters is who gets to be the first one inside of her. Everything else is just prep work for the real deal, the main event.

I spend some time on the bags, trying to punch out my frustration, while Dean and Jaxon lift. But it doesn't help much. I still feel jittery and keyed up, angry, and for the first time, pissed off that Athena was the one my father chose. I'd been happy about it a little while ago, soaking up the knowledge of everything I'd get to do to her to take my revenge. Now I can see the tension that it's going to cause between Dean, Jaxon, and me.

Ever since I saw Athena back in high school, she's been able to get under my skin. If it hadn't been her, I might have been able to get her out of my head, forget about her. I'd have been able to focus on whoever else the pet would have been, someone easy, some girl who wouldn't fight back, who'd just cry and beg until I shut her up with my cock.

Someone who didn't matter to me. Someone I could have fucked and forgotten.

Someone who wouldn't have made me feel as if I'm losing my mind with obsession, like a drug I'm already hooked on before I've even gotten a real taste.

ATHENA

*A*fter what happened with Dean, I couldn't make myself go to class. I have three more, but there's no way in hell I'm going to be able to focus. I can't bear facing anyone else who knows who I am and my place in the Blackmoor House and wants to either make fun of me or tell me how *lucky* I am. I don't trust myself not to go off and snap that one of them just jerked off into my mouth despite my begging him not to, so really, am I so lucky?

I've gotten my first taste, quite literally, of what it's going to be like to live with these three guys—and it's both better and worse than I'd feared. Dean wasn't cruel to me, exactly—his words were filthy and humiliating, and he didn't take no for an answer, but it could have been worse, and I know it. But it wasn't good for me, either, even though my pussy was drenched afterward. I might have been turned on, but I didn't get any real pleasure from it. It definitely was a one-way kind of deal.

His attitude is so fucking off-putting, I think as I wander down one of the cobbled paths on campus, flanked by borders of shrubs and flowers on either side. But, I have to admit, if it was coming from anyone else in any other situation, it might be a little of a turn-on, too.

Dean is cool and commanding, cold and arrogant, not cruelly frightening like Cayde or careless like Jaxon.

Jaxon. I let the image of him this morning flicker into my thoughts for a minute, standing next to his Triumph as he handed me a helmet. Under other circumstances, I think I could actually like Jaxon. Of course, it's hard to feel anything of the sort in these circumstances since he's complicit in this whole mess. But he's at least not cruel. He's handsome and feels familiar, even if it's just because he dresses like a biker—albeit a rich one—and rides a motorcycle. He doesn't terrify me like Cayde does. And I feel like I can figure him out a little bit, unlike Dean, who I really can't get a handle on at all.

My thoughts spin in a circle, going over the day again and again. I hate myself for even thinking of Jaxon in a positive way—I should hate them all, and I *do*, I really do. Even Jaxon. But I don't know how to get myself out of this situation, and the only thing I *can* think of is to try to go along with it until I can find some loophole to escape out of.

Today was just the beginning. I know it. I have no idea how much worse it's going to get. But I do have a strong feeling that Cayde is the one I'm going to have to watch out for, more than anyone else in the house.

I'm so caught up in my thoughts that I wind up wandering for far too long. I walk around campus until I realize that not only have I missed all my classes, I've gotten really, *really* far from Blackmoor House, almost all the way on the other side. The campus itself is huge and old, and many of the big Gothic stone buildings look the same. Add into that a late summer fog as darkness starts to fall, and there's a recipe for disaster.

For me, anyway. Because if I'm late for dinner, all hell is apparently going to break loose.

I hope against hope, half-running all the way back to the house and checking my map periodically to make sure that I'm not getting even more lost, that I'll somehow make it back before anyone notices that I'm late. *Maybe they'll just think I fell asleep in my room or something.* I break into a dead run halfway there, and by the time I reach the steps, I'm panting. I go to open the door, but before I can even crack it, it opens the rest of the way. Geoffrey is standing there, looking at me impassively as I stand sweating and gasping on the front steps of the house.

"Dinner is being served, Miss Saint," he intones. "And you're late."

Fuck. I'm in trouble now, and I know it. Whatever they have in store for me is probably going to be way worse than anything I've endured so far today.

The moment I walk into the dining room, my hair a mess and my face flushed, I can see the disgust on both Cayde and Dean's faces. Jaxon doesn't really look as if he gives a shit, as usual. Still, I can hear the deadly calm in Cayde's voice as he glances over at the maid—dressed in a normal uniform of black pants and a starched shirt, thank god—and tells her calmly, "Brooke, you can go."

She scurries out—no doubt she already knows that Cayde has a temper—and then he turns his attention to me.

"I'm disappointed, little Saint," he says, his voice still so calm that it's almost as scary as if he'd yelled. "You were told very clearly not to be late, and yet here you are. Late."

"I'm sorry, I got lost, and—"

"I don't want to hear excuses!" Cayde glares at me from across the dishes spread out on the table, a platter with roast and a bowl of mashed potatoes and others with vegetables, and gravy sitting next to it all. "You're going to be punished now, Athena. But you should have expected that already, after being unable to do something as simple as to keep track of time."

My heart is pounding in my chest again, but I just nod.

"You're going to serve us dinner," Cayde continues. "Go upstairs, and put on what you find on the bed. Do it quickly because we're all hungry. Oh," he adds, as I start to head towards the door. "Don't bother trying to refuse. If you don't put it on, you'll end up serving dinner completely naked."

Clearly, whatever I find upstairs is going to be something I won't like. I find that out quickly enough—lying on the bed is a piece of the skimpiest lingerie I've ever seen. I guess technically, it's a maid's outfit. It's just a black thong with a heart cut out in the center, a white ruffle attached to each side string, and then a black bra with heart-shaped nipple cut-outs and a matching white ruffle along the top of each cuff. My heart sinks just looking at it, but I know very well after this morning that Cayde will stick to his word and make me serve them naked if I try to come down not in the lingerie.

So I put it on.

It looks even lewder because I haven't shaved. The black hair between my legs sticks out of the heart-shaped gap, and my nipples harden in the cool air of the room as I put the bra on, jutting out of the cut-outs as if begging to be touched and tasted. The thought sends a jolt of heat between my legs, which confuses me more than ever. I don't *want* any of this. So why does thinking about it make me feel as if there's a growing heat between my thighs as if I might soak the thong like I did my panties earlier?

I swallow hard, tearing my gaze away from the mirror. I never pictured seeing myself in anything like this. I feel completely out of my depth, a stranger in my own body, and embarrassed and uncomfortable as hell. Nothing about this stupid outfit is *me*. It's not even what I would pick if I chose to wear lingerie. But I'm not being given much of a choice.

A sort of bitter resentment rises up in me as I head back downstairs, and I can feel myself starting to seethe. *Maybe this wouldn't be so bad if I were given any choices at all,* I think angrily. *I can't even choose the lingerie I'm forced to wear. I can't even wear my own clothes during the day. I don't have anything left. They could have left me* something.

I know Cayde wants me meek and quiet as I serve them their dinner. But I can't help it. I can feel their eyes on me as I walk into the room, even Jaxon's, burning into all of my exposed flesh. The lingerie seems pointless, stupid; it's barely covering anything at all and not even the important bits, really. My nipples are out for all of them to see, and the thong just barely covers my pussy lips, which are dangerously close to slipping out around the thin scrap of material.

"Fucking hot," Cayde says with a grin. "That's a good pet. Dressed for her masters' pleasure." He waves at the table. "Serve us dinner, little Saint. I'm fucking starving."

I should do it quietly. I *know* I should. I should save myself any more punishment. But I can't. I find myself slopping mashed potatoes onto their plates, flicking the pieces of roast, slamming Cayde's plate down in front of him. "There you go, *master*," I almost hiss, and I can hear the sarcasm in my voice that I can't seem to hold back.

Cayde is very quiet. So are Dean and Jaxon, and when I finally finish serving them their plates, Cayde's gaze doesn't shift away.

"Are you hungry, Athena?" he asks, his voice low. He begins to put food onto a fourth plate, and I look at it nervously. *I should have been better. I shouldn't have had an attitude. But how?*

"Yes," I say quietly, swallowing hard. "I am."

Cayde smiles then, but it doesn't quite reach his eyes. He sets the plate on the floor, next to his chair, as Dean and Jaxon watch. Jaxon's face is impassive, but Dean has a small smile on his face as if he's enjoying this.

"If you can't act like a lady," Cayde says, "then you can eat on the floor, like a bad pet. Come here, Athena."

Mutely, I walk towards him, feeling myself start to tremble. *No*, I think. *No, this is too much.* I'm not going to sit on the floor and eat like a dog. I look at the plate, horrified, and then back at Cayde.

"Sit." He whistles, and I stare at him.

"Sit, and eat your dinner if you're hungry. If not, sit and stare at it. I don't care either way. But get on the fucking floor."

I can hear the warning in his voice. It's the same warning I heard in Dean's earlier, when he reminded me about the contract. It means I've pushed the limits of what I can get away with, and now it's time to comply before things get much, much worse, much faster.

So I kneel down on the cold hardwood floor, next to Cayde's chair, and I look down at the plate so that he can't see the tears gathering in my eyes. *I won't do it*, I think. *I won't eat off of the floor like a dog.* Above me, I can hear the sounds of the guys starting to eat, their chatter as they enjoy their meals. They talk about classes, about rugby. Dean tells Jaxon he ought to see if anyone else on campus likes to ride, and Jaxon retorts that he prefers riding alone. They don't mention me, not even once. No one looks at me. No one speaks to me.

It's as if I don't even exist.

My stomach is hollow—I skipped lunch—but I couldn't eat right now even if I wanted to. I'm pretty sure I'd puke if I put a single bite in my mouth, and the last thing I want to do is throw up in front of Cayde again. He'd probably claim to have PTSD from the last time or some shit like that and punish me for that too. God only knows what kind of punishment he'd come up with.

It's the first day, I think, fighting back the tears. *The very first day and this is already what I'm dealing with.* I can't believe that the boys, especially Cayde, have topped out on their levels of cruelty after only one day. It's going to get worse, and I already feel as if I'm going to fall to pieces.

* * *

When the boys are done eating, Cayde looks down at me. "Not hungry, huh?" He shrugs, reaching down to take the plate away. "Your loss. Dinner was fucking fantastic." He pushes his chair back then, standing up. "Come on, little Saint. Your night isn't over."

Numbly I stand up, feeling the blood rush painfully back to my knees, which feel stiff and sore after kneeling for so long. Cayde tells me to follow him, and I don't fight for once, still too stunned from this last development to argue. Dean and Jaxon walk behind me, and we go all the way upstairs until we reach the bathroom that's just down the hall from my bedroom.

"Go in," Cayde says, standing to one side and gesturing. I look at him, trying to rack my brain for what he's going to do, but I realize that it's never going to be anything I'd guess. It will always be a shock because I would never have imagined any of these things before.

So I walk into the large bathroom, complete with dual sinks, a free-standing shower, and a soaking tub, only to see the maid from earlier—Brooke—standing next to the sinks.

"What is she doing here?" I croak, but Cayde just waves a hand at me.

"Get that lingerie off."

I hesitate. *What is happening now?* Will he force me to do something with Brooke while the guys watch and get off on it? That's my first and most obvious thought, but it's abruptly halted by Cayde's dark glare as he sees me hesitating.

"I'm already getting very tired of repeating myself, little Saint. Take it off, or Brooke will take it off for you."

Quickly, my fingers trembling, I undo the clasp at the back of the bra and let it drop to the tile, wriggling out of the panties right after. I can feel the gazes of all three guys on my naked body, taking it in, and a quick glance at each of them confirms what I'd already guessed—they're all already rock-hard, their bulges straining at their jeans. Cayde, as usual, is wearing joggers, so his is even more noticeable.

Three guys, all hard as hell from seeing you naked. It sounds ridiculous, like something out of a gangbang porno, but this is my life now. I shiver in the chilly bathroom, feeling gooseflesh pop out on my arms and legs, and Cayde surveys my naked body once more before nodding towards the apex of my thighs.

"I don't know about you guys," he says casually, "but I like my girls to have a shaved pussy. Especially a pet. What do you think?"

"I like a nice landing strip," Dean says casually. "But I'll never say no to completely shaved."

"Jaxon?"

I look over at Jaxon, eyes pleading for him not to answer. But he doesn't even look at me.

"Oh, I like it smooth and bare," he says, drawing out the last word, and I feel oddly betrayed that he joined in.

"Brooke, you heard the lads," Cayde says with a grin. "Let's get this pet shaved."

Brooke doesn't look thrilled with her task. I see what I missed before, the razor and the shaving gel next to her, and I flinch back. But Brooke, unlike me, has learned the wisdom of not arguing with her employers—or in my case, my *masters*.

"Sit down on the edge of the tub, miss," she says, gesturing. "I'll be careful, don't worry."

She turns on the tap for the bath, and I stare at the water in horror.

"Sit," Cayde says, his voice terse, and I know better than to keep fighting him. It's going to be worse if someone has to force this—and I have no doubt that it's going to happen, one way or another.

I sit.

"Spread your legs," Cayde says, and I can hear his voice thickening with pleasure. "Wide, so Brooke has an easy time of it. Lather her up, Brooke."

I feel as if I'm having an out-of-body experience, like I'm watching myself from above as I spread my legs in front of the three guys and a woman I met an hour ago, wide enough that I can feel my folds opening. I know that the guys can see everything all the way down.

"Wider," Cayde orders, and as I obey, I feel a cool brush of air over my clit, making it pulse. They can see *everything*.

Brooke takes a washcloth, running it under the hot water and then over my pussy. I flinch back, but she doesn't even pause, laying the washcloth over the side of the tub as she fills her palm with shaving gel and begins to lather the hair between my legs with it.

No one else has ever touched me down there besides my gynecologist. There's nothing intimate or sexual about what Brooke is doing, it's as clinical as it can possibly be, but this is still a far cry from a doctor's office. I'm on the side of a tub, in these guys' house, spread-eagled while a strange woman shaves off my pubic hair.

I feel like I must have entered some kind of alternate universe. Somewhere that this is normal and not the most insane mess of bullshit that anyone has ever had to endure.

All I want to do is clamp my legs shut, but I don't dare, especially once Brooke starts shaving. She does it quickly and efficiently, shaving away hair and running the razor under the water, adding more gel as needed, so it's not painful in any way. She doesn't even accidentally nick me.

But she can't help but touch me intimately—she's shaving my pussy, after all, and as she moves my lips out of the way and runs the razor over my skin, her fingertips brush my clit. Her breath is warm on my inner thigh. And to my horror, as she makes another pass with the razor, I can feel my clit starting to ache. I can feel my skin getting flushed, my pussy getting wet.

"Holy shit, I think this is turning her on," Cayde says. "Look at her skin. It's turning pink. I bet she's fucking wet right now."

"It's sure as hell turning me on," Dean says, adjusting himself in his jeans. "Fuck, I just want to come."

"Same." Jaxon rubs his hand over the front of his jeans. "Objection to us jerking it while she gets shaved?"

"Not now," Cayde says, waving his hand. "I don't want to see your dicks right now. And besides, do you want to ruin the surprise for her all at once? She's already seen Dean today. We should drag it out a little. Make her wonder about the rest."

"We could make Brooke eat her out," Dean suggests. "I'd watch that."

"No." Cayde's voice is harsh. "She's been a bad girl. She doesn't deserve a tongue on her pussy or an orgasm. She gets shaved, and then she goes to bed."

A fresh flood of arousal gathers between my legs at that, and I close my eyes, my humiliation complete for the night. Even if they can't tell how wet I am, *I* know. I know that I got wet while a stranger shaved my pussy, and the man who thinks he owns me talked about how I don't deserve to come, all as if I'm not even in the room. Like I'm just an object, sitting here on the side of the tub.

I don't know why it's turning me on. *It's got to be that I've just never been touched like this before,* I think desperately. *I don't really* like *any of it. I'm just reacting.*

But by the time Brooke finishes and wipes the warm washcloth over my smooth, freshly shorn skin, it's all I can do not to moan. She carefully washes all traces of the shaving gel away. When the rough surface of the washcloth rubs over my clit, I bite my lower lips hard, grabbing the sides of the tub as I fight not to arch up into her hand.

"Holy shit, she's horny." Dean laughs. "Look at that shit. She just about tried to hump that washcloth."

My cheeks flame red at that, and the second Brooke moves away, I clamp my legs shut, only to see Cayde glaring at me.

"Show us that shaved pussy," he demands. "No one told you to close your legs."

With my face on fire with embarrassment, I obediently open my legs again, letting him see all of my wet pink flesh on display.

"She's fucking soaked," Cayde says. "You know the rules, right, Athena?"

"Yes," I whisper.

"You can't touch yourself. Not even a little. You can't come without permission, so no humping your pillow to get off, either. If you come in your sleep, you have to admit it. No orgasms without permission. Say it aloud, so we know you understand." His voice is condescending now, patronizing.

"No orgasms without permission." I hang my head, feeling completely defeated.

"Good." Cayde smiles with satisfaction. "Now go to bed."

I can't get out of that bathroom fast enough. There's nothing in the drawers of clothes that I'd ordinarily wear to bed. Still, I also can't bear the thought of being naked while I sleep, completely vulnerable. Not in this house. So I pull on a pair of lace bikini panties, forcing myself to ignore how good the soft lace feels against my newly bare skin and how the gusset between my legs is instantly damp, and then put on one of the tight tank tops, slipping in between the cool sheets of my bed.

One day. That's all it's been, and already I've been stripped, swallowed cum, given a plate on the floor, and shaved.

What the fuck is tomorrow going to bring?

ATHENA

$\mathcal{T}$he morning following the humiliating shaving, I know I have a choice. Try to go along with what they want, or have the situation escalate rapidly.

Yesterday I'd worn something that inadvertently had appealed to Jaxon, and I know I should probably try to appeal to one of the others today. But the problem, of course, is that I don't want to. Dean is an arrogant asshole, and Cayde is—well, Cayde is fucking terrifying.

Not to mention the fact that he made me kneel on the floor while they ate.

Do what you have to, I tell myself as I get up and walk towards the closet. The smart thing to do would be to try to please Cayde, but I'm not entirely sure what kind of girl he's into, exactly. I remember that he used to go for the cheerleaders a lot back in high school, so I sort through the closet until I find a blue pleated miniskirt that reminds me of something a cheerleader might wear and pair it with a white halter top that buttons down the front that leaves my midriff bare, and white sneakers. I leave my hair down today and don't bother doing my makeup except for a swipe of mascara and some lip gloss.

I hate everything about my appearance, but it might be worth it if it makes Cayde less of a dick to me. I'm beginning to see that while there's no way I'm going to be able to avoid sexually pleasing these guys, it's possible I could strike up some sort of tentative truce. Or at the very least, not anger them unnecessarily.

If wearing a few stupid outfits will make that easier, then I know I should just do it. It's not the end of the world. It's not going to kill me.

I have to think about the big picture now—surviving these three guys and everything they have planned for me until I can figure a way out. A way to break the contract. A way to get my mother and me out of here without putting us both in too much danger.

The boys are already eating breakfast when I walk downstairs, and all three of them pause, their gazes raking over me almost...appreciatively.

"I see the little pet has learned to dress herself," Cayde says with a cruel smirk, his eyes lingering on my chest, which looks as if it's straining against the neckline of the top. It's a size too small, but of course it is. I don't think that's an accident, either.

"A little slutty for my taste." Dean frowns. "I like something a little more classy. But it'll do for you, Cayde. Tomorrow, Athena, you wear something I'd approve of."

"Like that stupid tennis dress?" I fire back before I can stop myself. *Great, Athena. I see the resolution to get along with them is going so well already.*

Dean's face darkens. "I see you haven't learned what your mouth is for yet."

I tense. *He wouldn't. Not here, in front of the other guys*—but if there's anything I've learned so far, it's that I can't predict how far they'll go or what they'll do. These three guys—or at the very least Dean and Cayde—are far more depraved than I would have ever guessed. And I know this is only the beginning.

Dean pointedly checks his watch, which looks ridiculously fucking expensive for a college student. He always dresses like he's in his twenties already, like he has some posh office job he goes to instead of English class and western civ. "We need to leave in a few minutes," he says. "Which is lucky for you, Athena, because even in that slutty outfit, you've given me a hard-on, and I should tell you to get under the table and take care of it for me."

"Ah, shit, man, I don't want to see that." Jaxon rolls his eyes, but I see them cut slightly sideways at me.

Is...is he trying to defend me?

"You don't want to see our little pet suck a dick?" Cayde laughs. "I want to see that."

"Maybe mine, and in private," Jaxon says, tossing his napkin down on the table. "But I'm not as into all this public shit like you guys are. Definitely not into seeing you two morons' cocks." He stands up, glancing over at me. "Come on, Athena, you want a ride to school again?"

I haven't eaten yet, but I'm not about to pass up an opportunity to get out of this room without having to strip or eat off of the floor or, worse yet, suck Dean's dick in front of everyone.

"Yes," I say quickly before Cayde or Dean can protest, and hurry out of the dining room after Jaxon as he strides out.

"You need to stop talking back to them," he says flatly as we approach the motorcycle. He hands me my helmet without looking at me. "You're only making this harder on yourself."

"I don't know how," I admit, buckling the helmet under my chin. "It's not in me to just roll over and take it."

"You're going to need to learn." Jaxon swings his leg over the bike, revving it up so that he has to yell over the sound of the engine to be heard. "They're not going to make it easier on you."

"Why don't you help me?" I look at him, standing next to the motorcycle as he waits for me to get on. "If you don't like what they're doing. Why don't you help me get out of it?"

Jaxon laughs. "That would be assuming I care that much."

"Don't you?" I lift my chin, leveling a challenging glare at him. "You've tried to help me twice now. You take me to school. I don't think you like what Cayde and Dean are doing."

Jaxon lets out a sigh, finally turning to look at me. "Athena, that contract is ironclad. Even *if* I cared enough to try to get you out of it, I couldn't. And who's to say I'm not enjoying it, too? I liked seeing you get your pussy shaved last night. That shit was hot. Just because I'm not into Cayde and Dean's mind games doesn't mean I don't see some perks in this whole situation." He jerks his head towards the back of the bike. "Come on. Get on before they come out and drag you back in there, or I decide to let you walk. You're wearing the right shoes for it today."

And the wrong shoes for riding a motorcycle, but I'm not about to let that stop me. I swing onto the bike, grabbing on to Jaxon for balance as he puts it into gear.

Jaxon seems like my most likely ally, I think to myself. *If I have any chance of an ally at all. Or is that just because I kind of sort of want to like him?* Even now, I'm having a hard time not wanting to scoot closer to him, wrap my arms around his leather-clad waist and lean my face against his back, the way I would if we were together and taking a ride on his bike. I'd breathe in the scent of his jacket and his shampoo, and I'd lose myself in the feeling of the wind whipping through my hair and the vibrations of the motorcycle under me, and—

"We're here." Jaxon's sharp voice jolts me out of my daydream. "Hurry up. I don't want to be late for my first class."

You're a fucking idiot, I tell myself as I get off the bike. *Stockholm Syndrome two days in? Come on. You're better than that.*

I don't know why Jaxon is the one out of all of them that makes me wish things were different. Maybe it's just because he doesn't seem to want to hurt me just for the sake of it—which isn't exactly a great reason to like someone. But I shouldn't count on him as an ally either, and I know it. Jaxon might not be as happy about all of this as Cayde and Dean are, but I also don't think he's going to stick his neck out for me.

And I have no reason to trust him. At the end of the day, the Kings are still one of the founding families, even if they've rarely been at the top of the food chain. And my family serves them. My father did as a member of the Blackmoor Devil's Sons, and my mother does now as a housekeeper.

I guess this was really always supposed to be my fate.

I manage to snag a seat near the back of the class in English, hoping not to have to be anywhere near Dean, but he still slips into the row behind me even though there's no room. He just fucking tells someone to move, and as soon as the dude sees that it's Dean Blackmoor telling him to, he gets up and hurries off to another empty seat near the front of the class like it's normal for someone to swagger into a lecture hall and demand your seat.

Dean's eyes are on me throughout all of class. I can feel it. And it's miserable. If I don't figure out how to pay attention even with that icy gaze freezing my back, I'm going to fail this class not because I don't care, but because Dean won't let me concentrate. All I can think about is him cornering me somewhere after class like he did last time and making me do something else to him. Maybe actually blowing him this time.

The moment we're dismissed, I'm out of my seat like a flash, blending into the crowd of students hurrying towards their next class with my heart in my throat. I'm just waiting for Dean to grab my elbow or to hear his voice behind me, but I don't. Still, I don't feel totally safe until I'm in my algebra class, in a corner seat where hopefully no one will notice my stupid outfit and comment on it.

English is the only class that one of the guys is in with me, thank god. I pay close attention to the time throughout the day, making sure that I'm headed back from my last class in plenty of time to make it for dinner. I don't want a repeat of the night before.

I stay in my room until dinnertime, and I change into a denim miniskirt and a ribbed white crop top that comes to just below my boobs, figuring that it's not what I'd wear, at least I don't feel like I'm auditioning for Locker Room Girls XXX. As soon as the clock hits five minutes to seven, I pad downstairs, only to see all three of the boys seated at the table before me. Still, I'm not late, and I go to pull out one of the chairs and sit down.

"Nuh-uh." Cayde shakes his head. "Down on the floor, pet." He points to the spot next to Dean's seat. "You can eat next to Dean tonight."

I stare at him. "But I'm not late."

"Don't talk back!" Cayde's voice raises. "My god, you're fucking hard to train. Maybe I *should* send you away, ask for another pet. A dog would be smarter."

Is that possible? I want to ask, but I can't. Because the consequences of me leaving would be the same, I'm sure, even if they chose to have me leave instead of me refusing.

"You can kneel on the floor, little Saint, or you can go upstairs and stay there until the morning. It's your choice."

I swallow hard. Everything in me screams to flee, to run upstairs to the tentative safety of my room rather than kneel next to Dean and eat off of a plate on the floor like a stray being given scraps. But I'm so hungry. I didn't have breakfast because Jaxon swept me out of here before Dean could come up with any other ideas about what to do with my "smart mouth," and I didn't have time to grab a packed lunch from the cook either. I don't have a debit card or money, so I couldn't get anything from the cafeteria. I hadn't had anything to eat since... lunch yesterday? I can't remember now. I feel almost dizzy. I'm so hungry.

"Athena." Dean's voice cuts through my train of thought, and for once, his tone is almost kind. "You need to eat. Come on. It's not that bad. I'll even feed you if you don't want to eat off of the plate."

I glance back and forth from Cayde to Dean to Jaxon, my mind racing. I keep hoping Jaxon will speak up for me again, but I know he won't. He meant it this morning when he made sure to let me know I shouldn't rely on him as an ally, that it would be a mistake. I can't afford to keep making mistakes if I'm ever going to get out of this.

"I'll eat," I manage to choke out, going to kneel down next to Dean's seat. The wood is cold and hard on my knees, and I wish now I'd opted for jeans. I blink back tears as I sit there, waiting for one of them to hand me a plate. It's not until all three of the boys have piled theirs high that Dean sets one for me on the floor in front of my face.

He doesn't even bother to give me utensils. It's just chicken breast and asparagus and sweet potatoes, but my choice is to eat it with my fingers or literally off the plate like a dog. I opt for my fingers, peeling off bits of chicken as the guys talk above me about random meaningless shit, classes, and hot girls they saw on campus and Friday's pledge party.

Wait, what?

"That's right." Cayde looks over at me, craning his neck to see behind Dean's chair. "You'll need to be back after your noon class finishes up, Athena. You're a very important part of the Blackmoor pledges' initiation. Make sure you shower and wash and blow-dry your hair, and wear very little makeup. Oh, and make sure your pussy is shaved smooth. I'll check, so unless you want to have Brooke do it again--"

"What outfit should I wear?" I ask, trying to keep my tone as neutral as possible, despite the sarcasm I want to infuse in every syllable.

"It doesn't matter," Cayde says, and I look up at him, surprised. "Just pick whatever you feel like."

Maybe this cooled him off a little. Eating on the floor is one of the more humiliating things I've experienced in my life, especially when Dean occasionally strokes my hair or pats my head like he would a puppy who is behaving particularly well. Still, if it's mollified Cayde, then it's worth it.

Two days until this pledge party. My stomach knots just thinking about it—I can only imagine what they have planned. Every day seems to stretch out in front of me now like an endless obstacle course, just waiting to trip me up with whatever trap or humiliation or punishment the boys decide on for me.

At least maybe after tonight, I'll get to eat at the table.

ATHENA

*T*hat doesn't turn out to be the case. Much to my horror, the next morning, at breakfast, I'm served on the floor next to Jaxon, and it rotates back around to Cayde by dinnertime. When I try to sit at the table at breakfast, wearing the stupid mini tennis dress that Dean requested, Cayde sharply tells me to kneel next to Jaxon. When I hesitate, he tells me that I have to earn my spot at the table back and not to try again until he expressly tells me that I can.

Jaxon, at least, ignores me while I eat my eggs and toast with almond butter. At least the eggs are scrambled—I don't want to think about how I would go about eating a fried egg—and Jaxon not making a big deal about it at least makes me feel less embarrassed. He gives me a ride to school as usual—it's become an unspoken thing, apparently—but by the time dinner rolls around, Cayde seems to be determined to make the experience as terrible for me as he can manage. He refuses to put a plate on the floor for me, making me eat from his fingers instead. Dinner is barbecued pork, and when he shoves a piece into my mouth, smearing the sauce around my lips and laughing, I choke.

"What are you going to do?" He sneers at me. "Puke it all up?"

I scramble to my feet and run upstairs to the bathroom, scrubbing my face over the sink. I don't cry—I haven't cried since I got here. It's less that I'm tough and more that I'm afraid if I start to cry, I won't stop. I wait for Cayde to come after me and impose some punishment, but he doesn't. The next morning at breakfast, my plate is at Dean's feet.

None of them have made a move to touch me sexually again, which I find interesting. Cayde, at the very least, seems more interested in tormenting me than getting off, which I honestly prefer if I had to choose. Dean seems happy to bide his time—or who the fuck knows, maybe they've agreed to take turns. Dean had his fun, so now he has to wait for it to come around to him again. I can totally see them coming up with some weird shit like that.

Although if that's what they're doing, they're going to have to skip Jaxon, it seems like, if Dean ever wanted a turn again. Jaxon doesn't participate in any of it. He might have enjoyed watching me get shaved—who knows, maybe that's a personal kink of his—but he doesn't take part in teasing me or force-feeding me when it's his turn to have me kneel by his chair for mealtimes. He doesn't try to touch me or even say much of anything at all to me.

But he doesn't try to befriend me, either. If anything, he gets colder as the days pass, silent during breakfast and then stalking out to his motorcycle. I follow him every day anyway, and he never tells me *not* to get on the back, but he doesn't invite me anymore either. He drops me off at the same spot and then zooms away without a word. That's it. I don't think I've heard him speak since the morning he saved me from blowing Dean under the table.

And all the while, anxiety churns in my stomach about what's going to happen Friday.

I don't dare try to defy them. I've seen how quick Cayde, in particular, is to dole out punishment for slight infractions, and I'm pretty sure fucking up their pledge party would count as way more than "slight." So as soon as my last class is over, I hurry back to the house as quickly as possible to follow the instructions Cayde gave me. The last thing I want is him coming up with some reason to think I haven't "obeyed" like I was supposed to.

I'm suspicious of Cayde's assurances that I can wear whatever I want—out of the choices I have here, anyway—but I opt for what I'm the least uncomfortable in any way, a pair of acid-wash low-rise jeans that at least seem kind of retro in a fun way, and a blue halter top that at least comes down to the top of my jeans, along with chunky brown heeled sandals.

When I walk downstairs, all three of them are waiting in the living room. Dean is reclining on the sofa, Jaxon is slouched in a wing chair, and Cayde is pacing in front of the fireplace. The moment I walk in, Cayde stops, his gaze landing on me like a hungry lion that sees its dinner for the night.

"Just in time," he says, his voice full of purring satisfaction. "I see you're learning something at least, little Saint."

I don't say anything. I've learned in the past week that silence is usually the better option when it comes to them, Cayde especially.

"Dean." Cayde nods at him. "Blindfold her, please."

I stare at him, open-mouthed.

"The pledges will be here soon; it's almost dark. Blindfold her and take her downstairs."

"What's the plan?" Jaxon asks, a slight edge to his tone, but Cayde ignores him. Dean gets up gracefully from his seat, striding languidly towards me with a strip of black cloth in his hand.

It takes everything in me not to flinch, to fight, to flee. I have no idea what is in store for me, but I know that whatever it is, I want to be able to see what's coming before it happens.

But I don't get that option. Dean wraps the blindfold around my head, his fingers sliding over my cheek and my hair as he knots it behind my head, tightly enough that it won't slide off. "Down to the basement?" he asks, and I hear Cayde's answering grunt.

"Come on, Jaxon," Cayde says, and this time, I don't feel a flicker of hope that Jaxon is going to save me. I'm on my own, whatever happens next.

It's hard to know exactly how much time passes. I know I'm taken downstairs into the basement below the manor house, Cayde and Dean at my elbows to keep me from falling, Jaxon's trudging footsteps

121

bringing up the rear. I regret not wearing shoes—the stone floor is cold under my feet and damp. God only knows what's down here. I certainly don't, I can't see shit through the black blindfold, and all I know is that it's cold, my skin prickling with gooseflesh as Cayde and Dean maneuver me through the room until I feel something hard and solid under the edge of my butt, like a table or a desk.

"Stay there," Cayde says sharply. I do, not moving, more out of uncertainty as to my surroundings than anything else. I stay right where they put me until I hear the shuffling of what sounds like endless feet for a few minutes, and I realize that the pledges must be coming in.

"Tie her hands behind her back."

What? I twist my head to one side, and my hand comes up to grab the blindfold—I don't like the sound of this at all. But before I can yank it off, a strong male hand grabs my wrist—too soft to be Jaxon's, too narrow to be Cayde's, it can only be Dean—and pulls both of them behind my back.

I feel something plastic-like tighten around my wrists, holding my arms solidly behind my back. My heart is hammering in my chest, my breath coming short and fast, and I feel dizzy with fear. There are too many strangers in here for me to be restrained like this, not knowing what's coming next, not knowing what the guys have planned for me.

I could have guessed what might come next.

Cayde's hands are on me now, and I feel something cold against my skin, sliding underneath my shirt. "Be very still, Athena," he murmurs in my ear. "I've got scissors right here. Wouldn't want to draw blood, now would I?"

I freeze, my heart in my throat. I'm sure he *would* love to draw blood. In fact, I think he'd really enjoy it, but I wouldn't. I don't move a muscle as I hear the soft *snick* of scissors through the fabric, and I feel first my shirt fall away, and then my bra.

I can hear Dean's soft groan from somewhere in the room.

There's the sound of Cayde setting the scissors down, and then his hands are at my jeans, tugging them open. I swallow hard, too frightened to move, too stunned at what's happening. How many people are watching this right now? How many more pairs of eyes can see my bare boobs right now?

It's not until my jeans and panties are stripped off that Cayde makes a low, pleased sound in the back of his throat. I realize with horror both what he meant about it not mattering what I wore and that he was going to know if I didn't shave.

Whatever is happening next, I'm going to be completely naked for it. A dozen awful scenarios run through my head, each one worse than the next.

"Open your mouth." Cayde's voice is harsh, rougher even than usual, and I'm too afraid to even think about disobeying. As soon as I do as he said, I feel the lacy material of my balled-up panties shoved into my mouth.

I want to choke. I want to gag. And it's not until Cayde undoes the blindfold from around my eyes and ties it around my face, securing the panties inside my mouth, that I see as my eyes adjust to the room what's really going on.

The basement is sparse and bare, just stone floor and stone walls. And in front of me, lined up in two columns and several rows, are the freshmen boys who must be the pledges. They're all blindfolded and stripped down to their underwear, the whole motley group of them— short, tall, chubby, thin, muscular, lean. Brunet, blond, red-headed. They're all staring straight ahead under their blindfolds with their hands crossed in front of them, and they're all shivering from how cold it is.

At least they can't see me, I think, with a small spark of relief. I glance sideways towards Dean and Jaxon, and I can see that Jaxon's face is hard, his brow creased as if he's not entirely sure what's going on. Dean just looks smug, his eyes trailing over my naked body, my stiff nipples, my gagged mouth.

"Pledges!" Cayde's voice rings out through the room. "Take off your underwear."

Oh god. Oh god. What is this? Surely Cayde isn't going to let them fuck me or make me do anything to them. I can't imagine him letting lowly pledges have what he hasn't even gotten to have yet. That doesn't make any sense. But if not that—then what?

All at once, the pledges do as instructed, pushing down their underwear and stepping out of them so that they're fully naked. Despite the clasped hands in front of them, I can still pretty much see everything—I've never seen so many dicks in one room. I look over at Cayde, but he's not paying attention to me anymore. He's grinning, ready to give his next order, relishing being in charge of these theatrics.

"Gentlemen," he intones. "You may remove your blindfolds."

There's a hum of excitement through the room as the blindfolds drop away, and they see me—naked, bound, and gagged in front of them. I start shivering, not with cold but with fear and uncertainty as one by one, I see their dicks start to rise as they get a good look at me, until every single pledge in the room is sporting a hard-on, from unimpressive to massive and everything in between.

"Cayde!" I hear Jaxon hiss, and I have a tiny flare of hope that he's going to put a stop to whatever nonsense Cayde and Dean have cooked up. His brow is furrowed, and he's looking at me, but Cayde ignores him, coming to stand by my side. He grabs my wrists, pushing me forward so that I'm forced to stand up straight, completely on display for probably fifty guys whose names I don't even know, who I've never even seen before today.

And not a single one of them seems to care that I definitely don't look like I volunteered to be here. They're all fully erect, with eager expressions on their faces, practically drooling as they rake their gazes over me. They've probably never had a girl on display like this for them before. Never seen one who has to stand there, letting them eat her alive with their eyes.

Hopefully, that's all they get to use.

"This is Athena," Cayde says. "I'm sure you've heard rumors. I'm here to tell you today that they're all true. This is the Blackmoor House pet."

There's an envious ripple of whispering through the crowded pledges.

"Yes, you heard that right. Our pet. Anything we want, she's required to do. If we choose to break her down, she must bend to our will. If we want pleasure, she provides it. If we want to toy with her, she allows it. She has no free will, no choices, except those we give to her. She belongs to us. Wouldn't you like that, gentlemen? A pet girl of your very own?"

The pledges all nod eagerly.

"Well, you won't have one," Cayde snaps. "Because you weren't born into the founding families like we were. But if you're lucky and find a place in the Blackmoor Fraternity, you'll have opportunities when you leave this university. Opportunities for power and wealth beyond your wildest dreams, to rise higher than you could have imagined, thanks to the connections you make here. And then if you decide you want a woman like this, bound and gagged and subservient to your every desire, you'll have one because no one will tell you no." He pauses for effect. "But first, you have to pass tonight's test."

This is hazing, nothing more. Some kind of sick test to determine who Cayde lets into the precious fraternity. I'd laugh if I could, if I didn't have panties wadded up in my mouth, but inwardly I'm choking with it. All of this is ridiculous. The power fantasies of a boy, not a man.

But a boy with enough power to break me, if he wants to. And I think he does.

"The test is this," Cayde continues. "When I give the word, you'll all begin to pleasure yourselves to the sight of pretty Athena here. But there's a catch," he adds, as the pledges look at him wide-eyed. It sounds too good to be true to them, I'm sure. *Jerk off to a pretty girl and get into the most desired frat on campus? That's just a reward for what they do three times a day anyway.*

"The catch is," Cayde draws the words out dramatically, his gaze drifting over the pledges and their eager, waiting boners. "You can't come until I say the word. Any one of you who comes before permission is given will automatically be disqualified. Nor can you stop once you start. If your hand leaves your dick for more than three seconds, you're disqualified. Understood?"

The pledges all nod in unison.

"I said, am I understood?!" Cayde thunders.

"Yes, sir!" They all shout it as loudly and eagerly as possible, and I wince from the noise.

"They learn quicker than you do," Cayde mutters. "Now stand here like a good pet, and wait for my next instructions."

Like I have a choice.

"Cayde—" Jaxon tries to interject again, but Dean elbows him hard, leaning down to whisper something in his ear. After that, Jaxon looks at me once, his jaw grimly set, and then turns away from the entire spectacle.

"Pledges! On your mark, get set—go!"

Under any other circumstances, this would be fucking hilarious. A bunch of dudes, probably all or mostly straight, naked and shivering in a basement because three rich kids told them to, hunched over their boners as they stare at me with wild, eager eyes. *These are the guys who are going to run businesses one day,* I think dizzily as I watch them start to stroke, their gazes raking over me, taking in every bit of my naked body, bared for their pleasure, to test the strength of their resolve. *The guy who runs a bank, or a real estate office, or a hedge fund, is going to be one of these guys who were in a basement jerking off to me.* It's so ridiculous that I'd be laughing my ass off—if I wasn't tied up and the object of fifty college students' feverish desire.

That's just fucking terrifying. They all look at me as if they want to rush me all at once, tear me apart in a mad dash to get to one of my holes. For the first time, I'm *grateful* for Cayde and his possessiveness, grateful for Dean and his snobbish arrogance, and Jaxon's mute objection to all of this because they're all that's between me and that fate. The fact that they own me is what's saving me from being meat for these boys, all of whom are completely insensible as to how human beings should behave now that all the blood has rushed to their dicks.

A few of them were doomed from the start. They're probably virgins, never this close to a naked woman before, because they blow their load in seconds, groaning as they stare at me while their cum shoots onto the stone floor.

"Out," Cayde says, and Jaxon opens the door. He looks glad to see them leave.

I watch it all numbly, like an out of body experience, as some of the guys slow down in an effort to last, some of them try to look away only for Cayde to bark out "eyes on Athena!" and a few stops for those three precious seconds before returning their hands to their swollen, angry cocks. One guy doesn't get his hand on his dick fast enough, the shaft bobbing up and down as it tries to leap back into his hand, and Cayde yells at him to get out. He loses it as he goes to grab his underwear, cum dribbling from his cock in the saddest orgasm I've ever seen as he stares at me like a lost puppy.

It seems to go on forever. A few guys just give up, widening their stances and jerking off hard and fast, determined to enjoy it, I guess, if they know they're going to lose. One of them near the front almost hits me with his load, and I flinch back, looking pleadingly over at Cayde.

"Don't get your filthy cum on my pet," Cayde hisses. "Get the fuck out. And that goes for the rest of you! Get any of your load on what belongs to us, and I'll make sure you fail every fucking class you ever take."

Eventually, it's down to about twenty guys. They're all sweating despite the cold, their hands moving at a glacial pace over dicks that must be painful by now, but I don't feel sorry for them at all. The room reeks of sweat and cum and warm male skin. Despite everything, despite how tired I am and how weirded out and scared, I can feel that lingering heat between my legs, as if the scent of maleness and testosterone in the air is making my body respond despite itself.

"You can take a break, gentlemen," Cayde says, and almost in unison, their hands leave their dicks, a sigh of relief going through the room. They all look painfully hard, cocks bobbing up and down as Cayde instructs them to make a single line.

"You've reached the second phase. Congratulations." Cayde turns to me. "Athena, sit on the desk."

127

I'm too tired to fight. The adrenaline surge in my body from earlier left me exhausted. So I just push myself up onto the desk with my bound hands, scooting backward a little so I can actually sit.

"Very good." Cayde smiles at me. "Now spread your legs as wide as you can."

I do as he asks. Dean comes around to stand on the other side of the desk, and I see Jaxon follow him, stopping behind me.

A groan comes from every single one of the pledges as I spread my legs wide, revealing my pussy to all of them. I feel a hot, embarrassed flush wash over me, heating my skin as their eyes all land between my legs, devouring the sight of me spread open like this. I know they can see everything—my clit, my entrance, probably even my asshole.

One guy lets out another, deeper groan as he starts to come with his hands still off of his cock. It jerks, spilling onto the floor, and he blushes bright red, his next moan one of disappointment.

"Fuck," he mutters.

"Go." Cayde shakes his head. "Get out."

"Now you'll start again," Cayde says. "You still are not allowed to come." He puts his hand on one of my thighs, and Dean's hand lands on the other, holding me open as the pledges wrap their fists around their dicks again.

"Go."

I brace myself against the desk, trying not to pay attention to how Cayde and Dean's hands slide up my thighs, coming dangerously close to my pussy. The pledges are all starting to stroke themselves again, and two more guys lose it. They've all got to be close to the edge, all of them are dripping pre-cum on the floor, and I watch as the field narrows down to twelve guys, the others slinking away with their boxers in hand and their dicks wilting.

"Stop!" Cayde calls out, and once again, the remaining pledges are left standing there, hands at their sides, watching Cayde with glazed expressions now. *They'd probably do anything at this point to come,* I think grimly. *They'd probably suck his dick if they were told to.* Who knows? Maybe that's going to be Cayde's next order.

"Jaxon, distribute the final test."

Jaxon lets out an irritated groan, but he does as Cayde asks. I realize with shock as he begins to hand something out to the remaining pledges that it's sex toys. Fake pussies, fleshlights, one for each guy that's left. Jaxon gives them out and then returns to stand behind me.

This just keeps getting weirder by the second. I can't believe what's actually happening here. It seems insane.

"You've almost made it," Cayde announces. "Congratulations. Now you're going to watch while we play with our pet. You will fuck the plastic pussy you've been given while we enjoy our real one. You can come at your leisure now. You are all members of Blackmoor Fraternity, and you've earned the right to finish while we allow you the pleasure of looking at our pet."

Oh god. Oh no. But there's no getting away. I squirm, but Dean and Cayde's hands are already firmly on my thighs, and I feel Jaxon's hands sliding around my ribs, squeezing my breasts. His hands are warm, gentler than the others, but still demanding, pinching my nipples as he groans near my ear. He pulls me backward, up against his chest, as Cayde's fingers tease my folds and Dean's find my clit.

I can hear the sound of the pledges fucking their toys, the wet sound filling the basement as they watch. "Look at her pretty pussy." Cayde spreads me wide, using his fingers to hold my pussy lips open, so they get an even better view. "I bet you'd love to touch her pussy. Lick it, even. She's so wet. She's enjoying this, even though she'd never admit it. But you can't. This pussy belongs to us. Only us."

The pledges are moaning now, grunting and groaning, and I close my eyes, close to tears at the feeling of Dean rubbing my clit. I'm getting turned on despite myself, my skin hot and aching, my clit pulsing under his touch. I *am* wet, dripping onto Cayde's fingers as he teases my entrance. I can't believe I'm actually aroused, so much so that I have to bite back a moan as Dean rubs my clit faster and Jaxon pinches my nipples, his lips rubbing over the shell of my ear.

I don't want to come in front of all these guys. I don't want to come at all. But I don't think I'm going to have a choice. It's too much, Cayde's fingers sliding inside of me as Dean expertly toys with my clit, Jaxon's breath warm on my ear as his tongue flicks over the lobe, his hands squeezing my breasts, rubbing my sensitive nipples. It all feels so fucking good, and I hate that they're the ones to touch me like this for the first time, the first fingers inside of me other than my own, the first guys to ever make me come. I know the pledges must be close, and I try to hold off because I'm sure this will be over once they've all shot their loads.

And then Jaxon starts to whisper in my ear.

"Just let go, Athena," he whispers, his hands cupping my breasts. "Lean into me; there you go. It'll feel so good if you come. Just pretend it's me making you orgasm, not them. Think about my fingers. I'd love to be rubbing your clit right now for you, feeling you twitch under me."

I gasp, and this time I can't stifle the moan. Cayde laughs.

"What a little whore," he mocks, looking across my squirming body to Dean. "All these guys, all strangers, and she's still wet and moaning for more. What a fucking slut."

No, I'm not! I want to shout. *You're making this happen, you're going to make me come, I can't help it!* I try to hold it back, but Jaxon is still whispering in my ear.

"Let yourself have some pleasure, Athena. Let it feel good. It doesn't have to be all bad. Come on, baby, just let go."

I can't stop it. It's too much, fingers inside of me, fingers rubbing my clit, faster and faster in tight little circles that send electric sparks over my skin, bursting through me, fingers on my nipples, three sets of hands touching me and toying with me and pleasuring me, Jaxon's mouth on my ear and then my neck, licking and sucking and biting, sucking harder, so hard I know it's going to leave a mark, and then something bursts inside of me, something like a firework, but bigger and brighter and so much better.

I scream with pleasure, the orgasm rippling through me as I throw my head back against Jaxon's shoulder, and I hear the pledges coming too, groaning and murmuring. There's a chorus of *fuck yes, fuck I'm coming, oh fuck, fuck, yes, oh God. I'm saying it too, my legs splayed open wide as my arousal drips down over Cayde's hand. My* hips buck up into

Dean's, and all the while, Jaxon is leaving a love bite on my neck, sucking hard at my flesh until my vision narrows at the edges from too much pleasure, and slowly the orgasm starts to recede.

The hands leave me abruptly. I sit up, dizzy, and suddenly it's all over. The pledges are discarding their toys, stepping around puddles of cum, looking slightly abashed at everything that's happened. With their orgasms finished and their sense returned, they can't quite look me in the eye. Someone is undoing my hands, undoing the gag. I spit out the panties, hot tears welling in my eyes as I realize everything that just happened, that I came, I had my first orgasm by someone else's hands. It was Cayde's fingers that were inside of me, Dean rubbing me to climax, in a dirty basement that smelled like sweat and cum, bound and gagged on an old desk.

I feel like I'm going to be sick.

It's too much. It's all too much, and I forget to care about what happens if I make the boys angry, what happens if I break the contract. I make a mad dash for the stairs, grabbing my clothes, pushing past the remaining pledges. Even though I hear Cayde and Dean and even Jaxon calling after me in varying degrees of anger and worry, I don't stop.

I drag on my clothes as I stumble up the stairs, my shirt still half undone as I run through the house and out into the chilly, early fall night. I run, and I keep running, nowhere in particular, just away from Blackmoor House, away from this awful place, away from boys who want to use my body and own me and make me eat off of the floor and call me *pet*. I want to run and never stop running.

I can't do this anymore. I just can't.

I knew I'd have a breaking point. I just hadn't expected it to come so soon.

I can't go back.

JAXON

*F*uck them.

     I'm so pissed I can't see straight. If I'd known—

Well, I don't know what I would have done if I'd known. I probably wouldn't have been able to change it. But I'm still fucking furious.

"What the hell were you thinking?" I round on Cayde the minute we're upstairs. The pledges all gone off to whatever afterparty they're throwing now that they're in the fraternity. "What the fuck was that?"

"A hazing ritual?" Cayde shrugs. "All frats have them."

"*All frats* don't tie up a girl and gag her while the pledges jerk off to her! *All frats* don't force her to have an orgasm in front of them. Jesus Christ, Cayde, I know you want to get revenge for something that happened years ago but use the one fucking brain cell you were given!"

"Jaxon." Dean's voice is a warning, but I ignore it.

"No. Not this time. You fucking idiots." I glare at Dean. "Did you know?"

He shrugs. "Sure. I figured it wasn't a big deal. Definitely not something that's been done before. No one will even believe them." Dean laughs.

"And if they do?"

"Then nothing." Cayde glares at me, seething. "*We're* in charge here. No one is going to do shit to us."

I let out a long-suffering sigh. "Cayde, she's a *virgin.*"

"So?" Cayde shrugs. "We didn't fuck her."

"No. But she's a real virgin, I'm pretty sure. Not one of those who gives head, takes it up the ass, but still has her cherry kind of virgins. I don't think she's ever had a guy touch her like that before tonight. She's probably the only person who's ever given her an orgasm. And now her first experience with it was…that."

"And why should I care?"

"Because she's not going to be any fucking good to any of you if you completely shatter her!" I throw up my hands, glaring at Dean and Cayde both. "Dude, she puked on us. She doesn't deserve this kind of torment."

"She embarrassed me in front of everyone." Cayde's jaw is set. "She deserves all of it."

"She just didn't slobber at your feet and beg forgiveness when you tried to embarrass her. We're not in high school anymore, Cayde. We need to start acting like men. And that?" I point down to the basement. "That wasn't how men treat a girl. That wasn't kinky. That was just fucking wrong."

"And what are you going to do about it?" Cayde crosses his arms over his broad chest, staring me down.

"I'm going to go after her," I say simply.

And then I proceed to do exactly that.

She got a running start, so I'm a little worried about whether or not I'll be able to find her at all. I get on my motorcycle and turn the headlight on bright, hoping that the roar of the engine won't spook her into hiding if she realizes that it's me coming after her.

I'm disgusted at what Cayde and Dean did to her. And yeah, I was a part of it, but I was just trying to make it better for her. Trying to give her some real pleasure, get her to let go and enjoy it, and not feel guilty about what her body was doing in a scenario that I'm sure she never imagined being in.

Hell, *I* never imagined that they were going to do that.

Cayde is a sick fuck. I always knew that, but this was really over the top. And while I don't think Dean had anything to do with the idea itself—it was all a little too dirty for his posh hands to have been in it—he was happy to watch and play along.

I'm worried about Athena. I'm worried about what will happen to her, out on her own and in the state of mind she's in, wandering around campus at night. I'm worried about the kinds of rash decisions she might make.

We might own her, but you're supposed to care for a pet. Treat it well. Even love it, as ridiculous as that sounds when it comes to guys like us. Cayde and Dean aren't even doing that. Cayde's so wrapped up in his revenge that he barely sees her as human, and Dean is just obsessed with winning the town back. If he could do it without Athena, he would. If he had to sacrifice Athena for real to win it, he would.

Sometimes I think it'd be better if this whole fucking town burned to the ground, I think grimly as I look ahead, trying to catch some glimpse of Athena. This obsession with ruling it, deciding which family gets to be in charge, and making decisions for a generation is a sickness. It should have been done away with a long time ago, in my opinion. All it does is chain us firstborn sons down to a life that we didn't choose, forcing us into a game that we didn't ask to play.

Athena and I have that in common, I guess.

It takes way too long, but eventually, I find her. She's collapsed at the end of the last road before you get off campus and onto the highway, crumpled near the grass, her shoes long gone, and her feet scratched up and bloody. I leave the motorcycle running as I knock the kickstand down and go to her, leaving the bright headlight shining out across the damp grass.

"Athena!"

She raises her head slightly, and I can see her tear-stained face and swollen eyes in the glare of the light.

"Shit," I mutter, squatting down and reaching to help her up. "Come on. Get up, Athena. Let me help you."

"No!" She pulls away from me. "I'm not going back. Not right now."

"You don't have to." I reach for her chin, tilting it up so that she's forced to look into my eyes despite the glare of the headlight. "I don't like what they did either, Athena. So come on. We're not going home right now."

"We're not?" She looks at me suspiciously.

"No. We're going to go get some food and go for a ride on the motorcycle. How does that sound?"

Athena purses her lips. "That sounds alright." She still doesn't look as if she quite believes me. "Why are you doing this?"

"Because I think Cayde and Dean went too far. And I want you to see that I'm not as much of an asshole as they are. So come on. Let's go for a ride, blow off some steam." I slide my hand around her shoulders, reaching for her arm with my other so I can help her up.

Athena wobbles unsteadily to her feet. I hand her the helmet and look at her bare feet. "Where are your shoes?"

"I lost them somewhere."

I sigh. "Be careful of the pipes. Don't burn yourself getting on."

She glares at me as she buckles the helmet, and it's reassuring to see that she still has some of the fire left in her. "I grew up around motorcycles, Jaxon. Don't insult me."

I like hearing my name on her lips way too much for my own good. I can't help but think that this entire situation sucks because I'd have been head over heels for a girl like Athena in another life, another world. She's gorgeous, smart-mouthed, just plain smart, tough, and witty. She's a match for me, the kind of girl who would keep me on my toes. She knows motorcycles, loves the feeling of the wind in her hair and the vibration of a good engine under her ass.

We could have been a real pair—if we weren't both chained to Blackmoor in different ways, if I hadn't already had my heart shattered beyond all repair, if she didn't also belong to the two men who are as close to me as brothers. If she were free. If either of us were.

I don't let myself think about her arms sliding around my waist or the warmth of her breath on my neck as she clings to me a little closer than usual. This time, she feels a little unsteady on the bike, and I reach around to touch her leg.

"You got it?"

"Yeah," she says softly, her voice breathier than I've ever heard it before. "I'm good."

I take her to the nearest diner I know of off-campus, a hole-in-the-wall place where they know me and won't give a shit if Athena doesn't have her shoes. It's my favorite place, a far cry from the posh restaurants and five-course meals I get at home and with my family. At this time of night, there's hardly anyone there, just an old guy who might or might not be off his rocker muttering to himself in a far corner, and an overly-made up girl who probably just got off her shift at the strip club sitting in one of the cracked vinyl booths. It smells like burnt coffee and grease, and I breathe in deeply as we walk in. I take Athena straight to one of the booths near the back of the diner, conscious as we go that the floor is kind of sticky and maybe not the best thing on her scraped-up feet.

She looks around as she sinks into the booth, stunned into silence. When I sit down, she finally finds her voice. Athena looks at me, her face a mask of confusion.

"Why did you—what is this place? This doesn't look like—"

"Like the kind of place I should be frequenting?" I grin. "Good, that's because it's not."

The red-headed waitress who usually works nights comes up to our table, wearing the blue polyester shirt and ill-fitting slacks that pass for a uniform here. "Black coffee and patty melt, Jax?"

"Sure thing, doll." I grin up at her. "And whatever the lady here wants."

The waitress looks at Athena suspiciously. "Where'd you drag her in from? She looks like a cat that got run over and still had one life left."

"Jesus," Athena mutters under her breath, and I can't help but chuckle.

"She's just had a hard night. Get her a cheeseburger and some fries. Maybe a soda for some caffeine. And water."

"You want the rest of the menu to go along with that?"

"Only if you make it with love, Diane." I grin at her, and she rolls her eyes at me.

"One day, you're going to find somewhere else to go, and it's going to be the best fucking day of my life."

"You'd miss me."

"Fat chance." She strides off, and I turn my attention back to Athena, who looks slightly dazed by the entire exchange.

"What—I guess you come here often?" She leans back in the cracked booth, her face suddenly very tired.

"As often as I can." I lean back, too, toying with the edge of a napkin. "There's a lot you don't know about me, Athena. But I can tell you that I'm nothing like Cayde or Dean."

"I figured that," Athena says softly. "Neither of them would have brought me somewhere like this, for starters," she adds, her voice full of dry humor. "I think Dean would have a fit just knowing a place like this exists."

"He does keep that lord title shoved all the way up his ass," I agree, and Athena's eyes widen, a sudden bark of laughter escaping her as she claps her hand over her mouth.

"I'm sorry," she says quickly. "I shouldn't have laughed."

"Athena." I know I shouldn't get too personal with her, too comforting, but I can't stop myself from reaching for her hand, prying it away from her face, and holding it in mine. "You don't have to worry about all that bullshit with me. All that stuff that Cayde and Dean get off on—the rules, the punishments, the humiliation, I'm not into any of that shit."

She narrows her eyes. "You liked watching Brooke—what she did to me."

I wince. "Yeah—sorry. That was kind of hot. That stirred up some shit I didn't even know turned me on." I shrug. "But come on. Making you eat off of a plate on the floor? Stripping you on the first morning? What they did to you tonight? None of that is my thing."

Athena licks her lips, and despite myself and the situation, I can't help but feel my dick twitch in my jeans at the sight of her soft pink tongue running over her lower lip. "So what is your 'thing'?" she asks guardedly.

"You mean my hobbies? Or what I like in bed?" I tease, trying to lighten the mood a little.

Athena winces. "I think I've had enough of the sex stuff for a while. Hobbies, please."

"I mean, you rode here on one of them." I frown, considering. "I like old cars, too. Tinkering with things, really. Fixing them. I'm an engineering major."

Athena's eyes widen. "Really? Wow. No wonder you aren't in any of my classes."

"What's your major?" I ask, and I'm actually genuinely curious.

"English." Athena shrugs. "I love to read, so it wasn't a bad choice. But the advisor, as soon as she realized where I was living and why, didn't really care about helping me sign up to any particular classes or figure out what major would be best for me."

I frown. "Why the hell not? That's her entire job."

"She said it didn't matter," Athena says quietly. "Because I'm going to belong to you three forever. I won't need a degree, or a career, or anything that matters, really. My whole life is decided for me already."

Not us three. Just one of us, I think to myself. But of course, I can't tell her that. It's part of the rules that she can't know we're competing for her and the town. Otherwise, she could throw the competition in the direction of the one she chose, and that would fuck everything all up. "That's bullshit." I cross my arms, staring at her across the table. "Who says you can't work just because you live on the estate after graduation?"

"Where would I work?" Athena shakes her head. "With an English degree? There are no publishing houses in Blackmoor. What, I'm going to use my fancy degree at the local bookstore?"

"I mean you could. But there's remote work. With our influence, we could make anyone allow you to work however you wanted. Who's going to tell us no?"

"Not me, apparently." Athena winces then, and I see her waiting for me to lash out at her. When nothing happens, she falls silent until Diane delivers our food and stalks off without another word.

Athena pokes at a fry. "Why don't you punish me? Why don't you get pissed?"

I shrug. "I'm not really into hurting girls. I mean—don't get me wrong," I add quickly, "I'm not against some good old-fashioned rough sex sometimes. A little bondage can be fun. But actually hurting a girl, making her do something she doesn't want to? That doesn't get me off."

"That's very different from the other two." Athena eats a fry after pushing it around in a pool of ketchup for a long time. "I don't know if I can do this, Jaxon."

"You have to." I lean towards her, letting her see how serious I am. "They're not going to let you out of that contract. And they're not going to hesitate to follow through on their threats if you don't comply. You don't have a choice, Athena. And before you could say I can help you, I can't. I can't even help myself." I point at her food. "Eat up while you're getting to eat at a table."

"Do you want out?" Athena looks at me shrewdly as she picks up her cheeseburger. "Do you want to leave?"

"What I want doesn't matter."

"Sure it does." She pauses, and for a second, I think she's going to say it matters to *her*, although I can't imagine why it would. But she doesn't. She just takes a bite out of her burger, and I'm left wondering how exactly we got this deep into a conversation. I haven't talked to anyone this much in a long time, let alone opened up this much.

"What would you do if you could do anything?" Athena asks, picking up another fry. "Anything in the world."

"Why do you care?"

"I just want to know," she insists. "You at least seem like a human. All Cayde wants to do is play rugby, and I'm pretty sure Dean wants to just—sign people's death warrants or something, who knows."

I look at her for a long moment. I know I shouldn't say anything more. I shouldn't open up to her any more than I already have. Letting

Athena under my skin is a bad idea. After all, I let myself be vulnerable with one girl. Once. Let myself envision a future with her. Even imagined escaping all of this with her, running off and having the life we'd planned together.

And look where that got me. Brokenhearted and bitter, and my life not one speck better or more like I'd want it to be than it was before.

But something about Athena's sad, open face makes me want to share, even though I know it's stupid. She's gone through hell tonight, and I know she's seeking comfort from me. I want to give it, even though I know how fucking stupid that is.

"I'd open a classic car and motorcycle restoration shop," I say finally. "They're expensive to own and run, and they're a money pit; you can't make money on that, really. It's why there are so few. But I've got a fuck-ton of money, even if my father fucking disowned me, I've got a trust fund from my mother he can't take away, that she left me after she passed."

Athena's eyes go wide, and I clench my teeth. *Fuck. Why did I say that?* I haven't told anyone about my mother's passing since Natalie. And now Athena is looking at me with those soft, sad eyes, the expression in them that I hate more than anything else.

Pity.

"Eat your food," I snap, harsher than normal. "We'll go for a ride after, clear both our heads. Just don't tell anyone back at the house about any of this, okay? If they ask, you ran really far and hid, and it took me for-fucking-ever to find you."

Athena nods. "Okay," she whispers. She doesn't say anything else, which I'm grateful for.

There are too many similarities between Athena and Natalie, my ex, I think as we finish our food and walk back out to my bike. Natalie was dark-haired and dark-eyed too, slender but not stick-thin, beautiful in that slightly sharp, edgy way that Athena has too. She was tough, like Athena.

Do you like Athena because she reminds you of Nat? Or because you just have a type?

It's not something I want to dwell on. I'd been a real rebel back then, determined to flout everything my father had planned for me. I'd given up on all that after Natalie. I'd decided to go along with my life as it had been planned. I was just going to make sure everyone knew I was really upset about it. I'd do as I was told, but I'd be sullen the entire time.

Now Athena is making me feel things again that I haven't felt in a long time. And I'm not willing to let myself go there. Not now. Not with her.

Probably not ever, with anyone.

But I still want her.

She feels fucking great, pressed up against my back with her arms around my waist, her black hair whipping around us both as I accelerate. We're going fast now as I pull out onto the highway, ninety, a hundred miles an hour, and most girls would scream in my ear to slow down, freak out, start crying, maybe.

Athena doesn't. She just grips me tighter, and I can feel her sigh as we speed down the highway into the night, the wind cutting cold against my face. *She's fearless*, I realize, but that shouldn't be a surprise, really. She's proven that already. She might have run out of the house crying tonight, but not until it was all over. She took everything they gave and endured it, and it both makes me proud of her and want to kill Cayde and Dean.

She deserves better than this.

I take her all the way up to a cliffside I know, where there's a wide grassy spread of field and plenty of stars, as far away from the house as I can get without actually leaving the boundaries of Blackmoor. Technically, we're not supposed to leave town until after graduation, and it's too risky to push that particular rule.

But we're well outside of town, where there are no artificial lights to blur our view of the sky, and I help Athena off the bike when I stop, killing the headlights. I hear her moan softly when her damaged feet touch the cool, thick grass, and the sound sends a bolt of arousal directly down to my dick.

I shouldn't want her as much as I do. The funniest thing about it all is that if I tried to take her virginity, I probably could. She's going to fight Cayde and Dean to the bitter end—hell, either of them might have to break the rules and force her in order for one of them to take it. *They might just do that,* the small voice in my head warns me, and I clench my teeth against the thought, instantly angry. The thought of either of them forcing that on Athena makes me even more furious than tonight's bullshit did.

All it would take is continuing to be somewhat nice to her, being the balm to Cayde and Dean's cruelty, and I bet by the end of the year, she'd give it up to me. Just a little consideration is all it would probably take. And the thought is so fucking tempting. I haven't wanted a girl like this in a long time. Since Natalie, sex has just been a release, a distraction. But with Athena, it would be *good*. Satisfying. *More.*

Which is exactly why I can't do it. And anyway, fucking Athena means accepting the responsibility of the town. For the rest of my life, I'd be bound to this fucking place. I mean, it's not like I'm not anyway, but at least as things are now, I can just half-ass back up either Dean or Cayde once they win. And maybe I can keep an eye out for Athena, make sure whichever one wins her doesn't treat her too badly.

I'm not cut out to run this place. And quite frankly, I don't want to.

"This is beautiful," Athena breathes softly as I lead her to a thick patch of grass.

"Come on, sit down. We'll just chill out for a while. Let everything roll off our backs."

"Do you come out here to do that?" She looks at me curiously. "Often, I mean?"

"Sometimes. When being at the estate, or the house, or my family's house gets to be too much." I shrug. "A long ride on a motorcycle can cure a lot. Wind in your hair, an endless road in front of you, the sky above you. Feels free. Like maybe everything else could disappear for a little while. If you let it."

"My dad used to say that," Athena whispers. She sits down next to me in the grass, and she pulls her knees up to her chin, wrapping her arms around her legs. "He used to take me out on the bike all the time when I was a kid."

She falls silent after that, and I don't know what to say. I should, really—I've lost two of the most important people in my life, and one of them was my mother. But I also know how and why Athena's father died.

He was a rat. He betrayed his brothers, his club, his family, every-thing that should have mattered to him. I don't know how Athena feels about that. And I know asking would insinuate that we're far closer than I should allow us to be.

"I miss him," she says softly. "I miss home." And then, as if she can't hold it in any longer, she starts to cry.

She doesn't cry like a lot of girls I've known. There's no wails, no hiccupping sobs. She bites her lower lip hard, breathing in short gasps as the tears run fast and thick down her face. Before I know what I'm doing, my arms go around her, and suddenly she's crying in my arms, with her face against my chest, soaking my shirt.

What are you doing? My mind screams at me, and I know this is a bad idea. I know I'm letting Athena think that she can trust me and rely on me, when in fact, that's the last fucking thing she should ever do. But something in me just won't let me allow her to sit there and cry without anyone to comfort her.

It feels like she cries for a very long time. I'm about to disentangle myself and tell her to get it together, that it's getting too late and we need to go home when suddenly she lifts her face from my shirt and looks up at me.

All the air is sucked out of my chest when her eyes meet mine. They're dark, and the whites are reddened from crying; her face is tear-stained and flushed—what I can see of it in the moonlight, anyway. I can see the teeth marks in her lower lip where she bit it, and suddenly all I want to do is suck that full lip into my mouth, crush her against my chest and let my hands run all over her body.

"Jaxon?" Athena whispers, and I lose all self-control at that moment.

I forget about all the reasons I shouldn't do anything with her, about why I'm staying out of this game, about why I shouldn't torture myself with playing with what I can't have. My cock is rock-hard in my jeans, Athena is soft in my arms, and I need to know what it's like to kiss her.

So my hand buries itself in her wind-tangled hair, and before she can stop me or I can stop myself, I drag her mouth up to mine.

I feel her hesitate for a split second. *Is this her first kiss?* I wonder, and then as she suddenly tries to kiss me back, I know it must be. Her mouth is clumsy against mine, her hands unsure as they go to my waist, but somehow it's better than any experienced kiss I've ever had. I've gotten so sick of the girls who just want to fuck me because I'm a King, who just want access to the world I'm a part of. I know dimly that part of the reason I want Athena is precisely because she wants nothing more than to be as far away from all of that as she can.

Just like me.

I can feel the war inside of her as she struggles a little in my arms, and I know then that some part of her wants me, too. She just feels like she shouldn't. She knows she shouldn't want any part of this, but she's drawn to me, just like I'm drawn to her.

And then she gives in.

There's a tiny moan as she suddenly leans into me, her hands going up to my face, rubbing over the light stubble there, and I pull her fully into my lap. She gasps when she feels my cock pressing against her ass, hard and aching for her. She moans for me, her lips parting, and I can't help but take full advantage.

I know, in a way, this is wrong. She's vulnerable, clinging to me because I'm the only one who's shown her even a little kindness since she arrived at the house. Still, I tell myself it's not that bad, that the others have done way worse, and at least with me, she'll have pleasure. At least with me, she's enjoying it.

"Jaxon." She whispers my name as she leans into me, her breasts pressing against her chest, and I know I can't try to fuck her. I can't imagine what would happen if I went back to the house and tried to tell Cayde and Dean that I've won, and I don't want anything to do with that fallout, or the town itself...or any of it.

But goddamn it, I want Athena, and there are so many other things we can do.

She tastes so good. Her mouth is warm and sweet, her small whimpers and gasps as I slide my hands over her driving my arousal higher and higher, and I grab her hips, pulling her down harder against my cock so I can grind against her, groaning from the pleasure of just that.

"Have either of the guys made you come?" I ask against her mouth, one hand going up to run through her tangled black hair. "I don't mean tonight. I mean for your pleasure when you'd actually enjoy it."

Athena shakes her head, pulling back slightly, and I can see the blush that stains her cheeks even in the moonlight. "No," she whispers. "No, they—I don't think they care if I enjoy it. Cayde likes it better if I don't, I think."

She's probably not wrong. My cock throbs at the thought of everything I could probably get her to do with me, everything she'd be willing to do just because I'd give back what I took.

"Well," I murmur, my hand sliding up to cup the side of her face. I rub my thumb over her bottom lip, and when her lips briefly purse around the tip of it, I groan from how hard my dick throbs in my jeans. "I do care. And if you please me, Athena, I'll please you. How about that? Cayde and Dean might not give a shit about a girl's pleasure, but I do. I want to eat that sweet pussy of yours, but you have to suck my cock after I get you off. How does that sound?"

Athena breaths in sharply. "I've—" she hesitated. "I've never given a blowjob. Dean jerked off into my mouth. But I didn't—I might not be good at it."

Shit. I want her to suck me just for the sheer pleasure of it, but I realize that I'm saving her in a way. Dean wouldn't be all that pleased if she didn't give him a stellar blowjob, but Cayde would make her life hell. "How about you get some practice with me, then?" I suggest softly. "I won't be pissed if it's not perfect. I just want to feel your mouth on my dick."

Athena squirms in my lap, and I can tell that despite how nervous

145

she is and everything that's happened tonight, she's turned on too. "Okay," she whispers.

I tighten my hand in her hair, pulling her mouth back to mine. "Tell me you want me to lick your pussy," I whisper against her full lips. "I like it when girls beg me to eat them out."

Athena wavers for a second, I can tell. My hips arch up despite myself, pressing my heavy erection against her ass, and she whimpers. "Yes," she moans, squirming more. "I want you to lick my pussy, Jaxon. I want you to make me feel good. Please—"

Oh fuck. I can't remember the last time I was this turned on. In a flash, I have her on her back in the grass, and I pull off my jacket, spreading it underneath her, so she has something to lay on besides the ground. "You're going to enjoy this," I promise her as I lean over her, my mouth hovering over hers. "But you have to relax. Let yourself enjoy it."

She bites her lower lip and nods. "Okay," she whispers. "I'll try."

Fuck. I'm getting so many of her firsts tonight, and I'm not doing it to get back at Cayde and Dean, but there's a part of me that takes a certain petty enjoyment in knowing that. I was her first kiss tonight, and I'll be the first man to lick her pussy and make her come, the first cock she sucks. And she's doing all of it willingly, even asking for it. *Fuck you,* I think to both of them. *Fuck you for treating her like dirt. And fuck you for thinking I'm less than you.*

Athena doesn't think I'm less. In fact, she thinks the opposite. And I know that I shouldn't be doing any of this because I'm digging myself a deep pit with this girl, one that's going to suck me down and be the ruin of me if I'm not careful. But I'm too fucking horny to stop now. I want her too goddamn bad.

She wriggles her hips when I pull her jeans down, and I breathe in sharply when I realize she's not wearing any panties. Of course not— those fuckers back at the house gagged her with hers. I slide my hands up her thighs, pushing her legs gently apart, and when I run a finger down the crease of her folds, she jerks upwards, moaning at my touch.

She's so fucking wet. My finger slides right between her folds, coated instantly with her arousal. When I drag my fingertip up to press against her clit she gasps again, squirming under my touch as I start to stroke her.

I warm her up slowly, rubbing her clit with my fingers in slow circles, feeling her grow even wetter as she presses her palms into the grass, gasping, her back arching as I bring her closer to the edge. And then, when I can't wait any longer, and I don't think she can either, I move closer, spreading her apart with my fingers and touching her with my tongue for the first time.

She cries out when I lick her, running my tongue from her entrance to her clit in a long, slow lick. "Oh my god, Jaxon," she gasps, one of her hands going to my hair. "Oh my god. I didn't know—"

"Feels good, doesn't it?" My words rumble against her, and she nods, gasping as I lick her again. I go slowly for a moment, and I realize as I start to increase my pace, swirling my tongue around her clit, that the guys back at the house are fucking missing out. They don't even have the slightest idea how much.

Because Athena, when she's horny, when she wants it, is fucking incredible. She lets herself go, her hand in my hair, her hips bucking upwards as I lick her clit faster, and when I suck the hard nub of flesh into my mouth, she almost screams. She's on the verge of coming, I can feel it, and I lick faster, swirling my tongue in tight circles around that pulsing bud until she starts breathing so fast that I'm almost afraid she's going to hyperventilate.

"I'm coming, oh my god, Jaxon—" she nearly screams it, her ass coming up off of my jacket as she comes hard on my tongue, grinding herself against my face as she tangles her hand in my hair. Her juices run out over my tongue, and she tastes so fucking sweet. It's all so fucking good, her pussy and her moans and her cries as she screams my name again, and I have to make her come again, even though my dick is fucking *throbbing*, aching. I've never needed to shoot my load so bad in my life.

But I thrust two fingers in her instead while she's still coming, feeling her pussy grip them in a way that makes me almost desperate to fuck her. She's so tight, so fucking *wet. I groan aloud, the vibrations running along her wet pussy and her pulsing clit as I keep licking, thrusting my fingers into her.* I curl them inside of her to find her g-spot, thrusting and licking until I hear her suddenly cry out, her voice nearly a shriek.

"I'm coming again, oh god, Jaxon, I can't, oh my godddd—"

Her body jackknifes on the ground, writhing as I feel her pussy clench hard around my fingers, a fresh wave of her juices coating my fingers and filling my mouth. I don't want to stop eating her ever. I want to have her pussy in my mouth every fucking day, and suddenly I hate Cayde and Dean with a ferocity that I've never felt before because Athena is everything I ever fucking wanted, ever since Natalie—

I pull back, panting, my fingers still buried inside of her, her pussy juices all over my chin. Athena's hair is a wild cloud around her face, her neck and chest flushed, and I can feel her still fluttering around my fingers. My cock is about to tear its way out of my pants, and I know if I wanted to, right now, I could fuck her. I could thrust into that sweet virgin pussy, and she wouldn't stop me. She's too far gone, too horny, and I could push her into that decision.

One that would ruin both of us.

"You promised to suck my cock," I say instead. It takes everything in me to pull my fingers out of her because she feels so soft and hot and good, squeezing around me, so tight, and *god,* I want to fuck her so goddamn badly.

"Okay," Athena whispers, still panting. "Do you lay down this time?"

I can't help but crack a smile at that. "Yeah," I say finally, and she scoots off of the jacket, pulling up her jeans. I feel a flash of regret as she pulls them over her hips, her pussy disappearing from view as she buttons them quickly. I've lost my chance to fuck her at least, but my cock throbs, reminding me that I'm still gonna get to come at least. Even if it's in her mouth.

It's the only thing I can do. I can't take her virginity. I just can't.

I lay back on the grass, watching Athena chew at her lower lip as she comes to sit next to me. She swallows hard, and it's on the tip of my tongue to let her off the hook, to just tell her we'll go home now.

But for one thing, I know she doesn't really want to go back. And for another, I'm too fucking horny. My cock is so hard it fucking hurts.

Athena pushes her hair away from her face, reaching for my belt. She looks way too innocent as she undoes it, still worrying at her lower lip as she slowly slides my zipper down. My cock throbs as her hand brushes against it, and I fight back the dangerous tightening I feel in my balls. I want this to last, a little while, at least.

The second she gets my jeans open, my cock springs out, thick and hard and already dripping pre-cum. And then Athena gets a good look at it and gasps.

"You're fucking huge," she whispers. "And—oh my god."

Oh, shit. I'd forgotten to warn her about that.

"You're pierced." She reaches out to touch the tip of my cock where the head is pierced, and I shudder, my cock lurching up into her hand. "Does it feel good? For girls, I mean?"

You could find out, I want to say. Instead, I just nod. "So I've been told," I say hoarsely.

She wraps her hand around me, then, her thumb rubbing over the tip, toying with my piercing and spreading the pre-cum around the head. When she finally starts to stroke me, I'm slick with it, the tight and straining skin wet against her palm.

"Your mouth," I groan. "Please, Athena, I need your fucking mouth."

She looks at me with those wide, dark eyes, and there's a look in them that I can't quite read.

And then she bends her head to take my dick in her mouth.

The first cock that's ever been in there.

It's almost enough to make me come on the spot. Her mouth is hot and tight, sucking almost immediately as she goes down, and I know there's no way in hell she's going to be able to take all of me. All I can think of as she slides down until the head hits the back of her throat and then immediately comes back up, her hand still stroking me, is that she's already pretty fucking good at this. That, and how much fun it would be to teach her how to really suck a cock.

I'm not going to last long. Even inexperienced, she's good at keeping her teeth out of the way, and when she moans as she slides down again, I almost lose it. A second later, she comes back up, her lips wrapping around the head as her tongue toys with my piercing, and that's all it takes.

"Fuck, Athena, I'm going to come." My hand goes to the back of her head, and I expect her to let go of me, to recoil from my load before I can shoot it into her mouth.

Instead, she keeps going. She's sucking me shallowly now, probably because she's not used to having something so close to her throat. Still, her tongue is playing with my piercing, her lips fastened tightly around my shaft as her wet, drooling mouth sucks at the head, and through it all, she's still stroking me, faster and faster, her saliva and my pre-cum making my shaft so slick that it almost feels like I'm inside of her, and oh...*holy fuck.*

"Oh god, Natalie!" I scream without thinking, my hips bucking up into her mouth, and I feel her stiffen, but she keeps going.

I haven't come so hard in literal years. The first shot hits the back of her throat, and she coughs. Still, she's back at it in a second as she sucks harder, her tongue flat under the head as I shoot my cum into her mouth, filling it with a load bigger than I've had in a long time. To my astonishment, she swallows every last bit of it. She keeps going until there's not a single drop left, licking and sucking every last bit away. Finally, I have to pull her away because I'm too goddamn sensitive, and it almost fucking hurts.

I can't speak for a second. I'm panting, my whole body twitching and shuddering, and I burst out laughing when Athena sits back on her heels and asks worriedly, "Was that okay?"

"Yeah," I manage when I can speak again. "Yeah, that was really fucking good."

And then, with a flash of realization that makes my blood run cold, I remember what I said.

I'm on my feet in a flash, yanking up my jeans and grabbing my jacket. I grab Athena's elbow, hauling her up to her feet too, and I only have a second to take in the startled look on her face at the change in my mood.

"Come on," I snap. "Let's get you home."

She follows me without a word, and I can see the suddenly sad expression on her face, but I can't do anything about it. I can feel myself shutting down, closing off, and I clench my teeth as I start up the bike.

How could I have been so fucking stupid?

ATHENA

I've never been more confused than I am after that night.

I'd run out of the house terrified, upset, and feeling more broken than I'd ever felt in my entire life. And Jaxon had come after me. Probably because the guys had told him to, true, but still. He'd come after me. He hadn't pawned it off on someone else; he hadn't told them to do it. He'd been the one to come and get me, and instead of taking me straight back to the house, he'd actually taken care of me. Taken me to get some food, given me space to breathe.

And then—

I'd never imagined that I'd actually *enjoy* doing something with one of the guys, much less that I'd want it. Even less that I'd *beg* for it. And I hadn't thought I'd kiss one of them. In fact, that had been one of the few things I'd been pretty sure *wouldn't* happen. They wanted to hurt me, punish me, force me. Kissing was romantic, loving. I hadn't expected kissing.

I'd never been kissed before.

And I'm *glad* it was Jaxon.

God, it had felt so good kissing him. He'd felt familiar, good, like we were meant to be doing exactly that. He'd smelled like leather and exhaust, his hair had felt soft, and his stubble had felt so good under my fingertips. He'd kissed like he'd wanted nothing more than to have me in his arms, like he could have kissed me all night, and never stopped.

I'd never known what it was like to be that turned on. That aroused. I'd *wanted* him. If he'd pushed, I might even have slept with him. I don't know why, exactly, but I feel like Cayde and Dean might not want me anymore if I wasn't a virgin. But that wasn't why I'd come close to asking Jaxon to fuck me.

It was just because, very simply, I'd wanted him.

Now that my head is a little clearer, I'm glad, of course, that I didn't push things further. I'm not ready for that, if it's my choice, and not with Jaxon King, of all people. Even if he is the best choice of the three—he's still one of them.

But everything else we did—

I'd never known an orgasm could feel like that. And he'd made me come not once but twice. He'd kept going, even after he could have stopped and demanded his own pleasure. His mouth, his tongue, his fingers, it had all felt so fucking *good*. So good that I already wish he would do it again.

And I liked going down on him, too.

I liked that he hadn't forced me into it. That he'd made me come first. I'd realized that if given a choice, I actually *like* giving head. I liked how he felt in my mouth, that he was pierced, the way he'd tasted. I'd even liked swallowing his cum.

But then he'd called out someone else's name at the end.

Who is Natalie? I wonder as we speed back towards the manor. Whoever she was, or is, Jaxon had been upset that he'd done that. Not because he was worried about hurting my feelings, I don't think—he might have been nice to me, but I can't forget that he's a King, a member of one of the families, and he's not a nice guy. He's just as hard-edged and rough as the others. Just because he doesn't like hurting me doesn't mean he's a good guy.

I'd felt him shutting down after that. And now we're on our way back to the house, and I can feel my stomach knotting, my blood turning cold as I see the manor approaching in the distance. I don't want to go back in. I don't want to ever see Cayde and Dean again.

"Go upstairs," Jaxon says as soon as we walk in, and I see that no one is waiting for us. "Quickly, before someone realizes you're back."

I do as I'm told. He doesn't tell me goodnight. He doesn't say anything at all. It's as if everything that just happened out there in that grassy spot on the cliff didn't matter.

I should have expected that, I know. But it still stings.

My body feels wrung out, exhausted. I fall into bed still in my clothes, and thankfully, I don't dream.

* * *

THE NEXT MORNING, I'm awakened by a banging on my bedroom door. I pry one eyelid open and see that it's five a.m., a full hour before I usually wake up.

"Athena!" Cayde's voice is loud and angry outside my door. "Get the fuck up and meet us downstairs. Don't bother getting dressed. Put a robe on and meet us in the living room."

I swallow hard. I know what "don't bother getting dressed" means by now—he expects me to be naked under that robe. Whatever is waiting for me down there, I know I'm not going to enjoy it the way I enjoyed last night. But I also know I'm not going to get a choice in the matter.

I try not to panic, and I fight back the tears that threaten to well up in my eyes. In a way, what Jaxon did with me last night was almost cruel, even though I know he didn't mean it to be. But he showed me what it could be like to enjoy fooling around with someone, to get pleasure out of it, and it's going to make it that much harder to submit to what the other boys want from me now.

There's no thick, fluffy robe in the closet for me. Just short silk ones, and I wrap a black one around me, tying it tightly around my waist as if that will help me at all. As if it'll offer any protection.

I know I'm stupid to think so.

I walk into the living room, and to my surprise, find that it's just

Cayde and Dean sitting there. I look around despite myself for Jaxon, and Cayde laughs. It's a short bark of a sound, unpleasant and sharp, and I wonder if he knows what Jaxon and I did last night.

If this is going to be some kind of punishment for that.

"You did very well the other night, little Saint." Cayde's voice isn't quite as angry now. Dean is sitting next to him, his face impassive, but he nods.

"You did well with the pledges," he agrees. "You were a good pet, Athena."

"Thank you?" I manage, unable to stop the slight question in my voice. I don't think they brought me down here early, before breakfast, just to praise me.

"But," Cayde begins, and I can feel my shoulders slump. There's always going to be a "but."

"We were all very aroused by what a good pet you were," Dean says, interrupting him. "Seeing you like that, naked and bound." He grins, a hungry, predatory expression on his face. "I could have fucked you right there, little pet."

Cayde shoots him an annoyed look.

"So, am I in trouble?" I venture, and Cayde's glare turns on me.

"Yes, little Saint." He stands up, walking towards me with his hands clasped behind his back. "You left your owners here instead of pleasing them afterward. You left us hard and horny, and you didn't bother to ask if we needed anything from you. You were too worried about your own selfish feelings to remember who you belong to. So now you're going to pay for that." He smiles. "Drop the robe."

I know better than to argue. I blink back tears as I untie the sash, letting the robe slip from my shoulders and fall to the floor. I can feel Dean's icy eyes burning into me as he looks at me, taking in my nudity, enjoying my powerlessness.

Cayde's gaze rakes over me; he's enjoying it too. "So now you're going to make up for it," he says. "I guess Jaxon must not have cared that much since he elected not to be here this morning. He's already gone to class."

My eyes widen, and Cayde laughs. "Yes, little Saint. Your savior is gone already. He won't be sweeping you out of here and taking you to class before we can get our hands on you. Now, you have a choice."

"I do?" I blink at him, startled.

"Yes. Don't say I never give you anything."

"What is it?"

Cayde grins. "You can choose which one goes first. What you don't get to choose is what we do. You're going to get each of us off in whatever way we choose to make up for leaving us with blue balls last night. So pick, little Saint."

I stare at him. What a fucking "choice." I'm going to have to get both of them off no matter what, but I want to get Cayde out of the way as fast as fucking possible. And maybe if I choose him first, he'll be gentler with me.

"You," I say, lifting my chin.

Cayde laughs. "Good, little Saint. It's nice to be appreciated." He glances over at Dean. "Do you want to watch?"

Dean snorts. "No thanks. Come get me when you're done. Voyeurism isn't really my thing."

Cayde smirks. "Your loss." He strides over to the couch as Dean gets up and walks out without so much as a glance in my direction, leaning back. "Come over and get my pants open, little Saint. And act like you're excited about it."

I don't know how to be seductive. I honestly don't know how to lie with my face. I've always just settled for looking angry. But that won't help me here. So I just settle for walking slowly towards him, feeling his eyes on my naked body as I sink down to my knees in front of him and reach for his belt.

Last night, Jaxon had made me feel beautiful. He made me feel good. But now I feel self-conscious about my breasts that aren't big or small, just somewhere in between, my pale skin, my hair that hasn't even been brushed yet. I can see Cayde is hard, bulging out the front of his joggers, but I don't think he's hard because he thinks I'm hot. He's hard because he has power over me, because I'm on my knees on account of the fact that he ordered to me, and because he can make me touch him whether I want to or not.

"You wanna see my cock?" he grunts, and I nod, licking my lips as I reach for his belt.

"Yes," I whisper, knowing what he wants to hear. And I have to admit, I *am* a little curious. I know what Dean looks like, long and thick and straight, and what Jaxon looks like, also long and even thicker, with a little bit of a curve and that piercing through the head. I shiver a little at that memory of how he reacted when I played with it with my tongue, and Cayde takes that as me being aroused by undoing his pants.

"What a little whore." He strokes my hair. "You can't wait to see my dick. I can see it in your face. Well, get it out, slut. I wouldn't want to make you wait."

I swallow hard, reaching into Cayde's boxers and pulling out his hard cock, trapped beneath the waistband, and I wrap my hand around it as he groans.

"Fuck yes, little Saint. Stroke that fucking dick."

He's shorter than the other guys but impossibly thick. His cock throbs in my hand, pre-cum sliding down the shaft, and I look up at him, wondering what he wants me to do.

"Well, hurry up." Cayde spreads his legs wider, reaching into his boxers so that his heavy balls are outside of them as well, hanging down underneath his dick. "Lick my balls, you little slut."

I lean forward tentatively, dragging my tongue over the skin. He tastes faintly salty, the texture strange, and I trace upwards with the tip of my tongue, not entirely sure what I'm doing.

"Fuck yes, lick my balls. Don't forget my cock—oh yeah, just like that."

He keeps talking like that as I stroke him, groaning as I run my tongue over him and then up to his shaft, knowing what he wants next. I fit my mouth over the thick, swollen head, and as his pre-cum coats my tongue, I realize I like how he tastes, too.

I feel dirty, knowing I just sucked Jaxon's dick last night, and now Cayde's is in my mouth, and soon I'll have to get Dean off too. I should feel embarrassed, humiliated, but instead, I feel that aching, blossoming warmth between my legs again, and as I slide my mouth down Cayde's shaft, I can feel the sticky dampness on my inner thighs that tells me I'm very, very aroused.

I shouldn't like this. But I do. I like the feeling of Cayde's thick cock stretching my mouth. I like the taste of him, the manly scent. I've never felt so confused in my life because I fucking hate Cayde. I hate how he's treated me, I hate his attitude, I hate how much of an asshole he is.

But I like how this feels.

"That's right." Cayde sighs with satisfaction. "Fuck, you're not so bad at this after all. Your mouth feels good." He grabs the back of my head, and I realize that he's not going to let me ease into it the way Jaxon did.

Instead, his hips buck upwards as he pushes my head down, his cock shoving into the back of my throat. I choke, gagging on his thickness, my throat spasming around his dick.

"Oh god, yes. This is what I wanted to give you back in high school. I'm gonna fuck your throat, little Saint." Cayde surges off of the couch, his hand still knotted in my hair, so that I'm kneeling in front of him as he looms over me, and he starts to do exactly that.

He thrusts hard like he might if he were actually inside of me, fucking my mouth with a force that might knock me over if he weren't holding onto my head. I can feel my gag reflex reacting violently, but I force myself not to let myself vomit because I know he's trying to force me into that again, trying to reenact what happened in the library that night, except this time I'm not going to get away.

I can feel him swelling in my mouth and throat, hardening, as he groans above me, his hand in my hair so tightly now that it's almost painful.

"Fuck. I'm gonna come, gonna pour it all down your throat, fuuuck—" Cayde groans again, shoving his cock all the way down until my nose and mouth are pressed against his groin and my eyes water. Then I feel his hips jerk and the hot rush as his cum starts to shoot down my throat.

I swallow convulsively, trying not to choke, to drown in his cum, as he holds my mouth tightly against him. I squirm, trying to get away, feeling as if I'm going to suffocate on his cock. Still, he doesn't let go of me until I feel the last spasms of his release shudder through his dick. Then he lets go of my hair, shoving me off of him so hard that I fall backward onto my ass on the floor, my eyes red and teary from how hard he fucked my mouth.

Cayde strides to the door, his softening cock still hanging out of his pants. "Dean! Your turn," he yells and then flops onto the couch as Dean walks in.

"Put that shit away, man," Dean says, walking towards me. "And get on your knees, Athena. I don't have all morning."

"Nah." Cayde holds his dick loosely in his fist, watching as I pull myself back up to a kneeling position in the middle of the rug. "I want to watch this."

Dean shrugs. "Have it your way, man," he says, reaching for his belt.

It feels absolutely surreal. I can still taste Cayde in the back of my throat, and now Dean is getting his cock out. "Finish getting it hard," he says, almost as if he's bored. "Hurry up. Actually, do me a favor, Cayde. Call the maid, and tell her to serve breakfast in here." He pulls away from me and strides towards the couch. "Stay there, Athena, until I tell you differently."

I stare at him, watching as he sits down, lazily stroking his cock as he watches me kneel there. A moment later, Brooke walks in, her face flushing as she sees the two guys sitting, Cayde on the couch and Dean in the wing chair, both of them with their cocks out. Cayde is already half-hard again, his balls cupped in his hand as he lazily plays with himself, and Brooke hurriedly puts a tray down and excuses herself, casting a sideways glance at me as she leaves.

"Athena." Dean whistles at me. "Come here."

I get up, walking slowly towards him as he takes the lid off the breakfast tray, sitting next to him on a small table. His cock stiffens as I approach, and Dean smirks at me.

"Jaxon interrupted me last time," he says. "But this time, I get what

I want. Get on your knees, Athena, and blow me while I have my breakfast."

Somehow, this is even more humiliating than what Cayde did to me. Cayde was rough and mean, but Dean is treating me like I'm not even human, like I'm just something he can stick his cock into for pleasure while he goes about his day.

Which is—actually, pretty much what I am. It's one of the worst feelings I've had since I got here.

I sink to my knees, reaching for him as he starts to eat his breakfast. He doesn't touch me, doesn't groan, doesn't make any sound. He just eats his breakfast and sips his coffee as if I weren't even there, his hips occasionally jerking as I hit a spot he particularly likes. I'm almost angry by the time I've been at it a few minutes, and I try harder, sucking and licking, teasing the head the way Jaxon liked, but I can't get a single response from him. He ignores me completely as I suck him, until finally, he pauses, one of his hands going to grip the side of the chair as I feel him stiffen. It's the only hint that I get that he's about to come, and in the next second, he leans his head back, his eyes closing as I feel his cock start to spasm, shooting his load into my mouth and down my throat.

"Swallow it all. Good girl," he mutters, petting my head as I swallow convulsively the third load of cum I've had in my mouth in twelve hours. I slide my mouth off of him, and Dean glances down at me. "Lick it clean," he says, and I flick out my tongue, licking off the last of his cum until he nods.

"Good pet." He glances over at Cayde, who is hard again, jerking his cock as he watches me swallow Dean's cum and lick him off. "Looks like Cayde has another load for you. Go take it like a good girl."

I stare at him, but I know by now he's not joking. Numbly, I cross the room and kneel in front of Cayde again.

"Stick out your tongue," Cayde groans, and I obediently open my mouth, letting my tongue slide out as Cayde rests his cock on it, still jerking feverishly.

A second later, his cum shoots into my mouth, and once again, I swallow every drop.

"I think she's earned a place at the breakfast table," Dean says casually, buttering a piece of toast. "If she's still hungry, that is."

* * *

As I walk to school, I decide that I can't bear to spend another day in a class with Dean. English is the only class that I have with one of the guys. The add/drop period hasn't quite ended, so instead of going to a class where I'll have to see him sitting somewhere near me and think about what happened this morning throughout the entire lecture, I go to my advisor instead and ask him to get it switched. I have to change a couple of other classes to fit in a later English class, but thankfully, it works out.

It's the only good thing that's happened so far today.

I can't help but wonder, as I walk into the class that I switched to, how many of the guys in my classes were in that basement Friday night. I hardly saw them all or memorized their faces, but I'm betting they'll recognize me if they see me again. I doubt they'd say anything to me—they'd probably be too afraid of getting their asses beaten by Cayde or Dean or Jaxon if they said a word about what happened down there—but that's somehow almost worse. I could be sitting right next to someone who jerked off to me in that basement, and I'd never know.

The best thing I can do is just not really look at anyone, so I just get my books out, sliding down into my seat and doodling in my notebook as I wait for class to start. Until I hear a bright, surprised voice next to me call out my name.

"Athena? Oh my god!"

I know that voice. I look up, startled. *There's no way.*

I can't believe it. Mia is standing there in front of the empty seat right next to me, her eyes wide as she stares at me. "Oh my god, Athena, I didn't know you got into Blackmoor!"

"Um…yeah." I scramble to collect my thoughts, sitting up quickly. "I—yeah. I did. I didn't know you were going here, either."

Of course, Mia actually got in. She's smart as hell, and she actually belongs here.

Unlike me.

She sinks into the seat, her face practically glowing. "I can't believe it took this long for me to find out you were here! I barely talked to you all summer, I know. We were in Europe, and my parents wouldn't pay for me to have an international plan, and—"

She's chattering on now about her trip and the countries they went to, and meanwhile, all I can think is *I have a friend here now, an actual friend, and I'm not going to let them take this away from me.* The guys can do whatever they want to me, but I'm not letting them take away my best friend.

Suddenly, I feel like there's a light at the end of the tunnel. Something to grab onto, something good here in this awful mess.

"Let's get something to eat after school." Mia smiles brightly. "My treat. Okay? We can catch up then."

I know that's probably going to make me late, and I know I'm supposed to go directly home after class. But at the moment, I can't bring myself to care.

So against my better judgment, after classes are done for the day, I meet Mia at a cute, quaint little coffee shop on the edge of campus, the kind of place that also serves tea and scones in china cups and on pretty little dishes along with the coffee and sandwiches.

"Get whatever you want," Mia says. "It's on me." Which is a relief because I still don't have any actual money. I'm sure it's to prevent exactly this, being out with someone who isn't in the guys' circle, who might not approve of what's going on.

"I got a scholarship," Mia tells me after our sandwiches and scones and coffee are brought to the table. "My parents were thrilled, of course—they have plenty of money for tuition, but now my mother can spend it on face-lifts instead of classes for me." She rolls her eyes. "I thought it should go to someone who needed it more, but whatever. I guess 'merit' scholarships are a thing. What about you,

Athena. Did you get a scholarship? Or is this Philip St. Vincent again?"

It's almost as if something shorts out in my head. I hear buzzing, garbled voices like I did the morning after I woke up in the bed in the manor, and I smell something coppery and damp.

And then, just as quickly, it's gone.

"Athena?" Mia peers at me. "Are you okay?"

"Yeah," I manage. "I'm fine. A little bit of a headache, that's all. I guess you could say I have a scholarship."

Mia frowns. "What dorm are you in? I don't even have a roommate yet. Oh!" She exclaims excitedly. "I know! Maybe you could get a transfer, or…"

"I'm in Blackmoor House." I just say it, flat out, my voice miserable. Mia probably knows what that means. Everyone else at the school seemed to. I wonder, numbly, if she'll still want to be friends with me after she realizes. Or if she won't want anything to do with the Blackmoor House whore. The *pet*."

Mia pauses, and she looks a little pale. "Oh," she says softly, setting her coffee cup down. "I heard stories about that. I'd always just thought they were that, though. Stories."

"No." I bite my lip hard to keep the tears from welling up. "There's a contract and everything. It's very real."

"So you agreed to it? For what…tuition? I mean, I guess I get it, but Cayde was such an asshole to you in high school—" Mia trails off as she sees my eyes shimmering. "Athena, are you okay?"

The compassion in her voice undoes me. I can't stop the tears then, and I wipe them away as fast as I can, sniffling as I try to get myself under control. And then, with Mia looking at me sympathetically, I do exactly what I know I shouldn't.

I let it all out.

I tell her about waking up not knowing where I was, not being able to remember the days beforehand. I tell her about the contract I can't remember signing and what happens if I break it. I admit to what my father did, tell her what would happen to my mother and me out on the street. And I even tell her about what Cayde and Dean have done to me so far, less graphically, of course. But it feels good to tell *someone*.

"Jaxon is the only one who's been somewhat nice to me," I tell her. "Not *nice*, but not an asshole, either."

"So he's left you alone?" Mia frowns.

"No. But what we did—it was nice. Good, even. He didn't force me." I tell Mia about the pledge party then, and by the time I finish, her face is completely white.

"Oh my god, Athena. How can any of this be legal? I mean, if you don't remember signing the contract—"

"I don't. But my signature is there, and it's not forged. I can only imagine they have some proof of me actually signing it. It would be my word against theirs that I was under some kind of influence when I did it—I must have been. But my word won't count for anything against them. You know that."

"I mean…" Mia hesitates. "It sounds awful. But maybe it could be worse? I mean, lots of girls have had sex at college and also have to pay for classes."

"They made me eat off of a plate on the floor."

Mia winces. "I've heard weird things about the families, you know. I mean, there are always rumors. But now that I'm here, there's even more. Especially since there are kids here from outside Blackmoor."

"What kind of rumors?"

She leans closer. "That the founding families are part of some kind of weird cult. That they do rituals and stuff. Blood vows and crazy shit like that. Isn't that wild?"

"That can't be true." I look at her, and Mia starts to laugh.

"Right? It can't possibly be real. I mean, can you imagine?"

"No, I really can't." I try to imagine Cayde and Jaxon in some kind of flowing ritual robes, chanting under the full moon. Dean, I can kind of see it, but the others I can't, especially not Jaxon. The entire idea is completely ridiculous.

We spend the rest of the afternoon talking about Mia's vacation to Europe, about how happy she is to be here at Blackmoor, and how she finally feels how she can be herself—nerdy, into her studies, excited to learn. It's a far cry from my experience so far. Still, I push her to talk about herself and not my situation—partly because I just don't want to think about it anymore, and partially because it feels good to vicariously live through her, to imagine a world where I still have two parents, where they can take me on exotic vacations, where I live in a dorm and go to sleep every night without wondering what fresh torments my "roommates" might have cooked up for me the next day.

Where I can just be myself—someone that I'm not even sure I recognize anymore.

I used to feel like I had a good grip on myself. But now I wonder if all that acting out, all that tough-girl façade, was just a cover to keep me from falling into exactly the kind of situation I'm in now, one where I have no control over my life, where men are trying to bully me into submission, where any happiness I have is subject to the whim of others.

If so, I guess I didn't do a very good job. And if so, then who am I now? Am I just the heirs' pet, just a girl whose entire identity will be shaped from now on around the men who claim they own her?

That's a really fucking depressing thought.

It feels good to lose myself in Mia's world for a little while, though, so much so that when I finally check the time, I realize with horror that I've stayed *way* later than I was supposed to.

"I have to go," I tell Mia, my stomach knotting with dread. "I'm going to be late. And they get really pissed when I'm late."

Mia frowns. "I'm really worried about you, Athena. This doesn't sound healthy—"

"It's not," I tell her flatly. "But until I figure out some way out of it, I've just got to try to survive."

She opens her mouth as if to say something else, but I'm already flying out the door, my bookbag clenched in my hand as I hurry down the cobbled path back towards the manor house.

The last time I was late, they made me eat while kneeling on the floor for a week. *What is it going to be this time?* If there's anything I know about the guys, it's that they like to escalate their punishments, particularly Cayde. I have a desperate, terrifying feeling that whatever is waiting for me this time, it's going to be way worse than just being fed like a dog.

This is *definitely* not something I could have imagined myself thinking a little over a week ago.

Geoffrey is waiting for me when I burst into the house, almost slipping on the foyer tile. His face is set in grim lines as always, his mouth thin and disapproving as he looks at me—hair tangled around my face from running, shirt riding up, sweating. I don't look prim and proper, that's for sure.

"Clean yourself up," he says, a hint of disgust in his tone. "The heirs are waiting for you in the study."

Fuck. The study is the only room I was explicitly ordered not to go into or even try. As far as I know, it's usually locked. If I'm being called in there, they must be really pissed.

Or maybe not. Maybe they're going to ask for help with their homework.

Fat chance.

The only way I usually know how to deal with things like this is gallows humor, but even that's running dry for me lately. My heart is pounding in my chest as I splash water over my face, cooling off my flushed skin as I wipe it dry and run my fingers through my tangled hair, trying to make myself at least a tiny bit presentable. So maybe they won't be quite so pissed with me.

Who am I kidding? Whatever they've decided to do, they've already made up their minds. Looking a bit less like I just bolted across campus isn't going to really help me.

Geoffrey opens the study door for me as I approach, waving me in. I walk inside a bit unsteadily, looking around.

It's an overly masculine room, all dark, old-fashioned wallpaper, and heavy wainscoting, with trophy animal heads on the walls and heavy furniture—dark mahogany and leather throughout. There's a stone fireplace with a wood mantle and a long desk at one end that has several full bookcases behind it. I think of the empty bookcase in my room and feel a twinge of sadness.

The room smells like cigar smoke and leather, heavily masculine scents that remind me vaguely of a very different setting, the biker bars that my father used to hang out at. I wound up just inside once or twice when my mother would come to drop off something for him, and I remember that scent viscerally. But there it was mixed with the scent of engine grease and beer and sweat, and in here, there are none of those things. It's all elegant, old-fashioned masculinity in here. However, I have a feeling whatever the guys are about to do to me isn't going to be very elegant.

Cayde is sitting on a caramel-colored leather couch, and Jaxon is slouched in a nearby armchair as usual. Dean is standing by the fireplace, and they all look at me in unison as I walk in.

"Well," Cayde drawls. "If it isn't our little Saint. Do you need us to buy you a watch, so you can learn how to be on time?"

I could use a cell phone, you fuckers, I want to snap, but I don't. They might have already made up their minds what they want to do to me as a punishment, but whatever it is, I'm sure I could make it worse by what Dean likes to call my "smart mouth."

"I'm sorry," I say quickly. "I just lost track of time, and—"

"You were talking to a friend." Cayde smiles nastily. "Don't you think we know everything that's going on? Don't think you can slip something past us, little Saint. It'll just be worse for you in the end if you try."

I bite my lower lip hard. "I—"

"Mia Grayson, right?" Cayde glances over at Dean and Jaxon. "Do we think she's appropriate company for our little pet?"

I stare at him in horror. "Cayde, please—"

"Shut up!" he yells, his face flushing. "You don't speak while we make decisions, Athena." My name in his hard, angry voice sounds terrifying, and I flinch back, clasping my hands in front of me to stop them from shaking.

Dean shrugs. "She's from a good family. I vaguely remember her from high school. Nerdy, nose always in books, doesn't party or even really date. I'd say as friends go, she's a pretty harmless one."

Something loosens inside of me, and I look over at Dean gratefully, but he doesn't even bother meeting my eyes.

"Should we allow a pet to have friends at all, though?" Cayde asks thoughtfully. "Won't it just make her dissatisfied with everything we give her here?"

"Oh, come off it, Cayde," Jaxon says, rolling his eyes. "I know you're really into this whole *pet* thing, but she's still a fucking person. She needs someone who actually likes her. Let her have this Mia girl. She sounds boring as hell. If anything, Athena will come running back here for some excitement."

"Fine." Cayde narrows his eyes at me. "But if she turns out to be a bad influence, or if your behavior is bad—"

"It won't be," I promise hurriedly. "I promise, Cayde. I'll be good. Thank you—"

"Well, you'll have your first opportunity to prove it right now." Cayde nods to the chair in front of me. "You were late, Athena, and you need to be punished for that. Put on that outfit."

I lick my lips nervously, looking at what's laid out on the chair. As I slowly step forward and pick up the items, I realize it's a short pleated skirt, a collared sleeveless white shirt with a bow tied below the bust, and thigh-high stockings.

A schoolgirl uniform.

Normally I would have argued, or at least thought about it, but after Cayde's allowance, I don't dare. *They're just going to make me suck their dicks in it or something,* I think to myself. *Nothing that I haven't done before. It'll be fine.*

Quickly, I slip out of the clothes I'd picked for today, ignoring their eyes on me as I strip down to my bra and panties and reach for the thigh-highs.

"Lose the underwear too," Cayde instructs. "No bra or panties."

I wince but quickly pull them off, too, tossing them onto the pile of my clothes. I shimmy into the tight schoolgirl outfit as quickly as I can, wanting to be somewhat covered—although it doesn't do much. The skirt hardly covers my ass, the bottom of my cheeks showing even with it tugged down, and the shirt is as always a little too small. I can't button it above the knot, so my cleavage shows fully, the rounded sides of my breasts pushing against the sheer, tight white material. My nipples are pretty visible through it, too—it's not really clothing. Fetish wear, more like it.

"Is this okay?" I ask meekly once it's on, hating myself as the words come out of my mouth. But I'm not about to lose my chance to keep my one friend.

"Put your hair in two ponytails," Cayde orders. "Like a schoolgirl."

It's all I can do not to roll my eyes, but I quickly obey.

"Very good. Dean?"

I glance nervously over at Dean, wondering what he's about to do. He glances once at me, heat apparent in his gaze, before striding towards a tall cabinet against the opposite wall that looks very much like a gun cabinet.

But when he opens it, I see that's not what's in there at all. Instead of guns, it's a variety of whips and other implements. A riding crop, a bullwhip, a long rattan cane.

The cane is what Dean takes out of the cabinet.

I can feel my face paling. "Oh. Oh no, Cayde, I'm sorry, I—"

"Bend over the desk, Athena," Cayde says sharply. "Go!"

I can feel helpless tears filling my eyes, but I know I don't have a choice. I look at Jaxon, hoping he'll intervene somehow, but he doesn't say anything. He won't even meet my eyes.

I've never been spanked in my life. I've definitely never been *caned*. I can feel myself starting to tremble with fear as I walk towards the desk slowly with legs that feel weighed down like concrete now, my heart in my throat as I slowly bend over the desk.

"Pull your skirt up with one hand and grab the desk with the other. Make sure we can see your whole ass. And keep your legs together, you little slut."

Blinking back tears, I grope behind me for my skirt, grabbing the hem and bunching it in my hand as I pull it up over my ass. I can feel the cool air of the room hit my bare skin as I hold the skirt up, gripping the other end of the desk as instructed.

"See, you can be a good girl," Cayde says, his voice patronizing. "Alright. You were a half-hour late, so I think thirty strokes—one for each minute you were late. Jaxon, you get to do the honors."

What? I twist around, my face going pale. "Jaxon, no—"

"That's another stroke," Cayde says. "And not on your ass."

What does he mean? "Jaxon, you promised—"

"That's two. Oh?" Cayde sounds interested. "What did you promise her, Jaxon?"

"I just told her what she wanted to hear to get her panties down," Jaxon says, sounding bored.

I stare at him in horror, but his face is blank and emotionless. *That's not true,* I think, but as he takes the cane from Dean, I feel the tears starting to slide down my cheeks. I can still remember him saying, *you don't have to worry about that with me. I don't like hurting girls; that doesn't get me off.* But there he is, walking towards me with the cane.

Out of everything that's happened so far, this hurts the most. I feel betrayed, hollowed out, as if something is cracking inside of my chest. All I can think about is what I did with Jaxon on that cliffside afterward, about how much I'd enjoyed it, how I'd opened up to him and let him do those things to me and done those things to him because I'd believed him. I'd believed he cared, just a little. I'd believed he didn't want to hurt me.

This is because he embarrassed himself. Because he called out that girl's name when he came. That, or Cayde, has something on him that forced him into doing this, but as Jaxon comes to stand behind me, I know that's probably wishful thinking.

He told you not to rely on him. Not to trust him. This is why.

"Turn back around, Athena." Jaxon's voice is flat and emotionless. "And count the strokes. Aloud."

I swallow hard, bracing myself for the first one. I don't want to cry, and I try to fight back the tears, not wanting him to see how hurt I am by this. But when the first stroke of the cane lands across my backside, I can't help it.

"Ow!" I screech.

"Three more, not on your ass. Athena, you better keep your mouth shut except to count," Cayde warns. "You're not going to like where the extras are going. Start over, Jaxon, since she didn't obey."

I bite my lip hard as the next one hits. "One!" I cry out, clutching the desk. It hurts so much. I'd thought Jaxon might go easy on me— my last thread of hope as to why he was the one doing it was that maybe he'd asked to spare me the thrashing the other guys would have given me. But clearly, that's not the case.

If anything, his strokes get harder as they go on and as I count. "Two! Three! Four!" I'm crying openly by five, my ass on fire. Still, as the cane hits, again and again, making a pattern across my ass as Jaxon alternates between the stroke coming down on different cheeks and then the base of them, I feel something else, too.

A growing heat between my legs and dampness. *I'm getting wet,* I realize with horror, as I whimper out "twelve." By fifteen, the halfway mark, I can feel my arousal sticking to my thighs, my folds drenched with it as Jaxon brings the cane down again and again.

By twenty, my clit is pulsing, and I feel my hips moving the tiniest bit against the desk as my body starts to seek out some relief, my back arching. My pussy is aching, and I bite back a moan as Jaxon brings down the twenty-third strike.

"Holy shit, did she just moan?" Dean asks, and I squeeze my eyes tightly shut, feeling my face flame with embarrassment.

"I think she did," Cayde says. "Jaxon, is our little slut wet?"

The strokes pause for a blessed moment, and then I feel Jaxon's fingers pressing against my pussy, sliding through my folds as his fingertips brush over my clit for a single, exhilarating second that makes me moan in earnest this time, my legs opening without my meaning for them too.

"Holy fuck, she's soaking wet," Jaxon says, his voice thick with obvious lust. "I think she likes it."

I feel his fingers slide into me for the briefest second, and I arch backward without meaning to, wanting more of them inside of me. I can feel my pussy clench around his fingers, squirming against his hand, and Jaxon pumps them twice inside of me before pulling them free.

"Seven more," Jaxon says. "Try not to come while I spank you, slut."

What the fuck is wrong with me? Hearing Jaxon calling me a slut makes me want to cry at the same time that my body reacts with a fresh flood of arousal, dripping down my thighs as he hits me again with the cane.

"Twenty-four," I moan, and by twenty-six, I feel like if I had the tiniest bit of stimulation, I might actually come.

"Twenty-six. Oh god, Jaxon, please—" I moan. My ass hurts, it's on fire, and I don't feel like I can take another stroke, but at the same time, I'm hornier than I've ever been in my life. My pussy is aching to be filled, and I'm pretty sure if Jaxon tried to fuck me right now, I might let him. The other two I'm not sure about, I still hate them—but my mind is at war with my body, struggling between my resistance to wanting any of this and the fact that I so obviously have a kink that I was never aware of before.

"That's four. Jaxon, give her the last four on her ass."

I honestly don't know how I bear it. My brain feels as if it's short-circuiting, caught between excruciating pain and the hot pleasure sweeping through my body. I feel like I'm literally teetering on the edge of orgasm, my pussy dripping with arousal, my ass arching up for each stroke as I cry out, my voice just a sobbing moan as I whisper, "twenty-seven, twenty-eight..."

The last two come down hard, and I can hear Jaxon breathing heavily behind me. When I moan "thirty," he pauses, and then with a voice so thick with lust that it sends another bolt of need through me, he tells me harshly, "Athena, open your legs as wide as you can."

For a brief, wild second, I think he's going to fuck me, and there's no way I would say no right now. I'm too foggy with confused desire and too overcome with the pain and shock of getting my ass caned for the first time in my life. I feel like I've entered some other dimension. I don't have the slightest grasp of what is about to happen until I feel the *whoosh* of the cane coming up between my thighs, and then my world splits apart with pain as it strikes my clit.

"One," Jaxon says. "Fuck, Cayde, do you think she can take four?"

"I think she'll come before you get to four. Wanna bet?" Cayde drawls.

"I'll take that bet," Dean says. "A thousand bucks says she doesn't. I've never seen a girl come from getting her clit spanked."

"A thousand says she will." Cayde groans. "Jaxon, hurry up. I'm so fucking hard my dick hurts."

They're betting on whether or not I'm going to come, I think dizzily, my brain muddled and foggy. *There's no way I will.* And I'm suddenly determined *not to,* just so Cayde loses his thousand dollars.

"Two," Jaxon says, and I scream as the cane hits my clit again.

"Three."

My world shatters. The cane hits my clit for the third time, and I feel a sudden wave of pleasure mixed with the pain like nothing else I've ever felt in my life. I grab onto the desk harder, my back arching, my whole body spasming, my legs splayed lewdly wide. I know the guys can see everything, my pink, swollen, dripping pussy, and my reddened ass. Even that thought only makes me come harder as Jaxon brings the cane up against my throbbing clit for the fourth and last time. I think I'm going to go insane with the mingled pain and pleasure that makes every inch of my body feel like a raw, shuddering nerve ending.

"Holy shit," Jaxon says, almost reverently. "She fucking came. I've never seen a girl come so hard."

"You owe me a thousand bucks," Cayde says from behind me, and then I hear zippers being pulled down as the guys come towards me.

"Play with that pussy, Athena," Cayde says, and I can hear the sound of him starting to jerk his cock. "I want to see your fingers on your clit. Spread with one hand, play with your clit with the other. Make yourself come again if you can."

There's no way. My whole body is still twitching, but as I move to obey, my body feeling slow and heavy with exhaustion, I can feel that flicker of heat still throbbing between my legs. My clit is raw and sore, but even as I touch it, I can feel the need rising up again as I hear the guys come to stand behind me, the slap of their hands on their cocks louder now as they jerk themselves off to the sight of my red, upturned ass.

I can't come again. I can't. But I can feel how wet I am, my fingers slick with it, soothing my abused clit as I rub it gently, and as I hear the first groan behind me and feel the hot splash of cum over my already heated ass, my clit throbs under my fingertips.

"Fuck, look at that ass," Dean groans, and I feel his cum splash on the other cheek, dripping down my thigh as he shoots over my ass and the small of my back. "God, that's so fucking hot," he moans, and I can feel Cayde still coming too, until my skin is coated with it.

Jaxon isn't going to join in. But as I start to move my fingers away from my clit, almost reluctantly, I hear his harsh voice from behind me.

"Get that hand back on your pussy, Athena. I'm not done."

I start to cry again because I'd thought for sure he wouldn't get off on it. But at the same time, my hand eagerly goes back to my pussy, rubbing faster, because suddenly I *want* to come, I want to feel another orgasm while Jaxon shoots his cum all over my ass, and as I hear him groan, I feel the first tremors of it starting to run through my body.

When I feel his first spurt hit my skin, I start to come. I cry out, moaning as I arch my ass upwards, completely lost now as I hear Jaxon groaning. "Take my cum, you fucking slut," he mutters. The words feel like a knife even as I come harder, feeling his cum trailing down the side of my ass, down over my fingers as I rub my clit frantically, bucking against my hand as the orgasm shakes my entire body.

Everything feels like a blur. I lay there, still shivering from the aftershocks of my orgasm, and I wait for Cayde, for someone to tell me what to do next. But then I hear their footsteps walking away and the heavy sound of the door shutting behind them.

Somehow, I pry myself off of the desk. With the pleasure fading away, all I can feel is the burning, aching, stinging pain of my freshly caned ass, radiating into the small of my back and my thighs. I stumble towards my pile of clothes, reaching for my shirt to wipe the cum off of my ass, and I cry out with pain as the fabric touches my raw flesh.

It takes forever for me to get up to the shower. I don't see the guys anywhere, the maids or Geoffrey, and I'm thankful for that. *They're probably eating dinner*, but I've never been less hungry in my life.

I get undressed in the bathroom, my movements slow and choppy, leaving all of my clothes in a pile on the floor as I step under the hot water. It burns against my caned skin but feels good at the same time, washing away the evidence of what the guys did to me. I can see that the water flowing down the drain is faintly pink, and I lean my head against the shower wall, starting to cry again in earnest in here, where no one can hear me.

I've never been so confused in my entire life. I feel like I'm having some kind of sexual awakening. If it were under other circumstances, it would be amazing. I experienced more pleasure in that room than I ever have in my life, but more excruciating pain, too. *If only it wasn't with three guys who want to hurt me more than anything else, torment me, and bully me until they break me.* I don't know how to fight back when my body wants to give in to them. And then Jaxon—

I start to sob, thinking of Jaxon. I'd *liked* him. I'd wanted to trust him. I'd thought that he'd really meant what he said to me.

But clearly, he lied. Not only had he been the one to punish me after he'd promised he never would, but he'd also *enjoyed* it.

I feel betrayed and more broken than ever.

And now I have no idea who I can trust, if anyone.

I've never felt so alone in my entire life.

ATHENA

The next day, the house is empty when I come down for breakfast in the morning, except for Geoffrey. He informs me very coldly that I'm required to be at the field after class to attend Cayde's first rugby game of the season. I actually have the option to sit down and have breakfast in peace at the table, which seems like a cruelly planned trick since I...can't actually sit.

I opt for a cheese Danish from the kitchen instead and walk very slowly to class, wincing with every step. I'd have given anything to just stay in bed, but although nothing has ever been said about what happens if I miss class, I'm fairly certain it wouldn't be good. I suspect there would be some sort of punishment for that—or who knows. Maybe the guys don't give a shit about my attendance or grades.

I think they'd take any excuse to get to "punish" me again, though.

Mia is already in English when I come in, and as I sit down gingerly, wincing, she eyes me curiously.

"Are you okay?"

"You don't want to know," I mutter through clenched teeth.

"Did they—oh my god." Mia's eyes go round. "Athena, they can't—"

"They did." I wince, settling into the chair. "Just...let's not talk about it."

I can tell that she has a lot she wants to say about it, but the lecture is starting, which I'm grateful for. I'm not prepared to explain to Mia that it was both the worst experience of my entire life and that I came twice, harder than I ever knew I could. I have no idea if Mia is still a virgin or not, but I suspect she is. I definitely don't think she's ever imagined getting bent over a desk while getting caned and then having three guys jerk off onto her ass.

God, just thinking about it makes me turn bright red.

"You know," Mia whispers, leaning very close to me. "I might not have had sex yet, but I read a lot of romance novels. A *lot*, so you might be surprised what you can tell me, and I won't freak out."

I whip my head around, staring at her. "Did you just read my freaking mind?"

"No." She laughs. "But your face is *really* easy to read if someone knows you at all. Like...*at all*."

I can't help but laugh then, too. "They caned me," I whisper, leaning close so no one else can hear us whispering.

"Ouch." Mia winces.

"Yeah, ouch is right. It really fucking hurt. And I was so angry and upset, but...it felt good, too. I kind of...liked it. I still hate Cayde's guts and Dean, too...and Jaxon for lying to me. But at the same time—"

"You liked being spanked."

"Yeah." I look over at her. "I didn't expect you to be so chill about it."

Mia shrugs. "I think it's kind of hot. But Athena, it's not okay if you don't want them to do it."

"I don't—but I also do. I wish it was anyone but them. But I don't have a choice—and in a weird way, that turns me on, too."

Mia laughs. "Girl, you have a *fucked* up life right now."

"I know."

The professor stops, glaring up at us. "Ladies, do you have something you want to share with the class?"

Oh god, no. "No, sir," I manage, and he nods.

"Good. No more talking, please."

After class, I invite Mia to come to the rugby game with me, and she agrees to meet me after our other classes. It's the most normal thing I've done since starting here—going to a sports game with a friend, and I'm oddly looking forward to it, even if it is Cayde's game.

The rugby field is on the opposite end of campus. Mia and I walk there with energy drinks that she brought for us, chatting about classes and her new roommate and anything, really, other than what happened to me yesterday.

"I guess we'll stand," Mia says with a snicker, and I can't help but laugh too. It helps, really, that she makes light of it because it makes it not feel as awful as it is, as completely and utterly overwhelming.

As we walk towards the sidelines where Jaxon and Dean are standing, I have a weird feeling, a shiver running over me as if someone walked over my grave.

"Who is that?" Mia asks, and I glance in the direction she's pointing, only to see an odd-looking girl standing away from everyone else, watching us as we walk over to join the guys. She's tall and extremely thin, almost scarily so, with long black hair that hangs around her face in a way that's reminiscent of that one girl from the Ring, stringy and unkempt. She looks fucking weird, to be honest, and not just because she's watching us so closely.

There's just something that feels...*off* about her.

"Do you know her?"

"No." I shake my head, trying to shrug off the creeping feeling crawling down my spine. "I've never seen her before."

"Weird." Mia watches the girl for a moment, and then suddenly, she turns, her expression brightening as she sees a tall, gorgeous blonde striding quickly towards us.

"Athena, this is my new roommate, Winter Romero. Winter, this is my friend from high school, Athena Saint."

"The Blackmoor House girl." Winter's voice has that hint of jealousy that I hear so often in anyone's voice who knows I'm living there, which I don't think I'll ever understand.

"Yeah." I give her the same once-over she's giving me, and I'm a little surprised that Mia seems to get along with her so well. Winter looks like the typical Blackmoor girl, with thick, highlighted blonde

178

hair that she has pulled back in a sporty ponytail. She is wearing tight yoga pants that leave very little to the imagination and a cropped workout tank. She doesn't look like she just came from the gym, though; her face is perfectly made up, right down to her glossy lips and false eyelashes coated in mascara.

"And are these two of the guys you live with?" Winter looks over at Jaxon and Dean, and as her eyes linger on Jaxon for a second too long, I feel an odd flare of jealousy, which I immediately feel all too weird about. *I should want her to take them off my hands,* I think, but the idea of someone else catching Jaxon's eye makes my stomach knot for reasons that I don't totally understand.

"This is Jaxon King and Dean Blackmoor," I say flatly, wishing more than anything that I didn't have to fucking introduce them as if she doesn't already know who they are.

"You're so lucky," Winter says enviously, her gaze raking over Dean now. She seems to like him even better, tossing her long blonde ponytail over her shoulder and toying with the end flirtatiously. "I'm Winter Romero."

"Nice to meet you," Dean says politely. Jaxon just ignores her, which I can plainly see irritates her and gives me a small, warm feeling in the pit of my stomach.

"God, I'd give anything to live with three guys that gorgeous. You must be the luckiest girl on the planet, Athena," Winter says, smiling at me, although it doesn't quite reach her eyes. "Just eye candy all day, every day."

"Sure thing," I mutter, knowing Dean is in hearing range and remembering very well how he reacted to me setting the girl in English class straight that first day. The last thing I need is some sort of voyeuristic "punishment" out here in full view of everyone, and I'm not entirely sure that they couldn't get away with it.

We wait by the sidelines as the game starts, the players running out onto the field. I can pick Cayde out immediately, and Winter sighs enviously. "God, he's jacked," she says, her gaze following Cayde as he crosses the field. "How do you even pick? They're all *so* hot."

I roll my eyes, making sure no one can see me, and try to pay attention to the game. I don't actually know anything about rugby or the rules, but it's a rough sport, which surprises me. I wouldn't have thought Cayde would be down for something so brutal—but I guess maybe he enjoys the violence of it. More surprising than that even is that his *father* allows him to do it, which makes me wonder about Cayde in a way that I haven't before. Maybe he has a rebellious side that I don't know about.

As Mia and I try to follow the game, I can see Winter sidling between the two guys, her gaze flicking between Jaxon and Dean as she says something to them in low tones. Jaxon laughs, and I feel that burning in my gut again, jealousy that I didn't even know I could feel. *I don't even want them*, I think to myself, but the sick feeling in my stomach says something else.

The truth is that I don't even really know what I want anymore. Everything I'd thought I'd had planned for my life was so totally upended, and now it feels like my life has just become a series of one confusing event after another.

Blackmoor's team wins the game, which is hardly surprising. It looked like they were murdering the other team the entire time, even to my inexperienced eyes. They explode into celebration, whooping and cheering and chest-bumping each other across the field. Then Cayde breaks off, heading in our direction. He's sweaty and dirty, grass stuck to him in several places, and despite myself, I feel a tingle of excitement as he strides towards us.

Winter looks as if she's glowing as Cayde ducks underneath the rope separating us from the field. "Cayde St. Vincent!" she squeals. "I've heard *so* much about you. I couldn't wait to meet you. Congratulations on the win."

Cayde glances at her, his gaze raking up and down her body once before he shrugs. "Can't say I've ever heard of you," he says bluntly, and then he grabs my elbow. "Come on, Athena."

"What—" I start to say, but he's already hustling me along next to him, and I realize with a start that he's taking me back to the guy's locker rooms with him. "I don't think I'm supposed to go in there—"

"You go wherever I say you do," he snaps. "Come on."

He's clearly in a mood, despite the win, and I wrack my brain for what I could have done to upset him. I don't have to wait very long, though.

The moment we're inside, he kicks the door shut and grabs me, swinging me around up against one of the lockers and shoving me up against it hard. It takes the air out of me for a second, and my eyes widen, looking up at him as he looms over me. "Cayde," I whisper, feeling my heart start to pound. "What's going on?"

"I heard you did something with Jaxon," he murmurs darkly, looking down at me. "Away from the house, off on your own."

"It wasn't a big deal." I wriggle in his grasp, but his hands are hard on my arms, almost bruising. "Cayde, you're hurting me."

"Good." His green eyes darken, hungrily sweeping over my face. "Don't bother downplaying it. I already know. We don't keep secrets from each other, the three of us. Jaxon told me he ate your pussy." His hips move against me, and I can feel how hard he is. He rubs against my thigh, and despite myself, a tiny moan slips from between my lips. My ass hurts, pressed against the locker, and Cayde's hands on my arms hurt, but I can feel myself getting aroused. "Do you want me to eat your pussy, little Saint?"

I shake my head quickly. "No," I whisper.

"Don't lie to me. Bad girls lie. Bad girls get punished." Cayde grinds against me harder, and I whimper.

"That hurts, Cayde. My ass hurts."

"What if I cane it again? Maybe I'll use a crop this time. You deserve it for lying to me."

"I don't want you to do that."

"I heard you sucked his cock, too. Found out about his little surprise. Did you like that, little Saint?"

"No." I shake my head, but my voice is far from convincing.

"Now I know you're lying to me." Cayde grabs my hands, pinning them over my head against the locker as his other hand goes to my breast. "I bet if I pulled those jeans down right now and fucked you up against this locker, you'd come all over my cock while you told me you didn't want it and begged me to stop. You're such a little liar, Saint. And you're going to pay for all these lies."

His hips grind into me again, his hand squeezing my wrists so tightly I feel like I'm starting to lose circulation. "Why haven't you behaved like that with me, little Saint? You act like sucking my cock and taking my cum is the worst thing in the world, but Jaxon says you begged for his. He says you would have let him fuck you if he'd tried. So why won't you ask me for it?"

I feel anger boiling up in my gut, heating my blood and pushing the confusing arousal aside. *Why the fuck not?* "Maybe because you're a fucking asshole," I spit, raising my chin and glaring at him. All of my frustration starts to boil over then, all of my anger at how strangely my body is behaving, at Cayde and Dean for being such jerks, at them for punishing me over the stupidest shit, hurting me just because they can. "Maybe I wanted Jaxon because he was a little bit nice to me."

"Oh, I know." Cayde grins darkly down at me. "That's why I made him cane you. You see, Jaxon isn't really different from us, Saint. And I needed to make sure you saw that. But now I want you to beg for the same thing, Saint."

"I'm under contract," I retort defiantly. "So why don't you just fucking make me? You can make me do anything? So just fucking take it, Cayde. I'm tired of all these stupid games. Just fuck me and get it over with. You're boring me."

I turn my head away, refusing to look at him. I meant every word of it, and I don't care if he beats my ass raw again for saying it. I'm tired of playing their stupid games. I'm tired of wondering who I can trust. Clearly, it's none of them, even though my heart still yearns to give Jaxon a chance.

Cayde grabs my chin roughly, turning my face back towards him so that I have no choice but to look at him. "Maybe I should," he says, his voice dark and gravelly.

And then he does what I never would have expected. With his hand still firmly on my chin, he surges forward, and his mouth crashes down on mine.

It's hard and firm, his lips full, and I feel as if he's eating me from the mouth down. There's nothing gentle or coaxing about it. He forces my mouth open with his hand, his tongue plunging inside, and he tastes like citrus, like sports drinks, his lips faintly salty from sweat. I feel something in me respond even as I squirm in his grasp, trying to wriggle away from him and the lockers. Still, he keeps me firmly pinned there with his mouth and his hips, his hard cock throbbing against me through his shorts and my jeans as he grinds against me.

"I should fuck you right here," he groans against my mouth, his fingers still digging into my jaw. "I should take that little cherry of yours hard and rough and split you open with my cock, and then let the rest of the team fuck you while you're still bleeding. Would you like that, Saint? All those sweaty cocks in your pussy and ass and mouth, tearing you open after I'm done with you?"

"No. Please, no," I beg, shaking my head. I'm terrified that he'll actually do it because I don't know what lengths Cayde will go to any longer.

"I bet you'd come all over their cocks like a little whore."

"No! No, I wouldn't. I don't want that."

"Then tell me you want my cock, Saint. Tell me how badly you want it."

I'm tempted to do it, if only so it'll be over with. I think that if I begged right now, he wouldn't be able to stop himself. He'd strip off my jeans, and my first time would be in a locker room that smells like jockstraps and feet, fucked by the guy I hate the most in the Blackmoor house. But I'm also too afraid of what comes after to say yes.

There's got to be some reason that one of them hasn't forced me yet. I've sucked their dicks, and they've jerked off on me and humiliated me, but none of them have made a move to fuck me yet. There's got to be a reason why. There's got to be some reason that Cayde, especially, is holding back and asking my consent when he hasn't bothered with that for any other goddamn thing.

And until I figure that out, I'm afraid to let go of the only thing I have that they want and don't seem to be able to take.

I lift my chin, jerking it out of Cayde's grasp as hard as I can, and look him straight in the eye.

"I don't want any part of you inside of me."

His kiss is even more punishing this time. His teeth sink into my lower lip, his hips grinding hard against me as he groans. "I'm going to tear your pussy open one of these days, Saint, and you're going to beg me for more."

I do the only thing I can think of then. I arch against him, giving him all the pressure he could possibly want against his rock-hard cock that's pressing painfully into my pelvis, and I bite him back, hard.

He yelps, pulling back.

"Don't fucking bet on it," I tell him. I taste a little of his blood on my lower lip, and something about it makes me feel savage and wild. "I'll never beg you for anything."

Cayde's eyes are blazing, his expression so furious that for a second, I think I've wildly miscalculated. His hand goes for my throat, grabbing me and lifting me up off the floor, and I have a moment of pure, sheer terror as I realize that while maybe he isn't going to fuck me against my will, he might do way worse.

I might make him so angry he kills me.

The sound of a slamming door comes from outside the locker room, and Cayde lets go so quickly that I drop to the floor like a sack of potatoes. The air goes out of me, and I stare up at him as he glares at me, his chest heaving.

"Get the fuck out," he says, his voice low and dangerous. "Before I change my mind and decide to fuck you in front of all of them."

I don't wait to find out if he means it.

I scramble to my feet, and I run.

CAYDE

*T*he last thing I want to do right now is go to the big party being thrown tonight in honor of the first big game of the season. But unfortunately, since I'm the team captain, I'm pretty much required to go.

That, and it's being thrown at my fucking house.

What happened with Athena in the locker room left me fuming, my blood boiling with the sheer magnitude of how angry I am, and my cock hard as granite even after she scrambles out of the room. I hadn't wanted to let go of her—in fact, I'd thought I might shoot my load by accident when I'd seen the fear on her face when I'd picked her up by her throat.

Goddamn, that was hot. I'll have to remember that.

The girl needs to learn her place. I'd hoped having Jaxon thrash her over the desk would have done it, but she seems determined to stay stubborn.

I'd come so close to fucking her, even though she wouldn't give in. It feels like she's driving me fucking insane. It's so much worse than it was even before coming to Blackmoor U because back then, she was out of reach unless I'd just fucking knocked her out and taken her— and where's the fun in that? Now she fucking belongs to me, and I still can't take what should be mine because I have to fight two other guys for it, and one of the stupid fucking rules is that she has to say yes. I can't just force her.

What the fuck is anyone going to do about it if I do? Tell me that I forfeit the game? Who's going to believe her over me?

The problem is the other two guys, really, especially Jaxon. They both know very well that Athena doesn't want any of us, and least of all me, so if I try to say she begged me to take her virginity, they're going to know it's a lie. Dean *might* back me up, or at the very least not stand against me, but I don't trust Jaxon. He seems to have a soft spot for the little bitch, even if he *did* cane her yesterday. And even if he doesn't want to win the town, I think he wants to win her.

Jerking off in the shower doesn't even bring me any pleasure. It just makes me angrier as I brace myself against the wall and furiously stroke my cock to a climax because I shouldn't be doing this. I should have my dick buried in Athena's mouth, her pussy, hell maybe even her ass. I fucking *own* her, and there's no reason I should be pleasuring myself in the shower. She should have gotten me off in that locker room. She should have fucking *begged* for my cum anywhere I wanted to *allow* her to have it.

"Fucking ungrateful bitch!" I yell as I shoot my load all over the wall, my hips jerking as I stroke my cock so hard I think I might accidentally rub it raw. *She's going to take it, and soon,* I think as I feverishly rub the last drops out of my still-aching shaft. Masturbating doesn't even hardly take the edge off anymore; it's just a necessary evil at this point, so that I'm not sporting a rock-hard boner around all of my teammates.

I'm going to fuck her, and soon, before she drives me fucking insane.

Everyone from the entire school is at the party. By ten p.m., the manor house is crammed full of people, and I make my way through the crowd with my red Solo cup in hand full of tequila and ginger ale, looking for Athena. I've got a good buzz from doing a series of shots with the team, and my simmering anger from earlier is reaching a peak again. *Where the fuck is she?* I think as I push past a couple that is practically fucking up against one of the manor walls, the guy tongue-deep in the girl's throat. *If I find her with Jaxon, I swear to fucking god.*

"Cayde! There you are, oh my *god*."

A bright, high-pitched voice interrupts my train of thought. I turn to see the girl from earlier at the game, the one who tried to hit on me while I was focused on dragging Athena off to the locker room. She's dressed even sluttier now, in tiny denim shorts that look more like panties frayed at the edges and a tight white crop top that shows the outline of her nipples clearly through it. Her tits are obviously fake, and her bouncy blonde hair just completes the overblown Barbie doll look. She's exactly the kind of girl I would have gone for back in high school—and hell, probably still would, if I wasn't so fucking obsessed with Athena.

But right now, I don't want Miss Blow-Up Doll 2004. I want a girl with black hair and a sassy mouth, a girl who I'm going to break if it's the last fucking thing I do in this world.

This girl, whose name I don't even remember, isn't about to let me go that easily, though.

"Don't you remember me?" She cocks her head to one side, smiling prettily at me. "I'm Winter."

Winter. Ah, yes. "I'm looking for someone."

"Well, I think you found her." She pushes closer to me, easy enough to do in the tight crowd, and her hand slides down between my legs to grab my dick through my joggers. "Oh, yeah. That's what I was looking for."

My cock, already at half-mast all the fucking time from thinking about Athena, reacts instantly to being touched. Winter leans into me, moaning as she feels me stiffen in her grasp, and she wraps her hand around my shaft, stroking me in the middle of the crowd through my pants. I can smell vodka on her breath, and I know she's got to be half-drunk already.

"Come on, Cayde, let me show you how impressed I was by that win today. You can do anything you want. You can have my mouth, my pussy, even my ass if you want it. Just fuck me, baby."

I'm about to push her off of me, but her warm breath is tickling my ear. Her hand is tightening around my cock, and I'm torn between the fact that I want Athena right now and the fact that I haven't actually gotten laid in way too fucking long. I had my cock down Athena's throat a couple days ago, but I need *pussy*.

And after all, there's nothing in the contract that says I can't fuck whoever I want. I remember how Athena looked at Winter today as if she clearly didn't like her, and that makes up my mind. *If Athena won't fuck me, she's going to find out that other girls will. Let's see how she feels about that. I'm Cayde St. Vincent. I can have any pussy I want.*

"Come on." I grab Winter's hand, pulling it off of my aching dick as I steer her towards the stairs. "Let's go see what that mouth does, then."

"Mm," she moans, stumbling a little, and I make sure she can't see the obvious disgust on my face. I don't like sloppy drunk girls. But right now, I just want to fuck.

I get her upstairs to my bedroom as fast as I can, slamming the door behind me as I push her towards the bed. She topples onto it, pulling at the button on her shorts. "Help me," she mumbles. "Want your mouth on my pussy, Cayde."

"Oh no." I grab the waistband of her shorts, yanking them open and pulling them down her skinny thighs as I flip her over onto her stomach. I jerk my own joggers down, just enough to get my cock and balls out, and I slap the head of it against her ass as she moans. "I'm going to fuck that pussy and shoot my load in your ass, Winter, like the little whore you are. Come if you want, or don't, I don't fucking care."

"Mm, yes, baby," she moans, spreading her legs, and I can see that she's sopping wet already.

And then, to my utter horror and frustration as she wriggles on the bed, her skinny ass pushed up as she begs for my cock, it starts to droop.

What the fuck?

I'm a red-blooded eighteen-year-old guy, I've never lost a boner in my life. The problem is usually getting it to fucking go away, even after I've jerked it raw or fucked all night. It always seems to want more.

But apparently, it doesn't want the very willing, half-naked blonde sprawled across my bed, begging me to stick it in her.

I grab my cock, stroking it feverishly. Thinking of Athena gets it to stiffen again, and I grab a handful of Winter's ass, shoving my erection into her all the way to the hilt. "Take that, you fucking whore," I snarl, pumping my cock hard into her.

"Yes, oh god yes, fuck me baby, mmm—" she moans, whimpering in a high-pitched voice that instantly makes me start to go soft again.

Her pussy feels sloppy, not like I imagine Athena's being, and her whiny voice, her blonde hair, her skinny body squirming around and begging for it, it's all wrong. I pull out of her, hating even her scent as I jerk my cock again hard, trying to imagine Athena instead, yelling at me to leave her alone and fuck off, daring me to fuck her.

There we go. In an instant, just remembering Athena defying me up against the locker today, my cock is raging hard again.

This time, I shove it in Winter's ass.

She screams in pleasure, and I fuck her ass hard, hoping I can hurry up and get off before I lose it again. "Shut the fuck up," I mutter as I thrust, but she's still whining out her pleasure, which can't possibly be real. I've never known any girl to love getting unceremoniously ass-fucked this much.

My erection is gone in an instant.

"What's wrong?" she pouts as she turns around, looking over her shoulder at me. Her mascara and lipstick are smeared, and I'm suddenly so furious that I feel almost dangerously angry. "Can't you keep it hard?"

"Get the fuck *out!*" I scream. I grab her by her hair, hauling her half-naked off of the bed, and yank the door open, throwing her out into the hallway onto her hands and knees. My cock is still hanging out of my joggers, flopping around uselessly. All of my fury boils over —most of it at Athena and just directed at Winter because she convinced me to come up here, and now my fucking cock won't even work. "Go suck off the rest of the team or something," I spit. "Give them that used-up pussy. I don't fucking want it."

And then I slam the door, my chest heaving as I shove my cock and balls back into my joggers, going into the bathroom attached to my suite to clean off.

When I finally emerge, Winter is gone. All I can think about is Athena and how I haven't seen her all night, and that's just pissing me off even more. I stride down the stairs and back into the crowd, determined to find her and figure out just what the fuck she thinks she's doing, ignoring me like this. *If she blew off the fucking party,* I think darkly—and then I round the corner and see something that makes me almost go nuclear with rage.

Athena is here alright. She's leaning up against the wall near the kitchen, a cup of something in her hand—and she's talking to a guy.

A guy who isn't Dean or Jaxon, either.

He's tall and way too handsome, with dark hair that flops over his forehead like a goddamn hipster, wearing a denim shirt with the sleeves rolled up and chinos, for god's sake. He doesn't look like Athena's type, but I don't fucking care.

She's not allowed to talk to other guys, and she knows it.

"What the fuck are you doing?" I stride up to them, and the guy looks at me, surprised.

"Hey. You can't talk to a girl like that," he says, and I feel the vein in my forehead bulge with anger.

"Don't tell me what I can and can't do in my house."

"Your house? Oh, you must be Cayde. Congrats on the win. But I'm busy here, as you can see."

"Not with my girl, you're not." I grab the front of his shirt, hauling him away from Athena.

"Cayde!" Athena shrieks. "It's not what you think—"

"Your girl?" The guy asks, surprised, but he doesn't get the chance to get another word out before I deck him in the jaw, sending him reeling back against the wall.

"Cayde!" Athena grabs for him, but I reach for her elbow, hauling her away as the guy reaches up and finds blood on his lip.

"Fuck this, I'm out," he says. "You can fucking have her." A second later, he's gone, disappeared back into the crowd.

Athena wrenches free of my grasp. "What the *fuck* do you think you're doing, Cayde?" she screams. "I wasn't doing anything wrong, and neither was he!" She twists away from me, running for the kitchen, and I follow her, determined not to lose track of her for the second time today.

She makes it all the way out into the backyard before I catch up to her, grabbing her elbow and dragging her up against me before she can get any farther. Over to the right, the deck is brightly lit, another crowd of people gathered talking and drinking and dancing around the pool, but we're in shadows, and no one is going to see what happens here.

"You're not allowed to be with other guys," I snap at her. "That's breaking the contract."

"I wasn't *with* him," Athena spits. "I was just talking. He's in my English class. He was asking me about the fucking *notes* from today, you absolute *psychopath*." She's hissing like a cat now, twisting in my grasp, and I can see that she's fucking done with me, and this, and all of it.

But that's fine because I am too.

"You can't talk to other guys either." I glare at her.

"OH, THAT'S FUCKING RICH." She rolls her eyes. "I can't even *talk* to them? Can't even say a polite hello, and oh, by the way, did you want to exchange notes about Robert Frost? Fuck off, Cayde. Talking about class isn't flirting."

It takes me less than a second to get my hand around her throat again. Before she can so much as breathe, I have her up against the nearest tree, my gaze boring into hers.

"You don't decide what's flirting," I growl at her, my eyes raking down her body. She's wearing a short leather miniskirt and a white halter top that stops just under her boobs. Although I know she doesn't have anything in her closet that doesn't show off her body, I'm still pissed at her for being dressed like this, for talking to *another man* dressed like this, for letting him look at what belongs to me. "I decide what's flirting. Whatever I fucking say it is, it is. You don't decide shit around here. And if I don't like the way another guy is looking at you, it's your problem to fix." I tighten my grasp around her throat, squeezing, and part of me just wants to choke the life out of her here. "So I say you were flirting, and you broke the contract."

I see her eyes widen, and I know it's not just because of the death grip I have on her throat. She squirms and kicks, and I loosen it a little, setting her down on the ground as she starts to cough. "I could call my father right now and tell him I'm kicking you out. Tell him to kick your mother out. And then what would you do, huh? How would you keep her safe? Guess what, little Saint, you couldn't. Because my next call would be to your poor dead dad's old biker buddies, letting him know that the Saint whores were back out on the street and ready for the taking. You'd wish I'd been the one to pop your cherry after that, baby."

Athena's face is horrified, and I revel in it, in the fear that I see in her eyes. *She's going to learn better than to defy me.*

"What do you want?" she whispers, her voice shaking.

I move closer to her, boxing her in against the tree like a predator trapping his prey. She flinches when my hand comes out again, but this time I use it to brace myself against the tree as I loom over her, all of my heavy, muscled bulk so close to her that I know she can feel the heat radiating off of my body.

"I want you to beg," I murmur, my voice a deep, low growl. "I want you to beg for my cock. Beg me to take your virginity. Beg for me to fuck you raw. I want you to plead and cry and open yourself up for me, and maybe then I'll see if there's even a shadow of mercy left in me for you."

Athena's chin is quivering. I can feel her shaking breath, her whole body trembling with fear as she looks up at me, her dark eyes meeting my green ones.

But I don't see pleading in them. I don't see begging.

I see anger. I see defiance.

And it makes me so fucking hard.

"Cayde St. Vincent," she whispers, her voice musical and sweet, drifting towards me in the space between our mouths, and for a brief second, I think she's actually gonna do it. She's going to beg me, and I know then as my cock threatens to burst the seam of my joggers that I won't even make it up to one of the bedrooms. I'll fuck her right here, up against the tree, in the grass, leaving her virgin blood smeared on the bark and the earth for anyone to see. I'll finally possess her the way I was always meant to, and if every fucking person at this goddamned party wants to watch, they can.

She smiles, and somehow her face looks even more beautiful like that, her full lips parting. My cock throbs as I'm reminded of how it feels to push between those lips, down that throat, to feel her gagging and choking around my thickness.

"In your fucking dreams," she whispers.

And then, before my lust-addled brain can register what she just said, that she just fucking *refused* me, she ducks under my arm, wrenching herself away from my body and stalking away across the lawn.

I spin on one heel, going after her like I'm on the fucking rugby field all over again, except this time she's the target and not the ball. I grab her elbow hard, wrenching her around so fast that she screams, and for a second, I think I might have actually dislocated her fucking arm.

Who the fuck cares. It's her pussy I want.

"You're going to fucking refuse me?" I snarl. "You know what that means, Athena. You know good and fucking damn well what I could do to you for this." My hand tightens on her elbow, dragging her up against me, and I grab a handful of her ass, squeezing it hard in my hand. I know it hurts, know the cane marks are still raw and red, but she doesn't even flinch. Instead, she leans into me for a brief second, her eyes glittering with rage as she clenches her teeth.

And then, before I can do anything, before I can say another word or force her down onto the ground or decide what I want to do next, she surges forward, bringing her knee up hard between my legs.

Directly into my balls.

I cough and gag, bending forward as Athena delivers a hard punch to my ear, knocking me sideways.

"You can shove your contract up your ass," she snaps.

And then she turns around, fleeing back into the house.

DEAN

I'm missing out on the big shindig at the manor house tonight.

Ordinarily, I wouldn't really care. Those frat parties aren't really my thing. Plastic cups, sticky mixed drinks, spills and vomit everywhere, sloppily drunk girls, everyone screaming over Cayde and his win today.

Not my scene at all.

But where I'm at tonight isn't my favorite way to spend a Friday night either. In fact, it's one of my least favorites—having dinner with my father and his friends at the supper club where he holds a membership. A real old boys' club, where everyone puts on dinner jackets and ties, and no women are allowed.

It could be a pleasant experience, really, if not for my father.

Tonight it's him, Mr. Romero, Mr. Bosworth, and Mr. Woodruff. They're all old, stuffed shirts, and I'm the one sitting there under a microscope, the one they've pinned all their hopes on.

"So, how are things going at the manor house?" Bosworth asks me, his eyes narrowing as he stabs a piece of salmon on his plate.

"To be blunt," Romero adds, "have you fucked the girl yet?"

The muscles in my jaw work as I remind myself to be calm. "Not yet. We're breaking her in. You gave us a spirited filly. There's a lot of work to be done to bring her to heel. Since we're not allowed to force her," I add dryly, slicing into my filet.

"You need to be mindful of the St. Vincent boy," my father says, looking at me harshly across the table. "He may force her anyway. He's obsessed with her. We all know that. That's why Philip St. Vincent insisted on her."

"I was under the impression it was because she'd be easiest to force into not questioning the contract. Since she and her mother are in danger from the Devil's Sons." Woodruff frowns. "St. Vincent has ulterior motives?"

"When doesn't he?" My father waves his hand. "His boy has been obsessed with the girl for years. Apparently, he tried to force her years ago, and she got away. Philip thought that by putting her in the house, it would give his son the necessary drive to push the girl into compliance and keep the town." He sets his fork down, his gaze steady and hard on me. "But *my son* isn't going to allow that to happen, is he?"

"No, sir." I set my fork down too. I didn't have much appetite in the first place, but this conversation is rapidly taking what I had away. "But the rules stand. I can't force the girl. The best I can do is try to convince her to give it up freely."

"Then figure out how to do that."

"I'm trying—"

"Trying isn't good enough." Romero's jaw clenches. "The St. Vincents have been a thorn in our sides for two generations now. The town, by rights, should belong to your family, Dean. It has your name on it. You have a fucking title, for god's sake. Act like a man, and do your duty to your family." He pauses. "What do you intend to do with the girl after you've taken her?"

I shrug. "Not marry her, like Philip did with his whore, that's for sure. Keep her as a side piece, maybe, if she's any good. Make her a servant in the house if not, like her mother. I know I'm responsible for keeping her, after," I add. "But I won't be making her the lady of Blackmoor, that's for sure."

"Good." Mr. Romero nods. "Because if you're successful, Dean, you'll have your choice of daughters to make your wife. But I'd be honored if you'd consider my Winter." He pauses. "She's loyal to the families. Beautiful. And she's been taught the virtues of being a submissive wife. She'll do anything you ask of her." He grins. "*Anything.*"

I feel slightly sick at that; my appetite fled entirely. I have my own twisted desires, just like Cayde and Jaxon. But hearing a father tell me about how his daughter will submit to me sexually in any way I want isn't among them. "I'll certainly consider Winter," I say politely. "But first, I have to make Athena mine."

"She's nothing." My father waves his hand. "She needs to learn her place. She should be grateful that we've taken an interest in her at all. If not for Philip's bleeding heart, she and her mother would be dead already. And once his son wanted her, well, there's nothing he won't try to give his son."

"He wants to keep the town. That's all there is to it." Woodruff shrugs. "But the Blackmoors should rule. It's time we take another look at the charter, honestly. This game of families should have been done away with long ago. The Blackmoor name is plastered on every institution and business, and statue in this town. It should be yours, in perpetuity."

"And that's why we're allies," my father says, a pleased smile on his face as he claps Woodruff on the back. "I won't forget the loyalty at this table. And neither will Dean. Isn't that right, son?"

"That's right," I murmur, but my thoughts are already far away. They're back at the house, wondering how Athena is faring at the party meant to honor Cayde, who is desperate to get into her tight, low-rise pants. How Jaxon is handling it. What my next move is, to try and ensure that I win the game and don't disappoint my father.

I learned a long time ago that my father isn't a man for whom disappointment is taken lightly.

"You'll need to try harder, son," he says, his gaze still drilling into me. "Don't let me down."

"I won't."

Jaxon's not the only one who likes long drives to burn off steam. I have my Ferrari tonight, and I open it up on the back roads, zooming down the open highway and sliding around turns as if I don't care if I live or die. The adrenaline burns in my veins, and as I feel my heart speed up, pumping blood faster, my thoughts turn to Athena.

Cayde thinks he should have the sole right to her because she humiliated him once. After all, revenge is all he's ever been able to think about. He's brutish, vicious, filled with rage. The perfect left hand for a man like me, who doesn't like to get his hands dirty. Who needs someone who can do that work for him.

As for my right hand? Jaxon is careless and reckless, but he's also smart. He'll realize, in time, that serving me is better than being thrown out on his ass. That doing my bidding and being my dog can get him the best of the scraps. That a lord doesn't forget those who are loyal to him—and out of the three of us, I'm the only one with a true title.

The only one with a real right to the town.

And the one who, by rights, should take Athena.

Long ago, English lords got the right to take the virginity of any girl they wished. That first blood belonged to them, and no one else, not even a husband. I have the right to take Athena's, not Cayde. Certainly not Jaxon.

By the time I make it back to Blackmoor House, I'm hard as hell, my cock raging from the frustration and adrenaline pounding through my veins.

It's in the wee hours of the morning, and the party is still going. But Cayde and Jaxon are nowhere to be seen. Neither is Athena. I push my way through the sloppily drunk crowd, going upstairs. I find Cayde in his room, a bruise blooming on the side of his face.

"What the fuck happened?" I demand. "Where's Jaxon? And Athena?"

"I don't give a fuck where Jaxon is," Cayde slurs. "And Athena is locked in the attic. Where she fucking belongs." He looks up at me, and the rage in his eyes is palpable. "She fucking did this."

"She attacked you?" I narrow my eyes. "Did you try to force her?"

"She fucking *hit* me!"

I know there's more to the story. Athena isn't stupid. Her compliance with a great deal of what we've put her through has proved that. This means that Cayde pushed her to her limits if she risked hurting him. He could declare the contract broken, and she and her mother could be fair game for the Devil's Sons if he wanted, although he won't. His brand of revenge will need to be delivered personally, and he won't give up a chance for that just because Athena got in a good blow.

"I'm going to find her," I snap. "This is going too far, Cayde. I know you're not telling me something. And I know you're obsessed with her. Get yourself under control. You won't win if you take her by force."

"I don't fucking care," Cayde snarls. "She kicked me in the fucking balls. She defied me. She humiliated me...*again*."

I shake my head. "Get a fucking grip, Cayde."

I know where the key to the attic door is kept, and when I find it and open the door, ducking in, I hear the sound of Athena scrabbling backward.

When I turn on the light, I see her on the far side near the window, blinking rapidly as her eyes adjust.

I also see the necklace of bruises around her neck—all of them plainly fingermarks.

"Fuck," I mutter. "Athena, did Cayde do this to you?"

She licks her lips. "He's really pissed," she whispers.

"Yeah, I know." I rub my hand over my mouth. "What the fuck were you thinking? Kicking him in the balls, punching him in the side of the head? Are you fucking insane?"

"He tried to strangle me!" Her voice comes out hoarse. "He was going to fucking rape me."

"No, he wasn't." I sigh. "Cayde won't do that. I know he *wants* to, and I know he threatens it, but he won't."

"Why not?" Athena challenges. "How the fuck could you possibly know that?"

"I just do." I look at her evenly. "Do you *want* to stay up here?"

"No." She narrows her eyes. "But it's better than being down there with you three assholes. What are you going to do next? Beat me with a fire poker?"

"Cayde might want to." I let out a long breath. "Athena, I'm not trying to hurt you. There's more to all of this than just you. What we're doing—it's for your own good. It's the best outcome for you, with your...past. With who you are. If you would just give in to me, things could be a lot better for you."

"I don't understand." Athena looks at me warily. "You're not making any fucking sense."

"I can't tell you more than that. But you'd be wise to let me be the one to take your virginity. Cayde won't want you after that. I can almost guarantee it."

"Just like I told Cayde," Athena sneers, shaking her head. "In your fucking dreams. All three of you. You can force me to do whatever, but something is stopping you from forcing me to do that. So fuck you. You're never getting it."

I shrug. "It's your funeral." I hold up the key to the attic door. "You can spend the night up here and tomorrow. Think things over. I'll let you out tomorrow night for dinner. Maybe you'll have come to your senses by then. At any rate, it'll give Cayde some time to cool down." I pause. "I'll do one favor for you. I'll make sure you aren't punished for tonight. I think those bruises around your neck were punishment enough. But don't make this mistake again. I won't go to bat for you next time."

Athena licks her lips, nodding. Just seeing her pink tongue running over that full lower lip is enough to make my cock throb. For a brief second, I consider forcing her to give me something in exchange. I could use a wet, hot mouth around my cock right about now.

But something about the necklace of bruises on her skin and the forlorn look in her eyes that I can see, even behind all the anger, stops me. So instead, I just leave.

When I lock the door again, I'm pretty sure I can hear her crying.

ATHENA

I already know I'm not going to sleep tonight. So instead, I spent my time poking around the attic that Cayde decided to lock me in.

My throat hurts where Cayde bruised it, my hand hurts where I punched him, and my body hurts from the flood of adrenaline that surged through me during the fight. My chest aches and my mind is spinning.

Dean wants me to give in to him. As choices go, he might not be the worst. I'll never give in to Cayde. And Jaxon is dangerous because my heart wants him too, not just my body. I'm drawn to him, and I need to avoid him for exactly that reason.

But I'm going to hold out as long as I can. Because I don't want to give *any* of them the satisfaction of having more of me than they already do.

There's not a ton of interesting stuff up here in the old attic. There's old furniture and some paintings that look expensive, but clearly didn't fit with whatever aesthetic the housekeeper was going for—or the guys. But as I poke around, pushing aside dusty rolled-up rugs and an open box full of what look like antiques—just thrown up here like they're Walmart tchotchkes—I find something far more interesting.

A small, heavily taped-up box, pushed into the corner almost like whoever stashed it up here was trying to hide it.

Which means, of course, that I'm going to see what's in it.

The tape tears away with a heavy, sticky sound, and as I sit in the corner, the light from the bare overhead bulb casting shadows all around me, I pull out the contents.

When I spread them out on the floor, all I can do is stare dumbly at them for several moments.

They're *pictures.* The last was taken a little over twenty years ago; I can see the date on it. There are a few photos from around the same date range, and then each spans about eighteen to twenty years between sets, going all the way back to when the photos were in black and white.

Each set shows a different girl. And in every set, on the earliest date, she's dressed in a white gown that would be almost bridal if it weren't so heavy and robe-like, with a thick veil covering her face. The background of the photo looks like stone, and then there's a closeup of the veiled girl, the front of it splattered with what looks too purplish red to be blood—probably wine. It's almost ritualistic, and a chill runs down my spine as I look at the older photos, which are even more creepy since they aren't in color.

In the later photos, though, the girls aren't covered.

They're in various stages of undress. In the older photos, even though they're bound and in some of them gagged, they're wearing lingerie that would now be considered basically clothing. But I catch a glimpse of a dick in a few of them, girls splattered with cum, bruised, crying. The newer ones are far more lewd—photos of the girls bent over, legs splayed, tied to beds fully naked. They're all different sizes—plump, thin, small-breasted, and large. In the older ones, they aren't shaved. In the newer ones, they are, or there's some design shaved into their pubic hair.

In the one from twenty years ago, the girl looks very familiar.

I turn the photos over, hoping for names, but whoever took the photos wasn't that stupid. Still, there's something creepy about there being a box up here in the attic full of pictures of girls, some of them weirdly ritualistic, others just plain pornographic. *Do the guys know these are up here?* I wonder, shuffling through them again. I wonder who the girls were, what happened to them, where they are now. Especially the most recent one, where I keep feeling every time I look at it as if I've seen the girl in the photo. Whoever she was, she seemed almost happy to be a part of it. In the photo where her hands are bound behind her back, her face is upturned, her eyes closed as she smiles almost beatifically, as if she's waiting for a blessing instead of some guy's load.

I've got to show these to Mia. I want to know what she'll make of it, if she'll think it's as weird as I do or if she'll have some explanation. She reads all the time, and she's always seemed to know more about the town than I did—or still do. She even tried to tell me about it a few times, but I didn't pay attention. I just didn't give a shit back then.

Now I kind of wish I'd listened more.

I scoot back into the corner, leaning up against an old dresser as I thumb through the photos again. My stomach rumbles, and I try to ignore it, focusing on trying to remember the faces in the pictures instead. I wonder if these photos were taken here, if one of these girls ever passed a night up in the attic like this.

Dean will let me out of here eventually. But until then, I'm going to use the time to plot my next move.

* * *

THE NEXT DAY, I hear the lock on the door turn. No one opens it, and I wait several minutes before I go over to it gingerly, turning the knob. It swings open, but there's no one outside, which makes me think Dean just unlocked it and left, not really giving a shit about what I did after that.

Which is fine with me. The house is quiet, and it's Sunday, so I won't be able to talk to Mia until tomorrow. I shove the photos under my shirt, kicking the box back into the corner and hiding it under a pile of old rugs. As soon as I manage to get down to my room, I put them in my bookbag behind all my other papers and notebooks.

I spend the rest of the day in my room. I'm starving, but I don't dare go down for food and risk running into the guys. No one comes to bother me, either, which is odd. I'd have expected at least Cayde to throw a fit that I've stayed in my room. Still, the hallway remains quiet, and I huddle in bed for the rest of the day, doing the homework that I'm behind on and hoping that this isn't just the calm before a much bigger storm.

But no one comes down the hall or knocks on the door.

I wait until I hear the guys leave the next morning before coming downstairs. I manage to find a couple of muffins and a sack lunch in the kitchen, which I stuff into my backpack before hurrying to campus. I'm almost late to English, and Mia looks at me surprised when I slide into the seat next to her, panting.

"After class," I hiss. "We're going to the coffee shop. I need to tell you something."

"What's going on?" she asks, but I just shake my head.

"Later."

We find the quietest corner of the coffee shop to huddle into, and when I'm sure no one is looking, I tug my scarf down to show Mia the bruises around my neck. Her eyes go wide, and I see the pinpricked flush of red on her cheeks that tells me she's angry. Mia never flies off the handle; she just gets that small red flush, and you know she wants to kill someone deep down. It's almost scarier than someone who screams and yells, to be honest.

"Who did that?" Her voice is hushed, angry. "Which one of them?"

"Cayde. He's on the verge of going insane, Mia, I'm telling you. Which is why I have to tell you what's going on."

I explain to her my theory, that something is keeping the guys from taking that final step and just outright fucking me. "Jaxon doesn't seem like the type that's down with rape, and I think Dean would consider himself above it, but Cayde isn't like that at all. He was *insisting* that I beg him for it… that I *ask* him for it when he was choking me. There's some reason that's the hangup."

Mia shrugs. "Maybe it's just his kink. Maybe he can't get it up unless the girl begs?"

I shake my head. "I don't think it's that. I think he'd like it *more* if I were begging him to stop, not give it to me. He gets off on the fact that I fight him. So I think there's some reason he can't just do it without my consent."

"I mean, it's a good thing that he can't."

"I agree. But look at these. I found them in the attic after Cayde locked me up there."

"He locked you in the fucking *attic?*"

I wave my hand. "Mia, they've done way worse shit than that. That's not the point. *Look at these.*"

I pull the photos out of my bookbag then and hand them to her. "They're in sets, all of them starting out with a girl in these weird white robes and veil and then getting progressively more and more pornographic. And they're all about twenty years apart. I found them hidden in a box behind a bunch of old furniture."

"Shit." Mia purses her lips. "Athena, this is some weird shit. Like— horror movie, serial killer shit."

"Right?" I take the photos as she's finished with them, stuffing them back into my bag before anyone else can get a look. "Some of them look like they might have been taken in the Blackmoor House. The one I'm living in."

"You think there are other girls like you? Girls before you, I mean? Like they've been doing this for a long time?"

"I mean, not the boys, obviously. But maybe someone else living there? Maybe it's some prerequisite for living in the house. The contract does call me the *house pet.* Not theirs, but belonging to the Blackmoor property. Like I'm a fucking chair or something."

"That's so weird, though." Mia flips through the last of the photos. "Like I've never heard of anything like that. I thought it was just some weird kinky shit that these guys did, like they got their parents to go along with it so they could have their fun with you. But this looks like —it's been going on for a *long* time."

"Didn't you say there was some weird stuff you'd heard about the town?"

"Yeah." Mia pauses, licking her lips. "But it's all rumors. And it's all *crazy*, Athena. Like batshit."

"Maybe there's something to it, though. Something more than just stupid rumors and gossip."

"I just—" Mia lets out a breath, quickly pushing the rest of the photos down into my backpack. "Be careful, Athena. These pictures— that's some freaky shit. Something bad might happen if someone even knew you'd found them. They might have been hidden for a reason, you know? Just—be careful."

"I will," I promise. "I'll see if I can get anything out of the guys, but I'll be sneaky about it. I won't let them know I found anything."

"Is there anything I can do for you?" Mia bites her lower lip, looking at me worriedly.

I think for a moment, and then an idea pops into my head. "Actually, there is," I tell her, a sly smile spreading across my face. "Can you go to my house on the estate and get some of my old clothes? Just tell my mom I asked for them. She'll be fine with it."

"Okay." Impulsively, Mia reaches out and hugs me, wrapping her arms around my neck. "I don't know what I'd do if something happened to you, Athena. You're my best friend."

I hug her back, feeling my chest squeeze tight. "I know," I whisper. "You're my only friend."

* * *

THAT NIGHT, I come down to dinner in my old clothes. Instead of low-rise tight jeans, I'm wearing my old black ripped boyfriend pair, rolled up around my ankles above my scuffed Doc Martens. I paired it with a loose white t-shirt knotted at my waist. I threw my hair up in a ponytail, dragging thick eyeliner over my eyelids without any other makeup. *This is the girl they're getting from now on,* I tell myself, looking at my reflection in the mirror. *And they can fucking deal with it.* I'm done playing whatever stupid game is going on here—or at least, I'm done totally playing it by their rules. There's some reason why they haven't fucked me yet, some reason why my mother and I aren't already out on the street after I fucking *punched* Cayde St. Vincent and kneed him in the balls. That contract isn't the end-all-be-all that they wanted me to think it is.

I walk down to the dining room, where I can hear the low hum of conversation. All three guys look up at once as I walk in, and I see a different expression on each of their faces—annoyed amusement on Dean's, sullen anger on Cayde's...and interest on Jaxon's. His eyes rake over me, and I can tell from the way the muscle in his jaw twitches that he likes this look on me. I reach up, pulling my hair loose from the ponytail and letting it tumble out around my face, and I see the small indrawn breath from Jaxon.

He likes me, I realize. *Me, the way I was back in high school. My style, the way I really am.*

It makes something flutter deep in my belly, something that's at war with the memory of him standing behind me with the cane, bringing it down hard across my ass. The memory of him jerking off after he'd sworn he'd never be aroused by hurting me.

But then, too, that memory comes with a flush of heat between my thighs, sending that old confusion rippling through me.

"This is me," I say flatly, lifting my hands palms up and letting them fall. "I'm tired of playing fucking dress-up. Take it or leave it, void the contract. I don't fucking care anymore. But I got some of my old clothes, and this is what I'm wearing."

I wait for them to lash out, to punish me, to order me down onto my knees or up to my room. But none of them say anything. After I stand there for a long moment, Dean and Jaxon return to their dinners as if nothing ever happened. Cayde is still looking at me, his jaw working with what I can tell by now is barely controlled rage, but he finally just sets his fork down, letting out a long breath.

There is *something else going on here,* I think, my heart speeding up in my chest. *They aren't going to just kick me out, no matter what the contract says. There's something deeper.*

"Stop acting like a child," Cayde says finally, and he gestures to the plate of food in front of an empty chair. "Sit down and eat your dinner."

I can barely breathe. My heart is pounding so hard as I flop down into the chair, reaching for my own fork. *I can't believe it.* I think, for once, I've actually won.

Whatever the truth is behind all of this, it's a damn good feeling.

Dean and Jaxon continue ignoring me as they eat, and I can tell that no one here seems to be in a very good mood. Finally, halfway through the rest of the meal, Cayde looks up at me.

"The guys and I have talked," he says slowly. "And we all agree you need to go home for the weekend. Back to the estate, where your mother is," he clarifies. "You can decide then if you want to keep behaving like a brat or if you want to come back and abide by the terms of the contract you signed."

Okay, maybe not a complete win. But my heart is still racing with mingled terror and excitement as I tell him meekly, "okay," and return to my dinner.

It still feels like a victory, even if it's a small one.

ATHENA

That small win gives me the courage to continue with the rest of my plan. I don't dare try to find out anything more from Cayde or Dean—Cayde is too unstable. Dean would just laugh in my face and then lie, and I'd never be quite sure if he'd actually been lying or not. But Jaxon—

Jaxon did lie to me, or at least I feel like he did, but I don't think he'd lie about something like this. If I could get it out of him, that is. And I feel like he might care about me just enough that I might have a shot.

Since that awful afternoon in the study, Jaxon and I have barely spoken. He doesn't look at me at meals, he doesn't give me rides to school on his bike anymore, and he doesn't save me from the machinations of the other two. It feels almost like our little interlude in that meadow happened a million years ago, in some other life. In some other freaking universe, even.

I can't square the Jaxon who tried to intercede for me with the other guys, the one who came to rescue me after the pledge party, who took me out to eat and kissed me like that on the cliffside, with the one in the study. The one who said he'd just done all of those things to get my panties down.

Which doesn't make sense because he doesn't have to do *any* of that to get them down. All he has to do is tell me, and I'm supposed to obey.

The only thing, apparently, he'd need permission for...is to fuck me.

So if I dangle that in front of him, maybe I can get him to open up.

He's in his room. I can hear some kind of growly music seeping out from under the door, and I knock hard, several times. "Jaxon? It's me, Athena. Can I come in?"

When the door opens, I can see a surprised look on his face. And I don't blame him—I've never come to one of the guys' doors before. I've never wanted to—and it's never seemed like a good idea. In fact, it's always been anything but.

"Yeah," he says gruffly. "Come in."

He hasn't shaved, and it looks pretty hot on him, the dark stubble decorating his chin and jaw and upper lip. I have a sudden urge to reach up and run my hand over it, to feel it rough and prickly over my palm, and I have to clench my hand into a fist to stop myself.

Jaxon pushes the door shut and looks at me quizzically. "What's going on, Athena?"

He's the only one that, when he says my name, it actually sounds good. Cayde rarely says it at all. I'm "little Saint" to him, not even worth using my actual name. It's condescending when Dean says it, like he's doing me a favor by even acknowledging me. But when Jaxon says it, it sounds good. Like a purr in the back of his throat, like thick chocolate rolling over his tongue. Like he wants to lick it up and eat it.

Just like he did to me.

I can feel that heavy warmth between my legs again at the thought, sliding through my blood and heating my body. It feels a little harder to breathe in here, and I tell myself that's just the incense he's burning by the window, but I know it's not that. It's the warm scent of his skin, the faint spicy scent of cologne, and the knowledge that his bed is *right there*. That this guy, out of all of them, wouldn't be so bad to have my first time with. He's even my type.

"What are you doing in here?" Jaxon asks, his voice a little rougher now. "You coming to get some dick?"

"Maybe." I lick my lips nervously, and I see his eyes flick down to my mouth. I can see the shudder of desire that runs through him. "But I have some questions for you."

Jaxon narrows his eyes. "Why me?"

"Because you're the only one I trust even a little bit." I blurt out the words, and Jaxon sinks down into his leather desk chair, sighing.

"Dean would just lie to me," I rush on, the words tumbling out of my mouth. "And Cayde wouldn't tell me anything. He'd just hurt me. So I came to you, because if anyone is going to tell me the truth, it would be you."

Jaxon's face is guarded now, careful. "And what truth are you trying to find out, Athena?"

"Why haven't any of you fucked me?" I ask the question bluntly, and I see the momentary surprise in Jaxon's face before it evens out again. "I haven't seen any other girls here besides at the parties. You guys are home every night unless Cayde has practice or a game. None of you are fucking anyone else. I'm pretty sure of it. So why don't you just take what you want from me? I know you want it."

I walk towards Jaxon, putting a little sway in my hips, letting my lips part. I can see it affecting him; he's as horny as the other guys. He's just better at hiding it. "Why don't you just take it? You take everything else. You've made me do everything else. So why not that?"

Jaxon stands up, and I'm close enough to him that when he does, he looms over me.

"I can't tell you," he says. His voice is low and deep, and the rumble of it sends a shiver over me.

"Why not?" I lick my lips again, more slowly this time, and as Jaxon takes a step towards me, I back up. "There must be some reason you're all fighting over me. Something more than just Cayde's stupid revenge and the fact that the two of you want me, too. You could have any girl on this campus."

Jaxon's eyes narrow, but he doesn't say anything. He just takes another step, and so do I, another and another, until my back hits the door, and there's nowhere else for me to go.

"Cayde could have nullified the contract after we fought," I whisper. "He could have raped me. But he didn't. He didn't do either of those things. There's something else going on."

"Maybe." Jaxon shrugs, his dark eyes fixed on mine. So close, I can see how very dark they are, almost black. His jaw is sharp and angled, his cheekbones standing out, the stubble making him look even more dangerous than usual. If Cayde is a predator, he's something brutal and big, a grizzly bear maybe, but Jaxon is sleek and feral, a panther in the jungle, a leopard waiting to pounce from the trees.

Just as deadly, but so much more beautiful.

"You have to wait for me to say yes to one of you to take my virginity," I whisper. "And that contract isn't as ironclad as Geoffrey made it seem. Because I punched Cayde, and I just wound up in the attic for a day, and I'm wearing my old clothes, but I ate dinner at the table. You all need something from me."

"Are you sure of that?" Jaxon braces himself against the door, his hand pressed to it beside my face, and with his other hand, he reaches for my face, trailing a thumb over my cheekbone. "What are you willing to risk on that bet, Athena? Your life? Your mother's life?"

"There's a reason you're all fighting over me. I know it." I look up at him, searching his face and finding nothing there to tell me what's going on, what's happening to me, all around me. "What about you, Jaxon?"

"What about me?" he repeats, his fingers trailing down my jaw. The caress feels too intimate, too good, and I have to force myself not to lean into it. *I want him to kiss me again,* I realize. I want to feel his full, soft lips on mine, to feel that hard lean muscle pushing against me, to feel the heat sweep through me that he rouses in my body. *If I were going to pick one of the guys, it would be him.*

"Would you fuck me if I asked? If I asked you to, right…now?"

Jaxon's body stiffens, his fingers at the point of my chin, and I feel him lean into me, just the way I wanted. He's hard, the thick ridge of his cock pressing against the fly of my jeans, grinding into my pelvis as he shoves me back against the door, his fingers tilting my chin up so that his lips are a breath from mine. "Is that what you want, Athena?" His lips are so close, and I feel myself reaching up, going up on my tiptoes because I *do* want it.

At the very least, I want him to kiss me.

Right fucking now.

A groan tears from his mouth as I strain upwards, my lips brushing over his. Then both of his hands are on my wrists, pulling my hands up, pinning them over my head as his mouth crashes into mine, devouring me as he grinds his hips into mine. "Fuck," he moans, nibbling on my lower lip as I feel him throbbing. I know we're both so fucking close to going over the edge, to me giving him my virginity without him even having to demand it. "You make me so fucking hard, Athena, fucking *Christ.*" He drags one of my hands downwards, presses it to the front of his jeans so that I can feel him, long and thick and so impossibly hard. "Feel how much I fucking want you. You're— Christ, you're *everything.*"

He groans out that last against my mouth as he kisses me again. I freeze for a moment in shock, registering those last words as his tongue slides into my mouth, and I can taste the hint of whiskey there.

My body feels as if it's melting, my veins lava hot, my entire being straining towards him with a need I never knew I could feel.

"I'm sorry," he whispers, his hand sliding down to my hip, touching the edge of my ass. "I'm so fucking sorry I hurt you, Athena—"

He's drunk, I realize as I taste the whiskey on his tongue. *Buzzed, at least.* But I know, somewhere deep down, that he means it.

I'm arching against him now. My hands are free and sliding along his face, into his hair, kissing him back. It feels so good to be doing it of my own volition, not fighting it, not being forced. I came in here to manipulate him into telling me what was going on, now I'm falling into my own trap, pulled under by the force of my attraction to him and the pounding, aching desire that I can feel radiating from his body into mine.

"I could end this right now," Jaxon whispers against my mouth, his body shuddering against mine. "I could end this whole fucking thing."

I look up at him, startled, wondering what he means. His mouth hovers over mine, and I can feel him on the edge of a decision, so close to taking my offer and my virginity.

I can feel the physical effort that it takes him to wrest himself away from me, stumbling backward with eyes that are dark and hazy with desire, his cock so hard that I can see the outline of it plainly through his jeans.

"Get out," he mutters, pointing towards the door. "Get the fuck out, Athena."

There's something in his voice that tells me not to test him, a wave of quiet anger like the one I've heard in Mia's voice that's somehow even more terrifying than Cayde's blustering, furious rage.

I yank the door open and stumble out into the hall, my entire body still pulsing with the awareness of how much I wanted him—how much I still fucking do—and turn to run towards my bedroom.

And directly into Cayde.

A second later, his hands are on my upper arms, shoving me backward into the wall. I look at him through dazed eyes, my mind still catching up, detangling itself from the aching desire I felt a minute ago into the new, fresh fear of having Cayde holding me up against the wall.

"Trying to seduce Jaxon, huh?" He sneers at me, his heavily muscled body leaning into mine, so different from Jaxon's leanness. "You must be desperate to get away from me if you'd let him fuck you." He leans forward, drawing in a deep breath as if he's sniffing me. "You even smell like him, you little whore. Don't bother denying it. I could hear the two of you. Panting and moaning like dogs in heat."

I don't say anything. There's nothing I want to say to him anyway. My eyes flick to the bruise on the side of his face below his ear, and I feel a warm glow deep in the pit of my stomach. No matter what happens, I'm glad I got that one punch in.

"What is it about him, anyway?" Cayde's eyes drag over my face, landing on my lips and then flicking back up. "I don't fucking get it. Why are you into him? Why does he get special privileges?"

I smile then, slowly, letting it spread across my face as I make him wait for the answer. "Because," I say sweetly, "he's not a dick. Like you and Dean are."

Cayde laughs then, low and bitter. "Oh, you don't know anything about dicks, little Saint. But believe me, I'd love to show you fucking everything." His hand slides to my face, cupping my cheek, and I don't feel the same urge that I felt with Jaxon, to lean into the caress. But I do feel *something*, something that I don't want to feel. There's not the heat of desire, but a pounding in my chest, the thrill of fear, of adrenaline, of the fight. I tense in Cayde's grasp, and I realize with a sick twist in my stomach that there's a desire here too, just of a different kind.

With Cayde, it's the fight that turns us both on, the fact that if we ever were to fuck, we'd be clawing each other all the way down, tearing each other to pieces until we were raw and bleeding and finished.

He leans into me, and I can feel the weight of him crushing me, not just his muscular body but everything inside of him too, his anger and need and something else, something that borders on desperation. He's hard, pressing into my thigh, and when he forces my hand down against it, I wonder if I could even take him for my first time, he's so thick.

"Just let me go to bed," I plead, but Cayde buries his face in my neck, breathing in my scent as he bites at one of the bruises he left there.

"Only if I come with you." He pulls down his zipper with his other hand, his shoulders and chest pinning me to the wall, still holding my hand firmly against his dick. A second later, I feel it out and against my hand, hard and hot and throbbing, and he wraps my hand around it.

"No." I turn my face away as he starts to stroke his cock with my hand, gripping it so tightly I can feel the bones grind together. "I'm not going to fuck you."

"You can't run from me forever, little Saint." He moves my hand faster, panting against my neck as he bites down, sucking hard until I cry out. I bite my lip, for some reason desperate for Jaxon not to hear me out here with Cayde, not to know what's happening. I don't want Jaxon to think of me like this, just a slut going from one guy to the next, my lips still tingling with Jaxon's kisses as Cayde forces my hand up and down his cock. "I'll have your pussy eventually. It's mine."

I shake my head, biting back tears as I feel him swelling in my hand, hard and throbbing, and I know he's close.

"You're driving me crazy," he groans against my throat. "You're like a fucking drug, some fucking witch. I can't stop thinking about—oh god, *fuuck*—"

I feel him go rigid against me, his teeth sinking hard into the flesh of my neck, hard enough that I'm almost certain he's drawn blood. His cum soaks the front of my jeans, spurting over the denim, hot and sticky against my skin.

When he pulls back, he's panting. I feel something warm trickle down my throat and see red on his lips, and I know I'm bleeding from his bite.

Very slowly, deliberately, with his half-hard cock still hanging out of his joggers, Cayde licks my blood off of his lips.

"That's not the blood I wanted on my mouth," he says darkly. "But don't worry, little Saint. I'll get the real thing soon enough."

I can't move. My hands are shaking, my neck is bleeding, and I can feel his cum cooling against my thighs, my jeans glued to my skin.

"Go home," he says coldly. "And don't come back until you've made up your mind to be good."

With that, he turns and walks down the hall. I can't move until I hear the slam of his bedroom door, and then, only then, do I flee towards the shower.

Only then do I finally let myself start to cry.

ATHENA

I haven't been home since I woke up in the bed at Blackmoor House that first morning, with a headache and no memory of what happened to get me there.

My mom knows I'm coming, and she's ecstatic about it. She meets me halfway down the drive, still in her housekeeper's uniform, her face flushed and sweaty and her black hair coming out of the bun she always keeps it in while she's at work.

I look more like my mom than my dad, or so I've always been told. I think my mother wishes I looked like him now, just a little, so she'd have some reminder of him other than the pictures she keeps everywhere. I don't know how she does it, honestly. One of the things I have liked about living at the house on campus is that there aren't reminders of my dad everywhere I look—reminders of his betrayal, his mistakes, everything we lost. I'd loved him very much, he'd been a good father and a good man, so far as I'd known, and I miss him desperately.

This means that the constant reminders of him around the house that my mother lives in now are like a hundred arrows to the heart every day.

My mom's arms around me feel so good that I almost burst into tears. This isn't my home, but it is *a* home. It's a place where my mother is, and that makes it more home than the place I'm living now could ever be.

She's made my favorite dinner, fried chicken and mashed potatoes and corn still on the cob. I eat more than I could have ever imagined eating before, putting down two plates of food before my mom serves up vanilla cupcakes she made for dessert with sprinkles in them and cream cheese frosting, looking almost shy as she pushes the plate towards me.

"I know you're a little old for cake with sprinkles," she says. "But I know you used to love it."

"I *still* love it," I assure her. "Thank you so much, mom. This is—this was the best."

"Aren't they feeding you enough at school?" She frowns. "It's not like you to eat so much—I'm not saying there's anything wrong with it, I'm just worried about you. You look pale, too. And…did you cut yourself?"

She reaches out to touch my neck, and I flinch back. I covered the bruises with makeup well enough, but it was hard to hide the wound that Cayde left last night. "Just had an accident at the gym," I tell her, hating myself for having to lie. "I've been working out a lot lately; that's why I'm so hungry." *And the guys I live with made me eat off of the floor for a while, and I've been avoiding mealtimes, so I don't have to talk to them.*

"You do look skinnier than usual." Her eyes are still crinkled at the corners, a clear sign of concern. "Are you enjoying it there, Athena?"

I can't tell her the truth, not any of it. She'd be horrified if I did. She'd insist I not go back, that I break the contract and that we survive on our own. Except the problem is we *won't* survive, the Devil's Sons will never let us go after what my father did. They'll enjoy us before they kill us, passing both of us around to all the guys in the club. It's no secret what happens to the daughters and old ladies of guys who roll over on the club. It's that, more than anything that would happen to them, that keeps the members in line.

Knowing what would happen to their families.

But I also just can't tell her because I can't imagine sitting here, in this small kitchen, breathing in the air still perfumed with fried meat and seasoned grease and butter and cake and telling my mother all the awful, humiliating, filthy things that I've done and been forced to do since I woke up in that bed. And even worse than that, I can't imagine admitting the rest of the truth—that I actually enjoyed some of it.

I was forced to do it—but I can't say I didn't like it, in a way, at the same time.

"It's been hard," I admit, because I know I can't just lie to her face. She knows me better than that—I might be able to make up an excuse about my hunger and weight loss, but not about being happy or unhappy. "It's an adjustment," I say, hoping she'll leave it at that.

"It was really kind of Mr. St. Vincent to arrange another scholar-ship for you," she says thoughtfully. "I want to tell you that if you're unhappy to leave, Athena, that you can just go to the public university like you'd originally meant to. But—" she hesitates, and I can see the struggle in her face, between the practical worries of her life and wanting to be a good mother, to give me anything I want or need to be happy.

"I think Mr. St. Vincent would probably be unhappy if you left, after all he did to secure that for you," she says softly. "I don't want you to stay somewhere that you don't like—but if he let me go, I wouldn't have a good reference for any other job. I didn't work while I was married to your father—this is the first job I've had since we were married. And without Mr. St. Vincent's protection—" she trails off, but I know what she's not saying. Without that protection, we're vulnerable to anyone from the Devil's Sons that wants to come after us. Anyone who wants to make an example of us.

We'd have to run very far away to escape them.

"It's alright," I tell her quickly. "It's just homesickness. But now I'm here, and I'm sure I'll feel all better by the end of the weekend. I'll be ready to go back and start a new week."

"Exactly." She beams at me, and I know that's what she wanted to hear—reassurance that it's not really that bad, that I'm just missing home, and that all I need is a couple of nights in my old bed and some home cooking and I'll be fixed right up.

I need a fuckton more than that. I need answers. I need help. And I need Cayde and Dean and, honestly, Jaxon too, to go straight back to hell where they came from.

But I'm not going to get any of those things, so I'm going to have to settle for a few good meals and a couple nights of sleep without wondering what fresh hell I'm going to face in the morning.

It does help a little. My mom practically glows while I'm here, happy to make food for me and sit and talk, telling me about what's been going on with the estate and a few friends she's made among the staff recently since Philip St. Vincent hired on a few more, and giving me suggestions of things to do while she's at work. I take her up on a few of them, going for long walks through the park, and one night after she's done, we go to see a movie together. It's like my old, normal life, and I'm almost able to put Cayde, Dean, and Jaxon out of my head for a little while.

Almost, but not quite. Because I know inevitably, I have to go back.

I have no choice. Even if I were willing to put myself in that kind of danger, I can't risk my mother. I did this for her in the first place, far more than myself, and I'm not about to turn back now.

I'm going to figure out how to beat them at their own game.

I could end this right now. Jaxon's words have been rattling around my head for days as I try to make sense of them. And I can only think of one thing.

Once I fuck one of them, something changes.

Which means the best way to beat them is to make the choice myself.

I know who I want, given the option. But he already pushed me away once when we were both on the verge of giving in. Still, I have to try one more time. Suppose I have the slightest chance of making my first time with someone that I don't completely hate, someone who my body at the very least desperately wants. In that case, the victory will be that much sweeter.

If he rejects me again—

So, therefore, I don't quite know what to do. I know that I don't want Cayde—or at least, nothing other than my traitorous body does —but Cayde's father is powerful, and Cayde is too, by virtue of that. His family has done a lot for mine, and it might be wise to solidify that by letting Cayde win.

But sex with Cayde will be vicious, and cruel, and painful. With Dean—I'm not sure what it would be. Humiliating, maybe, cold and probably emotionless. But possibly more pleasurable than with Cayde.

The truth is, all three of them have ways of turning me on, ways of creeping into the darkest, most twisted parts of my psyche and making me question everything I ever believed about myself. Everything I thought I knew about who I am and what I would put up with. What I would allow. What I would *want*.

I'm going back to Blackmoor House tomorrow, and I'm going to make my move.

And Jaxon is my target.

JAXON

*W*hen I walk into my room Sunday night, I find something waiting for me there that I definitely hadn't expected.

Athena, in my bed.

And not just Athena the way she normally is, either.

She's dressed for *me*. And what's more, she's dressed so perfectly for what I want that it's as if she got into my head somehow and found out things I've never told her.

If she'd come in here wearing lingerie, I'd have laughed. That's the kind of shit Dean's into, not me. But instead, she's wearing a black ribbed henley crop top, small enough that I can see the curve of her underboob and with the buttons open so that I can see the sides of her breasts too, pushing against the soft material. Her stomach is bare, smooth, and pale, and leading down to the black ribbed cotton thong she's wearing, the smooth globe of her asscheeks is bare.

I can still see the marks from the caning I gave her, and it makes my gut clench.

She's wearing thigh-high black socks, too, the soft flesh of her thighs just barely squishing over the tops, and the effect of all that soft, tight black material against her smooth, milk-pale skin and her thick black hair tumbling over her shoulders is enough to make me achingly, painfully hard the second I see her.

Enough that I almost lose all my good sense as soon as I shut the door.

She rolls onto her side, atop my duvet, the curve of her waist a gorgeous dip that I could lay my hand in, turning her onto her back, spreading her open for my pleasure. She wants me, I know it, or she wouldn't be here.

She's chosen me.

The problem is, she doesn't know what that means.

Would she still be doing it if she did? The question rattles around in my head, punishing me for the decision I know I'm going to have to make. I think she would if she knew. She wouldn't want either of the other guys to win, to inherit the town. Maybe she has a soft spot for Cayde's family after everything his father has done for her and her mother, but I don't think that extends to Cayde. I don't think she'd hand him the keys to the town if she knew she held them. In fact, I think she'd give them away out of sheer spite.

If not to me, then to Dean.

Which means if I refuse her, I'll be sending her to his bed.

It's almost painful to think about her there, about Dean's hands being the ones to unwrap her perfect body, stripping her bare. About him kissing those soft lips, opening her up, spreading her legs so that he can sink into that tight pussy for the first time. The thought of her crying out under him, in pain or in pleasure, makes my teeth clench tight, and every part of me rejects the idea.

But fucking Athena comes with a price, and I don't think I'm willing to pay it.

It's not just the responsibility of the town, either. I look at her in my bed, and I feel things I haven't felt in years. I walk towards her, drawn by what feels like a power outside of my control, and I know that it's more than just lust. More than just physical wanting.

I *like* Athena. I care about her. I have feelings for her, feelings that would only grow if I let things go this far.

And that comes with a pang of terrible guilt.

I've only ever loved one girl. And I lost her. Not to a breakup or some other guy, but to an accident.

An accident that took her life and left me brokenhearted in a way that I never imagined I could be.

I know that I can't live through that again. I can't allow myself to feel that way and then suffer that loss. And deep down, I know that I still love her.

If I were just fucking Athena the way the other two would, for revenge or to win this stupid fucking game, then it wouldn't feel like a betrayal of Natalie's memory.

But I wouldn't be doing it for either of those things.

I'd be fucking her because I want her with a need that feels as if it goes bone-deep, a need that leaves me aching and hard more often than not these days. A pounding, throbbing, painful need that makes me sometimes feel like I'm going to go crazy from it.

I only ever felt that way once before. And it feels wrong to want it again. To *give in* to it again.

If I go to bed with Athena, I'm going to be getting myself in way too deep.

But I still can't stop myself from going to the bed, from stretching out alongside her, reaching out, and touching her creamy soft skin. I can't stop myself from breathing in her scent, capturing her face with my hand, leaning forward to brush my lips over hers.

If I send her away, I might not ever get to do this again.

That thought hurts, piercing my heart and making my chest ache. But even if I could get past the guilt of Natalie, the rest of my reasoning still remains.

I can't run this town. I don't want it. I don't want any part of this stupid fucking legacy that our ancestors built and left to us, any part of the rituals that have grown men fighting over a girl's virginity every twenty years or so, tormenting and twisting and breaking her until there's nothing left except the keys to the kingdom. Then they take those keys and leave her behind, a broken doll that's been played with and used up entirely.

Even Philip St. Vincent, who married his pet, doesn't love her. That's easy enough to see. He's not faithful to her. So what's the fucking point? He might as well have discarded her, instead of leading her on and extending the torment for decades.

Or maybe that was the point all along.

My point is that I can't do this. I can't throw myself into the ring and claim Athena and a prize that I don't want and was never meant to have. And so even as my body strains towards hers, even as I feel her softness leaning into me and roll her over onto her back, feeling the heat of her pussy pressing against my cock as she wraps her legs around my waist, I shake my head and whisper against her lips:

"We can't do this, Athena."

She stiffens, her body going rigid against mine, and I see something in her face that I hadn't expected. Not just surprise...but hurt, too. And something else that I hadn't expected.

Betrayal.

"You could do it for me," she whispers softly, and that cuts me to the quick in a way that I'd never expected it would. Because I understand now what's going on.

Athena has decided to take control of the only currency she has. And she chose me to be the one she paid it to.

Because she trusted me not to hurt her. She trusted me to be gentle, to even make it good. And from the way I can feel her body still arching up towards mine, her breath coming in small delicate pants, her breasts pressing against my chest, I know something else too.

She wants me.

"I can't," I whisper regretfully, and I've never wished that I could change something more. "I can't do it, Athena."

"Why not?" She swallows hard, and I can see that she's trying to hold back tears.

"I can't tell you."

Her jaw clenches, and I see her expression shift to something else, from pained to angry...and then simply to resigned.

"Fine," she whispers, her voice shaking. And then she slips out from under me, her soft skin brushing against mine one last time before she runs for the door, slamming it behind her.

I've never regretted a decision so much in my entire life.

ATHENA

I'm shaking when I leave Jaxon's room; a part of me feels heartbroken.

I knew there was a chance he would turn me down. After all, he's been the hardest nut to crack. The only one of the three that seems to have truly complex layers, something deeper inside of him that I can't quite figure out. It made me like him, made me *want* him.

But he's told me no.

And I, of all people, have to respect that.

Not that I have much of a choice anyway.

In fact, there's really only one choice left to me.

I would have dressed differently for Dean. Part of me thinks I should go back to my room and change, but I can't. If I do, I'm afraid I'll chicken out. I'll go back to the relative safety of my room, back to the quiet, and I'll rethink this decision.

And then I won't have any control, again. They'll make all the choices for me. I can't let that happen, either.

So instead, I walk down the hall towards Dean's room. One foot in front of the other, like I'm walking to my execution.

It's not that bad, I tell myself.

It's Dean, not Cayde. He might treat you like you're beneath him, and you will be, but he won't hurt you. He's cruel, but he's not savage. It could be worse. He's handsome. He's got a nice dick. You could do a lot worse.

But they're all gorgeous. They're all hung. It takes more than a nice body and pretty face and a good dick for me to want someone—really want them, mind and heart and soul as well as body.

Right now, though, all that matters is the body.

The shock on his face when I open the door is almost worth it. He looks briefly stunned, and Dean so rarely loses his composure that I almost laugh. I manage not to, though, looking up at him with eyes as wide and innocent as I can possibly make them.

"Can I come in?"

His gaze hardens, darkens, sweeping down the length of my body as he takes in what I'm wearing, that I'm standing out in the hall in a crop top and thong and thigh-high socks.

"You just came from Jaxon, didn't you?" he asks, and his voice is so low and certain that I know I can't lie.

"Yes," I whisper.

"He's a fucking idiot," Dean says. And then he grabs my elbow and pulls me into the room.

When the door shuts behind me, I know there's no going back. My heart pounds in my chest as I look up at Dean's icy blue eyes, the sweep of his brown hair, the cruel line of his jaw. He looks handsome, regal, every bit the Lord Blackmoor that I know he is. I could be a maid a hundred years ago, being taken to bed by the lord of the castle.

But I'm not. I'm Athena Saint, in the present day, in a house that's old and dark and full of secrets that I'm determined to bring into the light.

"You're not very seductive about it," Dean says, his fingers sliding between mine as he pulls me towards the bed. He sits on the edge, legs spread, and he draws me in between his thighs as his hands rest on my waist. "But what else should I expect from a virgin?"

His hand slides down to my hip, his fingers tracing the edges of the cane marks. "This is a big deal, Athena, choosing who you'll give your virginity to. You almost fucked up. But you made the right choice, in the end." Dean reaches up with his other hand, stroking my hair. "Smart girl. Good girl."

"Just—be gentle?" I hate the quiver in my voice, but now that I'm here, now that I know Dean isn't going to turn me down the way Jaxon did, I feel a tremor of fear in my belly. I wonder if it'll hurt, if he'll make it feel good in any way, if I'll enjoy it or if it'll just be miserable.

"Oh, I'll be more than that," Dean murmurs. His hand slides up my waist, over the flat plane of my belly, underneath the crop top. "By the end of all this, you'll be begging for it. You'll be moaning so loudly that everyone in the house will know I've taken what's mine." His hand moves over my breast, squeezing, not so hard that it hurts, but hard enough that I know what he's doing.

His fingers toy with my nipple as his other hand goes to my thigh, and I let out a small sigh as he slides his palm up the soft skin there, up to the edge of my thong. "Strip for me, Athena," he says, his voice hoarse. "Take off your shirt."

I nod, licking my lips nervously as I reach down and pull the crop top up over my breasts and up over my head, tossing it aside onto the floor. I can see the appreciative glint in Dean's eyes as he looks at my chest, eye-level and closer to him than I've ever been before.

"I'll take these off," he says softly, reaching for the straps of my thong. I don't fight him, letting him pull it down over my hips, and he leans forward as he draws it down, brushing his lips over the flat of my abdomen.

"Do you want me to make you come first?" He looks up at me, his hand on my inner thigh. "You'll have to ask for it, my little pet. Ask me for your pleasure."

I almost don't. I have the urge to just go cold, to let him do what he wants, and refuse to take any enjoyment in it. But there's no point in that. It's going to happen anyway, and Dean at least will make it good for me if I play along.

Besides, if I have an orgasm first, it won't hurt as much.

"Please," I whisper, looking down at him. "Please make me come."

"When I've taken your virginity, I'll be your master," Dean says, his voice low and rough. "But for now, when you beg me, call me *sir*."

"Please..." my voice shakes, and I feel a tremor of desire run through me despite myself. He's so regally handsome, his hair gleaming and soft under the light, his face clean-shaven, his jaw strong, his lips full, his eyes that cold and icy blue. His looks are cruelly handsome, his eyes beautiful, even as they freeze you to death, and I feel my body responding to him as he slides his hand up, his fingers tracing the crease of my pussy.

"Please give me an orgasm, sir," I whisper, and the flood of arousal that sweeps over me, trickling from my folds down over his fingers, sends a rush of hot shame through me, turning my skin a flushed pink.

"You ask so nicely." Dean reaches down with his other hand, groaning as he undoes his zipper, allowing his already rock-hard cock to spring free. "God, it makes me hard. I'm going to teach you to beg your master for so many things, Athena," he murmurs, his fingers delving between my folds as he reaches up to pinch my nipple. "I'll teach you to plead, to ask me to do all the things I want to do to you. You'll beg to come, to suck my cock, to have me tie you up and tease you mercilessly. You'll plead for the crop on your ass, for me to force your orgasm and withhold it, for me to fuck you in every hole. You'll ask for your own humiliation, and I'll give it to you, along with my cum."

He's breathing harder now, and I can see the tip of his cock glistening, stiff, and ready for me. The sight of it sends a shiver through me, and I can feel the warmth spreading through me, reacting to his words even as I'm horrified by them.

I never thought I'd want any of those things. But the way he says them makes them sound dark and delicious, forbidden things that only he can draw out of me, taking my nascent lust and spinning it into a tapestry of sinful delights. His fingers slide into me, and I hear how sopping wet I am, the sucking sounds of flesh as he thrusts two fingers in and out of me, his thumb rubbing against my clit as he toys with my breasts.

"Spread your legs now, Athena," he tells me. "Spread them, and I'll suck your pretty little clit until you come."

I whimper, resisting at first, but I can't hold out for long. The thrust of his fingers, the rolling pad of his thumb, the dark growl of his voice, and the pressure of his hand are all too much. I see his cock throbbing, straining for me, and suddenly I want it, want him thrusting into me, filling the deep and boundless ache that I suddenly feel. His fingers aren't enough, they could never be enough, but I spread my legs, my back arching as he leans forward, pulling me swiftly onto the bed and moving down between my legs.

I cry out when his mouth fastens around my clit, when his fingers pump into me hard and fast, driving my body towards an orgasm that my mind doesn't want but that I'm desperate for anyway. He sucks at my flesh, and I can hear myself moaning, my voice rising to a high pitch as the hard, hot pressure in my belly starts to unfurl, burning through my veins. Suddenly I don't recognize the sounds I'm making. I'm coming out of my body, unraveling at the seams, and it's the best and brightest pleasure I've ever felt since that night Jaxon licked me to orgasm out on that grassy cliffside.

When Dean lifts his head, I'm still shuddering.

"I'm going to fuck you now, Athena." His voice is calm and sure, and I look up at him, still twitching with the aftershocks of my orgasm, suddenly terrified as I feel his hands pushing my thighs open wider.

"Wait!" I gasp, looking up at him. "Aren't you going to wear a condom?"

Dean laughs. "Athena, you're for our pleasure. You were given a shot for birth control when you were brought here. I won't be getting you pregnant." His eyes gleam as he looks down at me, dark with lust and the sure knowledge that in a moment, his cock will be inside of me. "None of us would miss out on the chance to fuck you raw." His hands stroke my inner thighs, pushing me open wide. "You're going to take every drop of my cum in that sweet pussy."

I'm breathless now with fear, gasping with it, but either Dean thinks it's arousal or doesn't care. His jaw is set, and I see his hips moving towards me, that huge cock angled towards my pussy. I want to scream out for him to wait again, to stop, but I know there's no point. It's time, I've made my decision, and there's no going back.

Dean Blackmoor is going to be my first.

I feel his fingers open my folds, revealing my entrance to the swollen head of his cock, and then he's pushing against me. I'm soaking wet, but I'm still tight, and when he pushes harder, and the head of his cock pops into me, I let out a surprised yowl of pain.

Dean's hands squeeze my thighs, his jaw set with concentration as he holds himself there for a second. *"Fuck,"* he grinds out between clenched teeth. "You feel so fucking good, so goddamn tight, oh fuck—"

And then he loses control.

I can see it in his face when he pushes forward another inch, and my pussy clamps down around him, both fighting him and trying to pull him in all at once. It's excruciating for me, but it must feel unimaginably good for him because he suddenly leans forward, grabbing the headboard behind me and plunging every inch of his thick, rigid cock into me in one hard thrust.

I scream. The pain is hot and immediate, and I swear I can feel my flesh tearing, feel myself separating around him as his thick cock opens me wide, splits me apart for him. He doesn't stop, either; he doesn't give me even a moment to adjust.

"Fucking...tight...pussy," he groans out, his hips jerking, his cock sawing in and out of me in long hard thrusts that seem to pierce me to the very core every time. I cling to the bed, fingers tangled in the sheets, looking up at him as he fucks me with his face hard and set, pleasure written across every inch of it as he cruelly takes my virginity.

"You're fucking...mine," he snarls, looking down at me with those icy eyes. "My pussy. My pet. Mine---*fuck!*" He pounds into me harder, groaning aloud, the headboard smacking into the wall as he drives me backward with the force of his thrusts. "God, it's so fucking *good*, I'm gonna fucking come, I'm gonna fill that virgin pussy up. Fuck, Athena..."

He throws his head back, and I feel my pussy spasm around him in the same moment that his hand grips the pillow by my head hard. "Take my fucking cum...*god.*"

I can feel it rushing into me, hot and thick, feel him shooting his load as he drives into me once more, sinking balls-deep as he arches backward, grinding hard against me as his cock spasms and pulses inside of me, emptying every last drop deep into my pussy. And I can feel my body clenching around him, feel strange electric shocks of pleasure along with the pain, not an orgasm but still good. I can't help but moan, squirming beneath him as I feel his hips twitch, reluctant to slide out of me.

"You like my fucking cock?" Dean groans, looking down at me with a possessive, triumphant grin on his face. "You liked taking my cum."

He pulls out of me then, and I whimper, feeling the soreness already where he was. He rolls onto his back, and when I try to move towards him, Dean puts out a hand, holding me off.

"I don't fucking cuddle," he says shortly. "But stay there. I might want you again before you leave."

His coldness feels like a physical blow somehow, but I obey mutely, laying there on my back as I feel his cum start to seep out, sticky and warm on the inside of my thighs. I can see traces of blood on his dick when I look over. As he turns out the light and the room goes dark, I take inventory of my body, trying to figure out if I feel any differently.

If I've changed at all.

It's over. I've won, or Dean has—I don't know which. Choosing who I wanted was a small victory, but if my theory was right, it was always going to be my choice in the end. Cayde was just trying to bully me into picking him to end my torment. Dean was arrogant in his belief that I should choose him regardless. Jaxon was always going to fight his own desires and turn me down, for whatever fucking reason.

So, in the end, I'm not sure if it was a victory. Still, it *was* my choice, or at least partially. I didn't give in to Cayde, and that counts for something.

I close my eyes, hearing Dean snoring softly beside me, and despite my attempts to stay awake and on my guard, I fall asleep.

My dreams are strange. I dream of the girls in the white robes in the stone room, of flickering torches and a goblet of wine. I dream of knives in the dark, of wine flowing through a thick veil, of the heavy feeling of being drugged, pulled under, fighting it but ultimately having no choice to give in.

I dream of fear and pain, and when I wake up, I feel Dean behind me.

He rolls me onto my stomach, seemingly not caring whether I'm asleep or awake. For a second, I'm terrified that since he's had my mouth and my pussy now, he's going to take my ass. But instead, I feel him pushing at my sore, ravaged entrance again, and when I cry out, he grabs the back of my head, shoving my face down into the pillow.

"This is your first lesson as *my* pet, Athena. Your pussy is mine now, for my pleasure, whenever I want it. I don't have to ask anymore. You're a sleeve for my cock, a toy for me to cum in. I woke up hard, and so you're going to lay there and let me get off." He positions himself between my folds, and when he thrusts into me in one long, hard stroke, I scream again, muffled by the pillow now.

"Maybe, if you're a good girl, I'll let you come too. Sometimes." He thrusts again, hard and deep, and I feel something wake up inside of me, a pleasure that tingles through my veins at the feeling of him so deep inside of me. "You were very good earlier. You begged for your orgasm, and you took every drop of my cum. I can still feel it inside of you. So you may come again if you want to. If you can, before I do. But—" his voice drops an octave, his thrusts faster now. "If I come first, you have to stop. I like these little games."

Without thinking, my hand slides underneath me, moving down to my clit almost frantically, rubbing quick and fast. His cock hurts, scraping along my newly raw flesh, but it feels so fucking good too, filling me up, stretching me, sinking into me all the way every time. I moan into the pillow, my ass arching up against him, grinding back as I play with my clit, and Dean laughs above me.

"That's right. My little fucktoy, my little slut. You love my cock in you, don't you? I can feel it squeezing around me. Hurry up and make yourself come. I'm almost ready." He groans. "Your pussy is too fucking good."

Somehow that feels like another tiny victory, that he's going to come too fast because it feels too good. I'm on edge too, and I rub faster, harder, spreading my thighs and grinding against him, my body wanting more, terrified that I'll still be on the edge of my pleasure when he comes.

"Gonna...fucking...come—" Dean groans aloud, and that, in the end, is what does it.

I feel the orgasm explode through me as he thrusts into me hard, holding himself as deeply inside of me as he can as he shoots his second load, his cum filling me up as I arch against him, my body shuddering and writhing beneath his as I moan helplessly into the pillow, ashamed of my orgasm even as it wracks my body with the most incredible pleasure.

Dean stays there for a moment, his cock twitching inside of me, and then he pulls out, flopping onto his back as he lets out a long sigh. There's a moment of silence as I lay there on my stomach, still panting, and then I hear his voice drift towards me through the darkness.

"Get out. I don't let girls stay the night."

His voice is so brutal, so cold. It chills me to the bone, and I don't even *want* to stay, but for some reason, it hurts. I don't give him a chance to tell me again. I'm too tired to deal with the anger, the punishments that might come from disobeying. Instead, I just get up, reaching for my clothes next to the bed and pulling them on in the dim moonlight.

I don't look back as I walk out. I don't care to see his face again. I've done everything I came to do, and now all that's left is to go to bed.

My chest squeezes tightly as I pass the door to Jaxon's room, and I can't help but wonder if he heard, if he knows what I did, if he knows that his chance to be my first is gone now. I feel the prickle of tears behind my eyes, and for the first time, I know I've lost more than my virginity tonight.

I lost my chance for my first time to be with the man I wanted, too.

I can feel my heart cracking in my chest, but I ignore it. I want to shower, but I can't risk the chance of waking up the guys, so instead, I just go to my room and lay down on my bed, feeling the stickiness of Dean's cum on my thighs and the raw soreness in my pussy, and hoping that I'll be allowed a break before he wants me again.

There won't be any relief from it now. Nothing to hold back, nothing he has to wait for me to give. That's over for good, now.

I still think I made the right choice. But I don't know what the days to come will bring.

When I fall asleep, I dream again. It's the same dream, white robes and stone walls, but now I'm the one in the robes, the one who feels like she can't breathe when the wine runs through the veil, filling my mouth until I swallow or choke. I'm the one slipping into a heavy, drugged sleep, looking up at faces I can barely make out through the fabric of my veil, but there are three faces there that I think I recognize.

Three faces that I see every day.

Dean, Cayde…and Jaxon.

DEAN

*W*hen Cayde calls a meeting in the study the next morning before breakfast, I know exactly why.

And I'm not about to play coy.

"Don't bother trying to figure out what the screams last night were about, gentlemen," I say cheerfully, whistling as I swagger into the room with all the confidence of a man who just had virgin blood on his dick the night before—and not just any virgin blood, either.

The blood that's won me Blackmoor.

"I nailed the sacrifice last night," I say with a grin, looking at Cayde and Jaxon's stunned faces. "And as I'm sure you figured out from her screams, she even fucking liked it. She came *twice*." I laugh, shoving my hands in my pockets. "You can go upstairs and check the sheets if you like. I'm saving them for the ritual, of course. Nice and bloody, just like they're meant to be. She's probably sore as hell today. I rode her hard." I shrug. "Blackmoor is mine. We can discuss the particulars later."

I don't even see the punch coming until I'm on the floor.

Cayde stands over me, shaking his hand as if the punch hurt his fist. "Fuck you and your particulars," he spits. "You fucking took what was mine, Dean Blackmoor. I won't forgive that. I can't. I won't be your fucking dog."

I rub my chin, feeling the blood trickle down from my split lip. I grin at him anyway, ignoring the pain. "You know the rules, Cayde. I followed you all these years. Now the tables have turned."

Cayde looks as if he's about to attack me again, but before he can lunge forward, Jaxon steps in, holding his hands up as he moves his body between Cayde and me.

"Hold up, man," he says. "Look, Dean won fair and square. I know you don't like it. But if she chose him, there's nothing we can do. It's the law. That's how the game is played. The blood of the sacrifice chooses the next lord of Blackmoor."

"There's no fucking way she chose you willingly," Cayde spits.

"Oh, but she did." I grin. "Want to back me up, Jaxon?"

Jaxon shifts uncomfortably. "She actually picked me," he says finally. "She came to my room, dressed up for me, tried to get me to fuck her. But I turned her down. And yeah, I knew where she'd go after that. Not to you, Cayde, you fucking terrify her. You've been the worst of us to her this entire time. I knew she'd go to Dean."

"And she did." I shrug. "Welcome to the new regime."

"Fuck you!" Cayde screams again, and then the study doors burst open.

"What the fuck!" Athena is standing there, panting, her eyes wide as she looks at the three of us. I have to admit we make a strange picture, with me on the floor bleeding, Cayde with his fist shaking above me, and Jaxon trying to play mediator. "What the fuck is going on?" she demands. "I could hear you fighting all the way out in the dining room!"

"Just a little disagreement over the legitimacy of last night," I say coolly. "Cayde seems to think that there was some foul play."

Athena licks her lips, looking among the three of us. "No," she says finally. "Cayde, he's telling the truth. I went to him willingly. To Dean, I mean." I see her eyes flick to Jaxon, but it's only a second. I see the hurt there, though—his rejection cut her deep. I file that away for later…you never know when something like that might come in handy.

"Why?" Cayde is shaking now, his face red with anger. "Why him?"

Athena laughs then, the sound low and bitter. "Isn't it obvious, Cayde? So that it wouldn't be you."

Cayde looks as if he might explode. "Don't you realize what you've done?"

"No," Athena says simply. "So why don't you tell me?"

Cayde freezes at that, looking at the two of us uncertainly. It's Jaxon that finally speaks up, unsurprisingly. He would be the one with a hard-on for the truth.

"It's over, guys," he says with a shrug. "She might as well know."

"Know what?" Athena looks at us, her gaze long and even, and I know then that this was a part of her own private game all along. She figured out that something was up, and she gave away the prize so she could find out what it was.

"There's a ritual, once every generation," Jaxon says, his voice almost tired. "Hundreds of years ago, 'virgin sacrifice' was taken very literally. In that, a virgin was sacrificed when the heirs of the founding families came of age, in the old Blackmoor back in Britain, and they drank her blood. But then we came to America, and things changed, and drinking human blood wasn't quite so doable anymore." He shrugs.

Athena has gone white to the lips, her face horrified.

"So instead, they came up with something different. Instead of literally drinking a virgin's blood, the blood sacrifice would be her virginity. They would give the girl to the three heirs to do whatever they liked with. It was usually always pretty kinky." Jaxon's mouth twitches. "Men get dark when they're given a girl they can use at their whim. But the catch was, the virgin couldn't be raped. She had to give up her virginity to one of them willingly—however they managed to convince her. Sometimes there was blackmail or coercion, sometimes there was seduction, sometimes just straight up tormenting her until she couldn't stand it anymore —Cayde's preferred method, I believe," he says sarcastically.

"And once she chose?" Athena's voice is shaking but wary.

"The man she chose would become the next lord of Blackmoor," Jaxon says simply. "Ruler of the town, until the next generation, and the law for everyone within it. The other two heirs would become his right and left hands."

"So I—" Athena swallows hard. "Oh my god. I just gave Blackmoor back to you." She looks at me, her eyes wide and shocked. And then her gaze flicks back to Jaxon.

"You knew this all along."

Jaxon nods slowly. "Yeah. I was there at the ritual."

"You were there when I—" she pauses, her arms wrapping around herself. "That's why you rejected me. You don't want the town."

"It's not as simple as that—"

"Shut the fuck up!" Athena shouts suddenly, her face pale and her eyes still wide and stunned and frightened. "Are you fucking kidding me? I was a pawn in this...this...patriarchal *bullshit* all along, and no one told me?"

"We couldn't—" I try to speak then, but she silences me with a glare as frigid as any I've ever given.

"I can't believe I fucked you," she whispers. "I can't believe I put you in charge of this whole fucking town, subjected everyone here to your fucking arrogance, because I didn't know." Athena shakes her head, walking backward towards the door. "I didn't know. I couldn't have made a decision because I didn't know." Her gaze flicks upwards. "I should have fucked Cayde. At least his family employs mine! At least his father helped us!" She swallows hard, shaking her head.

"Fuck all of you," she whispers. "I hate you all. Every single one of you."

And then the door slams behind her, and she's gone.

"Well, you've all really gone and fucked things up now," Jaxon says dryly, slouching into one of the chairs. Cayde steps back, some of the anger leached out of him, and I get to my feet slowly, feeling the soreness start to bloom in my jaw.

"What happens to Athena now?" Jaxon looks at me. "What are you going to do with her?"

"I don't really give a shit what happens to her," I say flatly. "I'll keep her around for as long as she's an interesting fuck, just as I'd always planned. I'll make sure she's provided for, as required, but other than that, she doesn't matter to me. She was always just a hole that I needed to fuck in order to win."

Jaxon's jaw clenches at that, but he doesn't say anything. Cayde has flushed red with anger again, and he shakes his head.

"This won't stand," he says, looking back and forth between the two of us. "You heard her. She didn't really choose Dean. She chose Jaxon, but he forfeited. There's no principle for that. So you haven't won fair and square." Cayde's lips press together thinly. "This isn't the end, Dean."

"What about you?" I ask Jaxon, after Cayde has stormed out. "Are you going to argue with it?"

Jaxon stands up slowly, running his fingers through his hair. "No," he says simply. "I turned her down. I already took myself out of the game, if I was ever in it at all." He shrugs, striding towards the door, and then he pauses, one hand on the knob.

"I have to say though, Dean..." he looks back at me, his mouth twisted in a half-smile. "I'm not altogether sure that the best man won."

ATHENA

I remember some of it now. Not all of it, but after Jaxon's confession, it's coming back in fits and starts. The initial drug, the one that got me into the robe and down those steps at all. The chanting, the robed bodies, the cold.

The wine. More drugs. And the blurred faces above me, the ones that I now know I've been looking at every day since.

They did this to me. They made me a pawn, a sacrifice, a plaything. I can feel my pain hardening in my chest, the hurt turning to anger, the hopelessness into a desire for revenge.

A desire to make sure that they don't get what they want.

I'm going to make sure that none of them win.

Dean Blackmoor doesn't deserve me, and he doesn't deserve this town. I don't think any of them do.

They picked the wrong girl.

I'm going to take everything away from all of them.

My virginity is gone, but Cayde still wants me, and deep down, Jaxon does too. I'll get them both into bed, make them fuck me, and then who wins? The one who came first? Not if I have anything to say about it. I'm going to destroy them.

I'm no one's toy, and I'm done being played with.
My mother named me after the goddess of war.
I'll never be anyone's sacrifice.

*ATHENA, **Dean, Cayde, and Jaxon's stories continue in the next install-
ment of the Lords of Blackmoor series: Savage Prince.***

243

Printed in Great Britain
by Amazon